KFIR LUZZATTO

I0618915

The Evelyn
Project

Pine Ten, LLC
205 North Michigan Avenue
Suite 810
Chicago, Illinois 60601

First publication: April 2012

ISBN: 978-1-938212-00-0

TABLE OF CONTENTS

CHAPTER 1

London, England. June 2009

London welcomed Franco back as he descended on the sunny sidewalk, right after the end of his weekly student reception hour, by cunningly thrusting upon him an elderly millionaire who spoke in riddles. It was a glorious day that brought back pleasant memories of a summer walk with his father in that exact same place. He loved the city and jumped at the opportunity to take a position there as a Latin lecturer. The first year of his two-year contract was about to end, but who knew – he might still settle down there permanently.

He had some free time on his hands. He resolved to take a short walk from his office building in The Strand campus of King's College to Covent Garden, but before he managed to start, a voice from behind him got his attention.

"Professor Lorenzi? Franco Lorenzi?" the voice inquired.

"Yes, oh, hello," Franco answered politely, turning around to see who was addressing him. What he saw was a small, elderly man, neatly dressed in what looked like an expensive suit too hot for the summer day. He couldn't place this person, who looked respectable and, obviously, knew him.

"I apologize for stopping you like this in the street, but I was on my way to see you. Oh ... but you don't know me, how stupid of me," he added. He searched his pockets feverishly, at last finding a small silver case. He opened it and handed Franco a business card. "You must forgive my muddle-headedness. At my age sometimes ..." he said. He shook his head apologetically, without completing the sentence.

"Don't mention it," said Franco.

He read the engraved card that said in golden characters, "Sir James Easby, G.F.C.D., M.R.L.D., Chairman, The European Historical Communication Society (EHCS)," and was impressed. He wouldn't have thought that this nice, unassuming man would be a big shot, but although he had never heard of the EHCS, the richness of the visiting card bore all the signs of importance.

"You said you were coming to see me. What can I do for you?"

"Yes. I tried to telephone you yesterday and then again this morning. When there was no answer from your office, I decided to come in person ... because of the urgency."

"Urgency?" Franco was mystified. What could be so urgent to send a stranger looking for a professor of Latin? After all, Latin had been a dead language for centuries. Whatever this visitor wanted from him could surely wait a few days.

"I'll explain ... but perhaps here in the street is not the best place to talk. Why don't we go and get some tea? I know a good place nearby," said Easby, and without waiting for a response, he started walking, followed by a bewildered Franco.

Five minutes later, they were seated in a quiet corner of the tearoom. Their orders were taken, and Franco's curiosity mounted quickly. Easby combed his gray hair with his fingers and gazed at Franco, and then he combed it again, twice.

"I owe you an explanation, Professor Lorenzi," he said at last. "This is an extremely delicate matter, so I hope you'll bear with me. What we've been doing ... I mean, the Society has engaged in an effort to help save a distant relative of yours, who is gravely ill. We have been working to help her for some time now. As a result, we have determined that to give her a chance to survive, we need to bring on board a blood relative of hers. That's it in a nutshell. That's why I've been chasing you."

"A blood relative, you say? Who is she?"

"I'm afraid that I'm not at liberty to disclose her identity yet. Privacy issues are involved that make that impossible at this point. Of course, if you decide to help, we will reveal her identity to you after the proper legal matters have been attended to."

"I know of no relative of mine who is ill."

"You two have never met." Easby shuffled in his seat and assumed an apologetic expression. "I appreciate that this is a bit vague," he said, "and I don't expect you to commit to anything before you have the full facts before you. At this stage, I wanted to make your acquaintance. I need to know whether you would be willing to help in principle and nothing more."

"Of course, as you say, I need to know more. I don't know who you're talking about or your role in all this, but if I'm needed to give a blood sample or something like that, you can count on me. On the other hand, if you're going to ask me to donate a kidney, that's probably going to be a much harder sell."

"I can guarantee that you will not be requested to make any sacrifice, except your time, and that your help is essential in saving your relative's life."

"In that case, I am certainly willing to hear more. Tell me a little about the EHCS."

"Certainly, certainly," said Easby, smiling, now clearly more at ease. Then he glanced at his watch, and his face darkened. "My ... is it really that late? I'm sorry, I must rush. I'm running terribly late for an appointment."

"Well ... now you really got me curious ..."

"I'm so sorry for teasing you, but I really must go. But don't worry, I'll get in touch with you very soon. We'll quickly take care of the formalities, and then I'll be able to give you all the details. I promise. Thank you so much for your patience and for your time."

Easby was already on his feet, gesturing to the waitress and obviously frustrated by her demeanor as she languidly presented the bill. He paid it, shook Franco's hand warmly again, and left murmuring some more words of apology.

Franco walked pensively back to his office. The circumstances of the encounter and the secretiveness of his visitor bothered him. He had liked the old man instinctively, but he needed to make sure that he wasn't walking into anything illegal before getting involved with him.

Back in his office, he turned on his PC and Googled "The European Historical Communication Society" and drew a blank. He then tried "EHCS," and the query returned some twenty-seven thousand entries, the least bizarre one being the "English House Condition Survey." After a while, he gave up on the acronym and Googled "James Easby." This time his search returned many references and articles with photographs of Easby taken on different occasions. The picture they gave of him was reassuring: the soft-spoken man was a millionaire and, until recently, the acting chairman of a large electronic industry. Over the years, his name had been associated with various charities and was frequently mentioned in social events reports. He was for real, and as he turned off his PC, Franco realized that he was now more intrigued than before. He knew that he would have to find out what it was all about, or his curiosity would kill him.

CHAPTER 2

Udine, Italy. June 1894

The Honorable L. stepped down from the unmarked carriage that had stopped in the dark and empty street. He wore a long black overcoat against the chill of the late evening but still shivered a little, standing before the closed door of a house that, judging by the state of its façade, had seen better days. His graying goatee made it difficult to guess his age, and the worries of the last months had carved his face to look older than his fifty-two years. Still, his lean figure conveyed an unmistakable innate strength that never failed to impress those who met him for the first time.

He felt uncomfortable standing there at the door of a house where he was about to seek help. He had never asked for help from strangers before and recoiled at the thought that his behavior might be viewed as a sign of weakness. To him, weakness was a mortal sin, but this time it was different; his whole world was at stake, and he had to go ahead and do everything in his power to save it. In reality, he thought, reassuring himself a little, the fact that he was willing to go through with something that other people might construe as a sign of weakness was in itself a sign of strength. Yes, that was bravery, and shying from the deed would have been an act of pusillanimity ...

The thought strengthened him as he banged the knocker on the door with three short, resolute strikes.

A young girl opened the door almost immediately. She stood there, wiping her hands on her apron. He eyed her briefly and immediately discounted her as irrelevant.

"I am here to see Mrs. Cecchi ..."

"Yes, Honorable L. ..." she started to say, bowing a little to emphasize the recognition.

"Shh! Don't you say my name, girl!" he admonished her.

"I'm sorry, Sir. Please do come in ..."

She moved aside, and he walked in, taking off his top hat. She closed the door, careful not to bang it, and bolted it, and then she turned to the Honorable L., who stood there rigidly, scanning the dark hall. When she saw that his gaze rested on her, she nodded briefly and walked to a door located at the far end of the hall.

"I'll tell Mother that you have arrived, Sir," she said. She disappeared through the door leaving the Honorable L. waiting in the hall. He looked around the dark, gray surroundings and sniffed the air. It was heavy with an odor that evoked the image of a room that has remained closed for the winter season. He shivered and reckoned that it was from the cold. The door through which the girl had disappeared reopened a few moments later; she curtseyed and said, "Please come this way."

The Honorable L. shifted his walking stick from his right to his left hand and walked through the door, which closed behind him. The room was large and poorly lit, with a fireplace where the embers of a small log were smoldering. Judging by the smell of smoke, the chimney wasn't drawing too well. Two high-backed armchairs were placed near the fireplace, and in one sat an old, wrinkled woman. She was dressed in black as befitting a widow, with a bonnet that she had surely put on especially for him. The black lace that surrounded it nearly covered her small, brown eyes. She didn't give any sign of being about to get up or speak, so after a brief hesitation, the Honorable L. walked up to her.

"Missis Cecchi ..." he said, not asking a question but stating a fact.

"Welcome," she answered with a high-pitched, croaking voice, "although your deed is not a happy one."

He didn't respond to her remark. Instead, he maintained a businesslike countenance that was too obviously designed to hide his emotions.

"My friend, who recommended you to me, said that you can be counted on to be discreet ..."

"Of course, but won't you sit down?"

He sat in the armchair in front of her but did not relax in it. Instead, he kept to the edge of the seat with his walking stick between his legs and his hat in his left hand, edging slightly forward as if about to sprint away. The only allowance to comfort that he made was to unbutton his tight overcoat.

"Thank you," he said dryly. "You will appreciate that my visit to you cannot be allowed to become generally known ..."

"Yes, I know ... you would be ashamed to admit that you have consulted with a witch."

Her bitter tone surprised him, and he hastened to disassociate himself from the accusation. This woman was his last hope, and he couldn't afford to offend her.

"No, it's not that. It's just that, you see, I'm a public figure, and this renders everything much more complicated ..."

"Never mind," she said, cutting him short. "I'm willing to help if I can. Your friend gave me a brief explanation of your problem, but I'll need to hear the whole story."

"It's about my daughter, Evelina. She is dying of consumption, and the doctors are not giving me hope. She's in Switzerland right now, getting the best medical attention that modern medicine can give and breathing the best air you can find, but she's getting thinner every day ..."

For the first time, he had trouble mastering his emotions, and his voice broke for a moment, but then he got hold of himself and continued.

"She keeps saying that she'll get better and that she knows I will choose the best cures for her ... as if the doctors knew how to treat this damned illness! She relies on me, and I'm powerless to help ..."

"You're not!" she said, sounding both determined and motherly, in a way that strangely contrasted with her appearance. "You're doing the right thing. You're here to help her. Did you bring the items as I said to your friend?"

"Yes," he said, hastening to take an envelope from his inner pocket and hand it to her. "Here I have her photograph and a lock of her hair that I always carry with me."

She studied the photograph closely, and then she laid back with it in one hand and the lock of hair in the other. She closed her eyes and remained motionless, except for the finger and thumb that kept smoothing the lock of hair in her hand and her lips that moved rhythmically as if trying to articulate a sound. He watched her intently, without shifting or moving for fear of disturbing her concentration, until minutes later, she shivered, shifting her body slightly, opened her eyes, and gazed piercingly at him.

"How far are you willing to go with this?" she asked him point-blank.

"To the end of the world and farther than that, if that's what I have to do," he answered, sitting up even more rigidly as if to emphasize his unbendable will. Her question had given him sudden hope.

"Then there is something we can do. I can't guarantee success. It will require faith, but all is not lost."

He got up, excited and unable to sit still. "Tell me what to do. I'm ready for anything. Anything!"

"That I will," said the woman, gazing at him and nodding with approval, "and may God forgive me."

CHAPTER 3

Udine, Italy. June 1894

The Honorable L. paced the huge rug impatiently, waiting for his friend, the mayor, to join him. The room was semi-dark, with heavy curtains that unceremoniously kept out the little light that made it through the deeply-set windows. Still, even in the dim light of the room, the large, dark painting that hung on the wall, portraying the martyrdom of an unidentified saint, created an oppressive atmosphere. Or perhaps it was simply his state of mind that painted everything in dark colors.

At last, the door opened, and the mayor limped in quickly, supporting himself with his cane. He was obviously so embarrassed that even his limp was apologetic.

"I'm so sorry to have kept you waiting. This meeting was going on forever ..."

"Well, it's my fault," the Honorable L. cut him short. "I should have given you forewarning of my visit, but there was no time."

The mayor gave his old friend a concerned look. Clearly, something was not as well as usual. "What's the matter? What has happened?" he asked.

"It's Evelyn ..."

"How is she? Is she back home?"

"No. The truth is she's dying, and I need your help."

He spoke flatly, matter-of-factly. He knew that otherwise, his old friend would have dragged him into a conversation that threatened to become emotional.

"Anything! Anything I can do, I will. You know she's almost like my own child."

"Thank you. I know that I can count on you, but some of what I am going to ask you to do for me may seem strange to you, and I beg you not to inquire into it."

"Go ahead ..." If the mayor was surprised that his long-time friend needed to prelude his request with such preconditions, he didn't show it.

"The first thing that I need you to do for me regards a document that I would bring to you in a sealed envelope. I need you to issue a decree that seals this document in the city archives for the next hundred years, to be made available to any of my direct descendants at the expiration of that time."

"Uhm ... I can do that, it's within my powers, but it will look weird to city officials unless I provide an explanation for it. Perhaps you can tell me what this is about ..."

"I told you I cannot, and you cannot ask questions. But you can make up the story for it, any story you like. It won't make any difference anyway."

"All right. Give it to me, and I'll do it."

"I don't have it yet, but I'll bring it to you soon. Thank you. The second favor that I am going to ask is more elaborate. There is a woman in town, a widow whose daughter is coming of age. I have promised her that she and her daughter will be invited to the ball you will give for your daughter's engagement. Pardon me for the liberty I have taken," he added in haste, seeing the pained expression on his friend's face, "but I had no choice. I had to promise her that her daughter would be introduced to society in that way."

"I don't understand ... who is this woman?"

"Her name is Cecchi."

"The Cecchi widow? Are you out of your mind? Don't you know who she is?"

The mayor's face had turned purple, and he was becoming greatly agitated. The Honorable L. put his arm on the mayor's shoulder, squeezing it lightly, and then he spoke soothingly.

"For how long have we known each other?" he asked, speaking in an undertone. He knew the answer very well and appreciated the power of that question.

"For the best part of forty years," said the mayor. He looked at his old friend inquisitively, as if taken by surprise at the question.

"Yes, since we were children. And in all these years, have I ever called a favor in?"

"No, and you don't have to remind me that I owe you my life. I don't want you to think that I'm ungrateful to you. Not even for a moment. If it weren't for you, I would've died on that damned hill in Sicily, where that bullet made me a cripple. I keep waking up at night with that pain in my leg that has never left me. The last thing that I remember from the dream that scares me awake is you, crawling toward me under fire and shouting to hang on. Oh, yes, I relive my debt to you day in and day out."

The mayor's face, which was never pale, had turned red under the excitement and the Honorable L. spoke apologetically.

"I wasn't suggesting that you were ungrateful or that I have any claim over you. That was a long time ago. I'm here because you are my friend, and a true friend is what I need now."

"I am your friend, you know that. But that woman ... it's not only that she is a common woman – one that my wife would never have at a social function – but you know what they whisper about her? They say she's a witch, a sorcerer, a woman without religion. Having her invited to my daughter's engagement ball would disgrace us. No, that can't be done."

"If I fail," said the Honorable L., his face hardening as he spoke, "Evelyn will never have an engagement ball. Then, you're leaving me no choice but to call your debt in."

His face remained expressionless, and his gaze was fixed on the curtains above his friend's shoulder. The mayor dropped himself onto the couch next to which they had been standing and, for a long moment, sat there gazing at his cane, which he held between his legs. Then, slowly, he raised his head and gazed at his friend, who had remained to stand.

"You really mean it, then," he said. When the Honorable L. merely nodded, he added, "My wife will crucify me for this."

"Tell her it is all my fault."

"I will. Sometimes I think she has more love and respect for you than she has for me. Still, she's not going to like this. She will make my life a living hell. We never discussed it, but convention has it that I am not to interfere with the preparations for the ball."

"I know. I'm sorry."

"You wouldn't reconsider telling me what this is all about, would you? You know you can trust me."

"You don't want to know. But believe me, this is the most important thing for Evelyn and for me, and I will be indebted to you forever for helping me."

The mayor got up and approached his friend. He gazed into his inscrutable eyes, and then he hugged him briefly without another word. The Honorable L. murmured brief words of thanks and left.

CHAPTER 4

Ambri, Switzerland. June 1894

"Evelyn, come! Quick! Your father has arrived."

Evelyn opened her eyes at the sound of the nurse's voice. She had dozed off on her bed, fully dressed. She was so tired ... But her father had arrived, and that was good news; she had missed him a lot in the last few days, even more so because she didn't know when he would be back. Lately, she had started thinking about death; her own death, which, only a few months ago, if she ever gave it a thought at all, was something in the distant future, nothing worth considering until her hair became gray and her skin started to wrinkle, had slowly become something worth worrying about right now. She knew she was in good hands, and her father was optimistic that the fresh air and the cures would help her get well, but she felt weaker every day that passed. As much as she didn't want to think about death or believe that she might really die so young, the thought kept nagging at her.

"Ev," her father's voice came from the door.

Evelyn stood up, panting slightly with the exertion, and faced her father. Another strong effort was needed to produce a smile of welcome, but she made it. She knew instinctively that her father needed the strength that only a smile from her and a lie that created an illusion of healing could give him.

"Darling Father ... I missed you."

The Honorable L. approached her quickly and folded her in his arms, kissing her cheeks, and then he took a step back. "You look so much better!" he said. He always said that, feeling that it was his duty to convince her of it. This was the only place where the absolute truth ceased to be sacred and no longer mattered to him.

"I feel a little better, but I'm so tired all the time."

"You must rest. That is your job; to rest and to leave all other worries to Doctor Schmidt and to me."

Evelyn smiled a weak smile and took a step back, and then she sat on the bed again.

"Are you staying for a few days, Papa?"

"I'm afraid that I have to go back immediately to attend to a few urgent matters, but I wanted to see you however briefly, and I need to speak with Doctor Schmidt, who is waiting downstairs. But I will be back again soon, don't worry. Now lie down to rest, and I'll come up again to see you before I go."

Too weak to respond, Evelyn nodded and lay down on the bed again, closing her eyes with a little sigh. The Honorable L. gazed at her for a long moment. She was so beautiful, so young, and so helpless that seeing her like this was tearing his heart apart. Still, it only strengthened his resolve to go through with the widow's plan, cost what it may.

Downstairs, the Honorable L. and Doctor Schmidt shook hands formally and then sat down by the unlit fireplace in the little sitting area of the chalet.

"I'm afraid that I don't have much to report, as far as progress is concerned," said Doctor Schmidt. "I have tried all the modern remedies and will continue to do so, but Evelyn is responding to treatment very slowly."

"What treatment are you giving her now?"

"Oh ... I'm not overlooking anything; please be assured. The best treatment that modern medicine knows requires keeping the breast and shoulders elevated, admitting plenty of fresh air, with a spare diet and perfect quiet. Evelyn is getting all that," he enunciated didactically. "Besides, I have consulted with one of the greatest physicians in Germany, Doctor Brehmer, and he has advised additional measures. Evelyn is now receiving chest-sponging treatment with vinegar and cold water, accompanied by a dessertspoonful of vinegar and half a glass of water. Yesterday we also started giving her oil of turpentine, about twenty drops in a glass of water. Tomorrow we will start giving her fifteen grains of gallic acid every four hours. Those are all recommendations that Doctor Brehmer gave me based on my medical report, and I am confident that they will be useful. But above everything else, what Evelyn needs is the calmness of mind, rest, quiet, and cool air."

The Honorable L. said nothing, and his face betrayed no emotion; it wouldn't have done to let Evelyn's physician know that he had little faith in the treatment. Doctor Schmidt paused for a moment, and then he pursed his lips and continued. "There is one more thing that I need to tell you. Normally it would be none of my business. I hope you won't think that I'm out of line ..." he hesitated for a moment before continuing, "... but I don't think that Evelyn's mother should be gone for as long as she has been. She hasn't been here for a week now, and Evelyn is restless, being here all alone with the nurse and, occasionally, myself."

"I appreciate your honesty, Doctor Schmidt. As you know, my wife and I have grown apart since Evelyn got sick. She blames me – me of all people!" he said, raising his voice for the first time with a show of emotion, "for Evelyn's illness. I haven't been able to talk to her or to reason with her for weeks now, and I don't know why she has gone away."

"I gather that she is interviewing other physicians, canvassing their opinions. I don't mind it. I take no offense, but I think that she should be here. I will talk to her when I see her next – with your permission, of course."

"By all means, do. I am very grateful to you, Doctor Schmidt. I am sure that Evelyn is in the best of all possible hands, and I don't know how to thank you for all your efforts. Now I have one favor to ask of you." The Honorable L. paused for a moment, weighing his words carefully. He had developed his approach meticulously on his way there, as he had educated himself to do in the political arena before delivering a speech of significant impact. "What I am about to say to you should not, in any way, be interpreted as lack of confidence in your treatment. As I have said many times before, I have full confidence in you and I'm happy that you're looking after my daughter. You must understand that."

"Yes ..."

Doctor Schmidt leaned forward attentively, looking perplexed.

"I have a friend in France who has heard about my daughter's illness. He knows a specialist who claims to concoct an efficient medicine using the patient's blood as a basis. I don't believe that such a magical cure exists, but I do not want to offend my friend who is taking my predicament very much to heart and, besides, even though I don't believe in it, one should not leave any stone unturned, don't you agree?" The Honorable L. averted his gaze, hoping that his eyes weren't exposing his lie.

Doctor Schmidt stiffened and shook his head in disapproval.

"That sounds like charlatanism to me. I follow every new medicine development, and I can assure you that I have never heard of such a preposterous idea. Nevertheless ... sometimes people need to believe in miraculous cures, and I certainly don't want to be the one to stop you from following every course of action that you think may be helpful."

It was clear to the Honorable L. by his stiff reaction that Doctor Schmidt was unhappy, so he spoke much more gently than was customary for his commanding personality.

"I am sure you're right, and, as I have said, I have full confidence in your medicine. But you understand that I must try everything. For my conscience ..."

"Of course, of course," said the doctor, now visibly mollified by his interlocutor's gentle way of speaking.

"Then I need your help, Doctor Schmidt. My friend gave me this vial containing a liquid – I don't know what it is – but I was instructed to fill it with Evelyn's blood and bring it back. I will ask you, please, to bleed her and bring this back to me."

The doctor took the vial and looked at it unhappily.

"She is not in a condition where blood-letting is going to be good for her, but since only a small volume is needed ..."

"Yes, only that small vial. But I must ask you not to tell Evelyn what this is for. I don't want to raise her hopes on the basis of what you clearly think is a futile exercise. Please make some reasonable excuse for it."

"I understand. I will do as you ask."

The doctor got up, picked up his bag, and walked upstairs without further ado.

"I must leave now, Ev. Be sure to rest and wait for me to come back. I promise to return as soon as I can."

The Honorable L. sat on the bed beside his daughter and took her hand. She was so pale, and her hand was so cold that his heart skipped a beat, but then she opened her eyes.

"I'm so glad you came. I feel better when you're here, and Doctor Schmidt is taking such good care of me that ..."

She started coughing and couldn't complete the sentence. She took her handkerchief from under the pillow and pressed it to her lips, but not quickly enough to prevent a drop of blood from staining her immaculate blouse. Her father waited patiently for her cough to subside, stroking her hand to infuse confidence. When she fell back onto her pillows, exhausted, shutting her eyes again, he felt that his strength was about to leave him and that he had to go before his despair would become apparent.

"Do rest now. Don't strain yourself," he said, heroically managing to preserve his usual calm tone of voice. "Doctor Schmidt was emphatic that you should rest and worry about nothing." He kissed her forehead, and then he turned his head toward the nurse who had appeared in the doorframe. "Please see that she is comfortable and keep the windows open, so she has all the fresh air she needs. I'll be going now," he added, speaking to nobody in particular.

With a last glance to the bed and to the figure of his daughter that looked so small and lost in it, he strode out of the room and down the stairs, quickly out of the house and into the yard where his carriage was waiting. He clutched the vial of his daughter's blood in his pocket and imagined that he was feeling some of her life energy in his hand. He wished that he could fill it with his own, the whole of which he would gladly have relinquished to her. He climbed into the carriage without looking back. Letting others see his emotions was a luxury he could ill afford.

CHAPTER 5

Ambri, Switzerland. June 2009

A paid vacation in a lovely Swiss chalet, with all her needs taken care of and fabulous pay, they had said. Sure, Sally thought bitterly.

She sat panting in the dark, gradually overcoming the panic that had gripped her and taking control of the shivering that had jolted her out of her dreamless sleep. Her nightgown was drenched with sweat despite the cool breeze that came in through the open window. For a moment, she had trouble remembering where she was, but as her eyes adjusted to the semi-darkness, consciousness returned to her and, with it, the recollection of it all.

She had a fever; she now realized it. Her hand went almost automatically to the bottle of Tylenol that she kept by her bedside. She took two capsules and swallowed them quickly with the bit of water left in her night glass – she didn't have the strength to get up and fill it – then she lay back in bed, trying to relax and letting the drug work its usual wonders. Gradually, at the thought that Doctor Benini would come in the morning, she started to feel better. Not only would he take a look at her and perhaps prescribe something for her fever, but they would also make conversation – something she really craved. The couple who kept the house and looked after her needs were efficient and polite – perhaps even too damn "Swiss polite" – but their conversation was limited to sentences of five words with as few syllables as possible in them. Sometimes she thought that they had been instructed to bore her to death.

Sally was wide awake now, still shivering a little as the breeze played with her wet nightgown. She pulled the light blanket over her, up to her neck, and propped up against the puffy pillows. Her mind went back to two months before, and she wondered whether she had been wise to take this summer job. She had been wondering a lot about that lately ...

The ad on her university's billboard in Florence had simply said, "Students wanted for a summer-long research project. No prior experience is required. Pay above the average." A cellular phone number was the only detail given, and Sally had jotted it down, unsure whether she would call.

She wasn't planning to go back to the States for the summer, though. Her parents – and their constant bickering – were a primary reason behind her decision to travel all the way to Italy to study Art. A small fund, established for her by her late grandmother on the occasion of her birth, had provided enough funding to support her modestly for three years. Still, she needed some additional income source, or she would soon be forced to ask her parents for help, which was the one thing that she really wanted to avoid.

So she had dismissed her plans to spend the summer vacations touring Italy; instead, she had called that cellular phone number and had interviewed for the summer job. The project had turned out to be an ambitious one; the professor who had interviewed her (she couldn't remember his name) had explained it to her. The aim was to study the effect of mental stimuli on the release of chemicals by the brain into the bloodstream. To that end, she would be given selected reading material and a reading schedule, and blood samples would be taken from her weekly. Because of the need to avoid foreign factors, she would be kept isolated from others for two months, except for severely limited contacts with persons working in the project. Twenty students from all over Europe would participate in the experiment, she was told, but they would never meet or talk to each other before the study was over.

"I'm afraid that's not for me, Professor," she had said right away. "I am a social animal, you see? I need people around me."

"Would you like to hear about the pay?" the professor had inquired.

The figure he had mentioned had made Sally's head spin. It was enough to see her through graduation and then some more. She couldn't afford to let this opportunity slip away, so she had agreed to continue the process.

The next stage involved physical testing run by a physician she had since learned as Doctor Benini. She was X-rayed and had blood tests done; she was then asked to inhale a foul-tasting aerosol and exhale into a plastic bag. She had answered what had seemed like a million questions. After a tense waiting period of three weeks, the answer had come: she had been accepted into the program.

Reading the agreement had been another ordeal. Sally's Italian was good enough by then to read a textbook, but the legal language escaped her. She had no trouble understanding the penalty clause, though; the study involved high costs and, therefore, should she drop out, she would have to pay a sum that by far exceeded all she had to her name. But by then, she had gone too far and, anyway, sorely needed the money. She had signed the contract, got a small advance, and the project had started. One month had passed already, and it seemed like an eternity, but she had no choice now – she had to pull through to the end.

"Do you think that you could get me some watercolors and drawing paper?" Sally had asked Doctor Benini during his last weekly visit to her.

"What for?" he had asked with surprise.

"I feel like painting. Perhaps it's the solitude here, or the beauty of the countryside, or a combination of the two, but I got this urge to paint ..."

"Are you any good at it?" Doctor Benini had asked, smiling a strange smile.

"I don't know. I've never tried before, but I have a feeling that I should. I study art history, you know, but I'm no painter ... not yet, at least."

"I'll see what I can do," Doctor Benini had said dryly. "Take this gauze and cough into it now," he had ordered.

Sally had gazed through the window following his car as it drove away and feeling a strange anger mounting inside her. They were pampering her, true, but her wishes seemed to count for less than nothing. She felt ... misplaced. Yes, that was it: misplaced, as if she wasn't there by right. And she had no idea what she meant by that.

The Tylenol had done its job, and Sally had finally dozed off. She had reached that strange, rare state when wakefulness and dream become one when you know with the clarity of daylight that you are dreaming and that what you see is not really there. But she was there. She was in her bed, in that room, and was talking to someone who was not in the picture—a woman.

"I am not well," she said. "I feel weak."

"It's because you exerted yourself too much, Evelyn," the voice said. "You shouldn't have stayed out so long to paint."

The Sally in the bed furrowed her brow. Why was this woman calling her Evelyn? That wasn't her name. But she heard her own voice answering.

"But the painting came out well, didn't it?"

"Yes, very nice, indeed. But you should be more careful. It gets humid late in the afternoon. Promise me that you'll be more careful."

"I promise, Mommy," her voice said. Her head was too heavy and, in her dream, she fell asleep. *A dream in a dream in a dream,* she managed to think before she sank into a deeper, dreamless sleep.

CHAPTER 6

London, England. June 2009

Franco dropped his pen and eyed with dislike the little pile of unchecked exams that refused to become noticeably lower despite his hard work. He had gotten up early that morning in the hope of finishing grading all of his students' tests, but the time now was past 11 AM, and he had made little progress. He read the maxim that he had placed on the top of the questionnaire's first page: *Non pote non sapere qui se stultum intellegit* – A man must have some wit to know he is a fool. Judging by the test results, some of his students did not have enough wit to suspect how stupid they were.

He decided to make coffee and take a break before going back to his grading work. His one-bedroom apartment was comfortable for a bachelor, and he liked to keep it tidy, so he picked up the cup of the morning coffee and what remained of the chocolate-chip cake that had gone with it. The cleaning woman came twice a week, but Franco himself invested time making the place hospitable; only the day before, he had refreshed the flowers in the vase that occupied a good portion of his small tea table. He was midway to the sink when the phone rang, so he placed the cup and plate back on the round dining table that doubled as a working space and then hastened to pick up the phone.

"Franco," said Zoe's voice.

"Hi Zoe," he answered somewhat guardedly. Their last date had ended on a jarring note, and he hadn't expected to hear from her again.

"You didn't call all week," she said. She sounded accusing.

"You broke up with me, remember?"

"Listen," she said, ignoring Franco's last remark. She had the annoying habit of listening only to her side of the conversation. "You have issues. You must deal with your mother complex if we want this to work out." Zoe was a psychology graduate student and never allowed anybody to forget it.

"I don't have issues, Zoe. Give me a break, okay? And there is no 'we.' We've been through this argument already."

"Yes? Then what was all that 'I won't ruin my life as my father did to himself' crap?"

"I don't want to discuss it again, okay?"

"You're screwed, Franco. Totally."

"And why would you care? We're not together anymore."

"You're right," Zoe said after a short pause. "We aren't," she added, and then she hung up.

Franco sighed and replaced the receiver, shaking his head with regret. He did like Zoe, the last of a long string of girlfriends, in many ways. She was smart and beautiful, but love? That was out of the question. The phone rang again, and he lunged for it.

"This is persecution, Zoe. It must stop!" he said, trying to sound severe.

"Professor Lorenzi?" said an unfamiliar voice in his ear.

"Speaking," said Franco. He was embarrassed for barking at a stranger, but the conversation with Zoe had left him in a combative frame of mind in which anything was prone to annoy him, so he didn't mind sounding unwelcoming.

"Good morning. I hope I'm not calling at a bad time. My name is Kathia Ramirez, and I am with the European Cult Watch

Committee, the ECWC. I would very much like to speak with you about an urgent matter."

Lately, everybody seems to have urgent matters to discuss with me, Franco thought bitterly. He had never heard of this committee and had no particular desire to hear about it now.

"Is this some kind of survey? Because if it is, this is really not a good time ..."

"Oh, no. No survey. This is a serious matter of great concern to the European Community."

"All right then, go on," said Franco with a sigh. He resigned himself to the interruption. The sooner he let her speak, he hoped, the quicker he would get rid of her.

"This is not a matter for the telephone," she said. She now spoke in a louder voice that betrayed a slight but unmistakable Latin accent, which, given her surname, came as no surprise to Franco. "I need to speak with you in person, please."

"Okay, then. We can meet in my office tomorrow afternoon. I'll give you the address ..."

She cut him short. "I really need to speak with you urgently," she said. "I am in the neighborhood right now. May I come up to see you?"

Franco hesitated. She knew where he lived and wanted to see him immediately. That started to sound a bit creepy. "I will have to see some credentials to make sure that this is an official call ..."

"Of course, I understand your concern. I assure you that this is not a crank call and that I am indeed approaching you on official matters. You will understand when I explain. I appreciate your cooperation. I'll be there in five minutes," she added, and then she hung up.

Five minutes! She must be parked right under my window, Franco concluded. He picked up the cup and cake plate again and placed them in the sink, and then he returned to the table to organize the papers that were spread on it. He didn't have time to sit down again before the doorbell rang.

He opened the door cautiously, unsure what lay behind, and was reassured to see that his visitor was petite – almost a head shorter than he – and dressed in a gray business suit with a white shirt, as was fashionable with young London female lawyers. She was in her late twenties or early thirties, with black hair and dark eyes that contrasted with her light complexion. She was smiling.

"Hello, Professor Lorenzi," she said. "Here is my badge."

Franco took the document that she was handing to him and glanced at it quickly. It was an official-looking document with the European Union's seal. He decided that, at least provisionally, he had no reason to doubt its genuineness. He handed it back to her, feeling embarrassed for keeping her on the mat while he inspected it.

"Please, do come in," he said with belated politeness. "Would you like some coffee?" he asked after closing the door behind them.

"Oh, I don't want to inconvenience you."

"I was just about to make some when the phone rang. Please take a seat while I brew it."

It took Franco five minutes to come back and sit down in the armchair next to the sofa where the young woman had seated herself, armed with coffee cups and more cake. He had felt self-conscious in the tiny space of his apartment, with her surely watching his every move as he made coffee. The atmosphere was tense, and he sipped his coffee without looking at her.

"I appreciate your agreeing to see me at such short notice," she said, speaking in a conciliatory tone. "And you make great coffee," she added, smiling.

"I'm Italian, so I better make decent coffee," he said, joining in the effort to lighten up the atmosphere. "Now, could you please tell me what this is all about?"

"Of course. What do you know about the ECWC?"

"Nothing, really. I've never heard of it."

"It is an organ that was established in nineteen-ninety-eight by the European Parliament's Civil Liberties and Internal Affairs Committee, following a report it produced addressing various problematic aspects of dangerous cults. I assume that you're familiar with the fact that many different cults have been spreading throughout Europe in the last decades. Some of them are innocuous, but others are deadly, such as the Europe's Solar Temple cult. You may remember that in nineteen-ninety-four more than sixty members of that cult were induced to mass suicide in France and Switzerland."

She paused for a moment, apparently to gauge Franco's response.

"I think I read something about it a few years ago, but I can't remember the details," said Franco.

"Many other examples of dangerous cults have been reviewed by the committee – which are not known to the general public – and the conclusion was that a pan-European effort was needed to investigate them and to preempt any acts of mass folly by their members. That's why the ECWC was formed. The committee reports to the European Parliament committee. It cooperates with other law enforcement agencies, such as the FBI and Interpol.

"Five years ago, the ECWC realized that to deal with certain more acute situations that cannot be fought by education and administrative measures alone, an organ with broader powers and means was needed. That's when the department to which I belong was formed. Its existence is not publicized, and most of our work is done under cover. We deal with the most dangerous organizations and with the more complex situations."

"This is all very interesting," said Franco, "but I still can't understand why you are telling me all this. I know nothing of any cults, and in fact, I've never heard of one in the university where I teach. I'm afraid you've got hold of the wrong person."

The young woman's smile disappeared, making her look at once older; she put down the coffee cup with which she had been toying, her back stiffened, and her voice took on an official timbre.

"Quite the contrary. We know that you were contacted by Sir James Easby two days ago. Is that correct?"

"You obviously know it is," said Franco. This breach of his privacy irritated him, and he grew aggressive. "But what is this? Have you been spying on me?"

"I can see that you're upset, and I understand you but please calm down; nobody is spying on you, but Easby has been under surveillance for quite some time now. That's how we came to know about your meeting."

"You can barely call that a meeting. He came to see me, and we had tea; that's all that there is to it. Why are you following him? As I understand it from looking him up on the web, he is some kind of benefactor. What business do you have tailing him?"

"I'm not at liberty to disclose details right now. I can tell you that Easby is one of the key persons in an organization – potentially a cult – that is currently rated as extremely dangerous. We believe that he has contacted you to further the interests of that organization. This could be very dangerous for you if you got in the way of those fanatics."

Franco put down his cup, and his face brightened. He now saw that he had been wronging this well-meaning public servant.

"Wow! That's really something. Well, thank you very much for warning me. I would never have suspected him of foul play. He is such a distinguished old gentleman ... anyway, now that I know, I will avoid him, and if ... when he calls me again as he said he would, I'll tell him to stay away from me. I really appreciate your committee's work and your efforts in coming all the way to warn me."

"Yes ... But that's not why I have come to you. In fact, we want you to get involved with Easby and learn as much as you can about what he is doing."

Franco gazed at her incredulously.

"You must be kidding!" he uttered at last. "I don't work for you, you know."

"Not yet, but we were hoping that you would," she said. She spoke as if that were a natural thing to say, and, exploiting Franco's speechlessness, she continued. "You see, we need inside information to find out what Easby's cult is up to, and you are the perfect candidate to help us because you have been chosen by Easby, so you are above suspicion."

Franco got up and took a step back. He gesticulated as he spoke. "Do you hear what you're saying? You want me to get involved with what you imply may be a bunch of murderous lunatics. And why would I want to do that? You must leave, please."

Kathia Ramirez gazed up at him without showing any sign of leaving. She spoke patiently as if talking to a child.

"Would you please sit down? It's hard on my neck to speak to you looking up."

She paused and waited for Franco to sit down, which he did after a moment's hesitation, and then she continued. "I could give you many reasons why you would agree to help us. For instance, the Home Secretary is always supportive of our efforts, and a word from us would suffice to end your work in the UK – but I would not use such that leverage on you. I could also appeal to your sense of justice and tell you that you are in a unique position to help us in our worthwhile war against evil. But the truth is that you have an excellent reason to help us out, an extremely good personal reason. This cult needs you badly for reasons unknown to us so far – the fact that Easby himself has contacted you is a clear sign of your importance – and they will never leave you alone. If you don't cooperate, they will get what they need from you, whatever that is, by force, and I can assure you that it won't be pretty. If you go to them without our support and try to cooperate, they will be happy but may choose to dispose of you at the end, when you have outlived your usefulness."

She paused again for effect and avoided looking straight at Franco, who had sunk deeply in the armchair, absorbing her words. When he said nothing and the silence became too oppressive, she put out her hand and touched his knee. He raised his head and focused his alarmed gaze on her face.

"I'm sorry, but I had to tell you the truth," she said, speaking for the first time in a less authoritative tone. "And now you can see that working with us is your best chance of getting through this unscathed. Do you understand?"

"Look here, Ms. Ramirez ..."

"Kathia," she interjected

"I'm not saying that I'm buying your story. It all sounds like a fib – cults, murder, old gentlemen turning into thugs ... I'm willing to listen some more, but you'll need to convince me."

"I assure you that all I'm telling you is real, and so is the danger to you. Please assume that I will be able to produce convincing proof that I am a genuine agent, working in a European law-enforcement agency, okay?" Franco nodded, and she continued, "So let's skip that part and get down to the important issues, Agreed?"

Franco nodded, resigned to the need to deal with this unexpected twist in his life. "Tell me more," he said, speaking as in a dream.

"It's like this ..." she began.

CHAPTER 7

London, England. June 2009

Kathia had to make an effort to keep her annoyance from showing. It had taken her much more than anticipated to convince this subject to cooperate once the initial shock had passed. She felt that Franco was being obsessive with his questions and all the "what ifs," but on the other hand, his frightened, needy behavior was sort of cute and made her want to protect him in a motherly kind of way. Until he became insistent and demanded to meet with Authority, that is. True, he was gentlemanly enough about it, and the reasons he gave for it were definitely plausible. Still, it was plain that he thought her too young and too feminine to be trusted – the macho pig!

She had had no choice but to call Richard Hawthorne, her liaison at Scotland Yard, and tell him that he would have visitors. Richard had been less than enthusiastic on the phone, adding to Kathia's general annoyance.

"I need to come and see you with Professor Lorenzi," she had said.

"Why?" he had asked dryly.

"He wishes to make sure that the operation that I am supervising has all the official support it needs."

"So what am I, the official spokesman? Yours? You know I'm swamped, and I don't have the time to chat with your friends. I couldn't find the time even if I thought that this was really important, but you know how I feel about it, so please take your professor elsewhere."

Kathia listened to this tirade, smiling all the time but tightening her cell phone to her ear to prevent the sound of Richard's voice from getting through to Franco.

"Thanks, Richard," she said, still smiling. "I appreciate your making the time to see us at short notice. We will be there in half an hour."

"Kathia ..." he tried to protest, but she hung up.

"Richard is a great chap," she said in a tone meant to reassure. "Let's go."

At Scotland Yard, they had to walk along a seemingly endless corridor. The last office, located in a quiet and dark corner, had a sign that said, "Superintendent Richard Hawthorne, International Operations Coordinator." Kathia knocked once and unceremoniously opened the door without waiting for an invitation to come in. A small, stocky man of about forty in a dark suit jumped up from behind a desk that overflowed with stacks of documents. His hair was meticulously combed. One immediately noticed that his hands were manicured; he obviously was particular about his appearance. He looked grumpy, but that did not deter Kathia from being sociable.

"Richard, dear, this is Professor Lorenzi."

The two men shook hands in silence, and Richard pointed to the chairs in a resigned invitation to his visitors to sit down.

"What can I do for you, Professor?" Richard asked.

"Please, call me Franco ... I'm not here as a teacher. In fact, I don't really know why I'm here. I know, I've heard the official explanation, but I find it hard to digest. I'd like to know what protection Scotland Yard can give me, and what is my official position as an alien resident in this country if this thing ... this so-called operation, creates any complications, legal or otherwise."

"Kathia ... you are more familiar with all the details, and perhaps you should be the one to explain what assurances are needed from us."

"I have explained everything to Franco – I too can call you Franco, right? And please, call me Kathia," she said, and when Franco nodded in assent, she continued. "As you know, we suspect James Easby to be one of the leaders of a dangerous cult that may already be responsible for murder. We want Franco to play along with them, to learn what they're up to, and give us as much information as possible, so we can stop them in time from doing whatever they're planning to do. Things may move very fast, and we have no control over it because we are clueless regarding their plans. All we have are bits of information received from anonymous informants."

"You see, Franco," said Hawthorne, speaking slowly, almost measuring each word, "Scotland Yard is not really active in this operation, which is run by Kathia's European organization. I have many other tasks and operations on my hands," he added, throwing a significant glance at Kathia, "and I don't intervene unless a need arises."

"That's all very well," said Franco, showing signs of impatience, "but what concerns me is my personal safety and how you are going to guarantee it."

"Kathia here is in constant contact with us and with police departments in other European countries, and we are here to assist, as well as to monitor her operation to ensure that everything is done legally and according to proper procedures. I have the power to use our resources according to my own judgment to serve these purposes. If you ever need our protection, Kathia will get in touch with us to obtain the required resources."

Hawthorne was clearly being evasive on purpose. Kathia was exasperated and could have kicked him. Instead, she decided to get Franco out of there before the conversation took an even worse turn. She got up and said to Franco, "I think you've got the assurances you wanted, and we shouldn't be imposing on Richard's time anymore. Let's go back to your apartment and get down to work."

Franco nodded, not looking really convinced. He got up heavily, thanked Hawthorne for his time, and followed Kathia out of the office.

In his office, Richard Hawthorne stood in silence behind his desk for two full minutes after the door closed behind his departing guests. Then he sank into his chair, picked up the phone, and dialed a number.

"They just left," he said, speaking quietly into the mouthpiece. "She has made things more complicated."

Without waiting for an answer, he hung up and then lay back in his chair. He closed his eyes. He could feel his migraine coming back to hit him with full power, herald to bigger headaches that, he knew for sure, awaited him.

CHAPTER 8

Udine, Italy. June 1894

The Honorable L. dropped the pen on the writing-table and sat back with a sigh. His hand hurt from the muscles' tension and from the pressure that he had applied to the pen without even noticing. He felt exhausted, both physically and mentally, and winced when the Cecchi woman spread drying powder on the page, and he saw how the tiny crystals became tinged with his daughter's blood that had been mixed with the ink.

She seemed satisfied that the page was dry. After shaking and blowing away the powder, she stood beside him and read slowly and silently. Every now and then, she would nod in approval. The Honorable L. was convinced that unless he kept his gaze on her at some point, she would smile and, for whatever reason, he found the thought unbearable. But he knew that he had to keep his anger to himself.

"Why the blood?" he asked.

"To help make the connection."

"What does that mean?"

"It means," she explained, speaking patiently, "that when the day comes to connect with your daughter and to pass healing strength on to her, someone will have to reach out to her from the future. He will have your letter, and the instructions, both written in her blood, which will help him or her make a connection. You understand?"

"I hear what you say."

"Good. The letter is just fine," Mrs. Cecchi said. "You can simply copy it."

"Why do we need a second copy?" he asked, not for the first time, but this time he got an answer.

"We must make sure that the letter is found. It may not be sufficient to have it sealed at City Hall, so we need another place to leave a second copy. The first copy of the letter doesn't give me sufficient vibrations to tell me it will be found for sure. I'll have to find an appropriate place for the second copy ..."

"What kind of place?"

"I don't know yet. Please, let's waste no more time now. Every minute may be critical."

The Honorable L. took the letter that she was handing him and placed it beside the writing paper. His expression was inscrutable as he picked up the pen and dipped it into the bloody ink. Inside, he was in turmoil, torn between the hope that this witchcraft would work and his practical and logical nature that told him to expect nothing at all from it. Evelyn's round face that maintained its childlike features despite her twenty-six years of age, with her smooth and milky-white skin, kept haunting his vision. In the last few weeks, she had grown thinner. Her skin had surrendered that baby-face look to her illness and exchanged it for a haggard, unhealthy complexion. However, he still continued to see her as before and worried about the significance of that vision. Was he already saving an image to be cherished when she would no longer be there for him to see? Was he already giving her up? He chased those thoughts away constantly, but they kept coming back to plague him.

He read the letter's words as if they had been written by somebody else. Then he transcribed them onto the clean paper in his neat, angular handwriting.

Sir,

When you read these words, I will be long dead. However, it is in your power to save a life if you can bring yourself to believe what I know is true – that the present and past are interconnected and that your Actions can mend the trouble of the past. I beg you, Sir, to keep reading to the end, with an open mind and heart, and to enjoy the power of Life over death, of defeating death and donating Life, and to rejoice in the incomparable power that you will acquire.

This I beg you to hear ...

"This is black magic," the Honorable L. muttered almost to himself. He put the pen down and gazed ahead, straight in front of him, to a point infinitely far away.

"This is the only hope you have to save your daughter," said the Cecchi woman viciously, breathing heavily down his neck from behind.

The Honorable L. turned around and gave her a frosty look that made her take a quick step back. No matter what was at stake, certain lines would not be crossed, and liberties would not be taken.

"I know, and I am doing what it takes even though it is burning what remains of my soul. But don't you expect me to like it ... or you. And don't worry, I'll do what I have to do, and you will get your reward."

"You understand that results may not be immediately evident, and the ball is in two weeks ..."

"I know. I gave you my word as a gentleman that you and your daughter will be invited to it, and that should suffice."

He spoke haughtily, without attempting to hide his distaste at the need to discuss such matters with her. Without waiting for a reaction from her, he picked up the pen again and started writing. Two lines down, he paused for a moment and said again, pointedly, "This is black magic," and then he kept on writing.

CHAPTER 9

London, England. June 2009

Kathia Ramirez was thirty-three years old. She was born in Barcelona to a Russian mother who had married a Catalonian architect. Her parents had two daughters, Kathia and Clarisa, one year younger than Kathia. The family had lived happily and comfortably until seventeen-year-old Clarisa had gone on a summer trip to Austria, never to return. The police had traced her movements until she left Vienna with a forty-five-year-old self-proclaimed messiah and three other girls of various ages. A two-month-long chase had ended at the outskirts of a small village, in the house he had rented under an assumed identity, when one morning, called in by the neighbors, the police found that he had shot his four concubines, his two dogs, and a cat, and had disappeared. People who had met him said that he had a magnetic, hypnotic personality and truly believed that God was talking to him. He had never been found, and the police believed that he had climbed the nearby mountains and found his death in some crevasse there.

Kathia's family fell apart after her sister's murder and her parents separated. Whether consciously or not, she decided to devote herself to fighting the particular brand of evil that had destroyed her once idyllic world; she went to study criminology in London, away from her parents, but returned to Spain and enrolled in the local police where she earned immediate respect from her superiors. She had joined the ECWC in its early days with one mission in mind: to crack down on dangerous cults anywhere. And she would not use half-measures while doing it.

Kathia knew more about Easby than she would admit to Franco – or, at least, she thought she knew. However, the bulk of her knowledge could only be inferred from bits and pieces of information. Franco worried her; he was so gentle, so ... vulnerable that she wondered how much she should tell him. She had to balance his need to know so as to be able to appreciate important information when he saw it, with the danger that he would freak out when he heard what he was letting himself in for. She wondered about him; he surely was bright – he had to be, to become a professor – but that was no guarantee that he would behave sensibly at the right time. And judging by the way he had reacted when she had told him about the possible dangers, she feared that he was perhaps spineless as well. Those were idle thoughts anyway since she had no better option.

Coming back from Scotland Yard, they parked close to his apartment and sat in the car.

"Are you hungry?" she asked.

"Famished, really. You?"

"I wouldn't mind a bite of something." She hadn't realized how hungry she was until she had asked the question.

"I know a little restaurant nearby. It's not expensive, and I eat there sometimes. Would you like to ..." Franco hesitated.

"I'd love to, but we can't," she hastened to say. "We must not be seen together in public because that could put you in danger. I think that Easby's people don't know me, but you can never be sure. You will think I'm fresh, but perhaps you can fix us something in your apartment?"

"I'd be happy to, really, but I don't have any real food, only cakes, and stuff. I never eat at home; most of the time, I eat at the university or at that restaurant I was mentioning."

"That leaves us only one choice, then." She switched on the engine and shifted into gear. "I'll fix us lunch at my place. Don't expect anything fancy," she warned him. "The apartment belongs to the ECWC, and it's rather bare, but I've got food there."

She smiled encouragingly as she drove through the traffic, and Franco sank back in his seat without speaking. He was sort of lifeless, Kathia thought as if he was past caring. Something would have to be done about that.

Franco moved around in the small living room, fidgeting with the few articles scattered around and waiting impatiently for Kathia to return. She had disappeared into her bedroom to change into something more comfortable, and he was ill at ease in the unfamiliar surroundings. Kathia's apartment was only slightly larger than his own and much less hospitable, he thought, but that came as no surprise; after all, it was an impersonal service apartment.

Kathia returned before he grew too impatient. She had changed into blue jeans and a flowery blouse that made her look both younger and less threatening.

"I'm a messy cook," she said, sounding apologetic, "and I can't spare a business suit."

"Don't worry about me; I don't care about conventions and political correctness," said Franco.

"Good," said Kathia. She pulled dishes from a small refrigerator without wasting any time and rejected Franco's polite offer to help. In ten minutes, the microwave oven produced a quite reasonable stew. They sat at a small Formica dining table. Kathia poured wine, and they ate in silence, neither one trying to make conversation. As soon as the hunger had been taken care of, Kathia got up.

"Can I get you something else, or should we get down to business?" she asked.

"No, thank you. That was very good. I'm full."

Kathia sat down again, pushed her plate aside, and leaned forward conspiratorially. "Okay, so here's what we are asking you to do. When Easby contacts you, we want you to play along with him. We need you to find out what he and his cult are up to, and we need you there with them to pass that information on to us in real-time or as close to real-time as possible. You must be very careful not to sound too eager to please them because that will immediately arouse suspicion. You must sound skeptical but open-minded. You need to take your time converting to whatever conviction they are going to sell you. Once you have converted, you must come across as an enthusiast – that's essential because if they feel that your faith in what you're doing is faltering, your life will be in danger. These cults have no room or compassion for wavering members. Once again, you must be extremely careful to avoid being overzealous because that will immediately spark suspicion. Do you think that you can do that?"

"I ... I don't know. I've never engaged in deception, which is what you're asking me to do now. I will have to weigh my options. If anything develops, I will obviously do my best, but first, I must be sure that if something goes wrong, you'll get me out of there."

"You will have to memorize two cellular phone numbers: mine, which is the first one you should call, and Richard Hawthorne's, which you should call if for any reason you can't reach me. We can't risk having you wired because if they find a bug on you ..."

She didn't complete the sentence, but its significance got across to Franco clearly, and he winced.

"Now for the difficult part," she continued, speaking softly as if to cushion the blow that the hardness of the facts could give him. "We don't know what they're planning, but obviously human lives may be in danger, and you may be asked to take part in activities that may endanger, or even harm, a person. You will have to use your own judgment, and sometimes you may need to go along with acts that you will find repulsive because otherwise, you will blow your cover. In fact, we can expect them to test you with some rather extreme situations to see if you're acting or if your faith in their cause is firm. You will not be found legally responsible for anything you do while working for us under cover, but of course, there is a limit to that too. Again, it will have to be a judgment call on your part."

"It's a hell of a choice that you're giving me here. Either behave like an insane fanatic or get myself killed. Wonderful!"

Kathia got closer to Franco, put a hand on his arm reassuringly, and spoke with a warmth that wasn't all an act. "I understand that you're upset right now since all this is new to you, but you're bright, and you're honest, and I'm sure that you'll do a great job. And when all this is over, you will be proud, very proud of yourself for helping us fight the forces of darkness on which this cult feeds."

Franco shook his head, swallowed twice to ease the dryness in his throat, and got up. "I'll go home now," he said moodily, "if you don't mind taking me."

He needed time to let everything sink in. He realized that perhaps he had no choice, but no one was going to make him like it.

CHAPTER 10

London, England. June 2009

James Easby beckoned to his old friend, Arturo Benini, who closed the door quietly behind him and approached without speaking. He joined him, standing next to the glass case that housed The Letter. They stood in silence, watching Maria and the precious document that she held between her fat fingers. She had taken it out of the case but wasn't reading it; her eyes were shut, and the large armchair in which she sat had room barely enough for her heavy body, which bulged from it at spots. Her lips moved as if in silent prayer, showing her missing front tooth and swaying two thick, long white hairs that protruded from her chin. Easby found her extremely distasteful but knew that she was a necessary evil and that they had to put up with her.

"She gives me the creeps," whispered Benini.

"Shh ...," Easby admonished him.

They watched her for a few more minutes, without moving or making a noise, and only relaxed when she stirred and opened her eyes.

"It's not time yet," she said, speaking with a heavy Italian accent.

"What did you see?" asked Easby, speaking softly and invitingly.

"I told you, it's not time yet."

"But when ...," Benini intervened.

"*Sono stanca*. I'm tired now," she said.

Without giving either man a glance, she got up, dropped the paper on top of the glass case, and walked ponderously out of the room. As soon as the door closed behind her, Easby picked up the letter, holding it carefully, almost reverently by one edge, and put it back in the glass case.

"How long are we going to stand her? When is she going to give us some practical help?" asked Benini when his friend's attention turned back to him.

"I might ask you that question. You know her better than I," Easby reminded him. "You are the one who brought her here."

"I know, I know. I'm not questioning the need to keep her, but I can't help feeling that she's taking advantage of her position and playing with us."

Easby turned his head to hide his worried expression and studied his friend from the corner of his eye. Benini was the initiator of the Evelyn Project and a vital link in the delicate chain of events that would lead to success. He could not be allowed to lose faith in their quest. He had to be encouraged. Pep talks were Easby's turf, and he was used to showing the way to those who lost sight of the goals.

"So far, she has been reliable, Arturo. I don't think that you have anything to worry about. All the facts in the letter that her mother passed on to her, and everything else she has given us, checked out. I have no reason to doubt her. True, she's not my cup of tea – or yours – but we need her."

"Unfortunately ..."

"Yes, unfortunately. So now tell me, how's our surrogate doing?"

"She's proceeding according to plan. The latest lab results show that the disease has reached an advanced stage. Fevers have started to appear, and she attributes them to a bad spell of the flu. I've given her palliatives, but soon she'll start noticing blood when she coughs, and then she'll begin to worry. That's why I'm getting edgy. We don't have much time, and Maria behaves as if she had all the time in the world. I'm pretty sure that she knows more than she's telling us. Besides, why can't we go ahead when we are ready? I see no reason to wait for her permission to proceed."

"And who's going to make contact, Arturo? You know as well as I do that she's essential to the project. We don't have the time to find someone else that is good enough to take her place."

Easby remained pensive for a while and then showed his resolute character, the exact trait that made him a born leader, whose leadership so many people accepted unreservedly.

"I'll tell you what we'll do, Arturo. We won't wait for Maria to give us the sign. After all, it's our project as she's merely a piece in the game. We'll effectively start with Stage Three. I'll step up the recruiting of Franco Lorenzi so we'll be ready when the time comes. I'm sure that when Maria sees that we are going ahead, she'll stop acting like a prima donna and will start being a team player."

"Great idea, James! I'll feel much better knowing that we have him on board. I have to go now. Talk to you tomorrow."

Easby watched with concern how his friend's back looked bent as he left. He hoped that he wasn't cracking. They simply could not afford any weakness on that point. Still, he realized that the responsibility that weighed on Benini's shoulders was tremendous and that only the faith in the righteousness of what they were doing helped him bear it. That faith could not be allowed to falter.

CHAPTER 11

Rome, Italy. June 2009

The tall man stood in the shade of the bus that disgorged a mass of camera-crazed tourists, ready to tackle yet another Rome church. He watched the sweaty mass with dislike, and only after the human serpent started streaming through the church's doors did he stir and walk quickly to join it.

His back was slightly bent in an automatic attempt to belittle his height to avoid standing out in the crowd – a habit that he had acquired early in his life and that now, at the age of sixty-one, was second nature to him. He fell naturally in step with the elderly couples that whispered their admiration of the majestic ceiling and of the beautiful stained glass to one another until he reached a roped opening with the sign "Keep Out," which blocked the access to a short and poorly lit flight of stairs. With the natural nonchalance of someone who had done it many times before, he slid behind the rope and walked quickly down the stairs. He stopped for a moment before an antique wooden door that seemed too low for him to consider opening, and then he turned the handle and passed through it, head down.

The room was bare; a small table and two uncomfortable-looking wooden chairs were the only furniture if one didn't count the slanted candlestick with five freshly lit candles that added little to the pale light shed by a solitary light bulb that hung from the ceiling. A strong smell of incense thickened the air and almost turned it into a living thing. He knew that the other door of the room led into the church's inner meanders, and he noticed with a quick glance that it was closed.

The room had nothing attractive in it, but Heinrich von Stoffen loved it. It was where many of his business transactions with the Vatican Bank had taken place – those which the bank officials didn't care to have generally known – and had helped him amass a considerable fortune. He had done very well and had become a rich man – but not nearly as rich as he would be once the deal that he had carefully planned for a year now went through. If it did go through, he mused bitterly. The bank had grown careful lately. Its officials were under close scrutiny, which seemed to be turning everything from a set of simple processes into a heap of insurmountable obstacles.

The echo of steps coming from outside heralded Monsignor Le Fevre's arrival and von Stoffen got ready to greet him. Although it would have been exaggerated to call it a "friendship," the relationship that had developed between the two men over the years was one of mutual respect and sympathy. Le Fevre's rise to a position of power within the Vatican had clearly been aided by the successful deals that he and von Stoffen had concocted together when Le Fevre was still a relatively junior officer of the Vatican Bank. Their relationship had worked out well for both of them. The years had helped them develop mutual trust, although von Stoffen had no illusions about the ultimate strength of their ties; he knew that Le Fevre's loyalty was due elsewhere.

The door opened, and Monsignor Le Fevre walked in with a welcoming smile and an outstretched hand.

"My friend ... good to see you," he said, with a genuine ring of pleasure in his voice.

"Good to see you too," von Stoffen echoed. "It's been a while ..."

"Yes," Le Fevre acknowledged quietly. He gestured toward the table, and they both sat down on bare wooden benches that allowed no room for comfort. Without more small talk, the conversation turned to business.

"I got your message, and I gather that the matter is urgent," Le Fevre prompted von Stoffen.

"Yet, it is. My current contact at the bank is not moving forward, and I need your help. As you know, the deal on the table is one of great impact, and time is of the essence. I don't know what's keeping him from going ahead, but it can't wait much longer."

"The situation is very delicate," said Le Fevre, gazing at von Stoffen and smiling in a way that contradicted his statement. "I can't blame him for being cautious; you know that the bank is being watched very closely these days. But I'll make inquiries and see what I can do."

Von Stoffen eyed him in silence for a moment and then made an impatient gesture with his hand. He wasn't buying Le Fevre's distanced attitude.

"Pardon my bluntness," he said, "but I know you well enough to be sure that you already have all the details at your fingertips. Very little escapes your attention where Vatican business is concerned."

"You're right ... as usual," Le Fevre said, smiling. "The truth is that there is something we ... you can do to get things moving. It has to do with the information you gave me during our last meeting."

"Easby's silly quest? I just related it to you as a curiosity. What relation may that have to the deal that I'm proposing?"

"Well, no direct relation, of course. But the Holy See is concerned. Very concerned. The sentiment is that this heresy must be stopped at all costs."

"I'm not following you ..."

"That's because you're not a true believer," said Le Fevre, smiling again. "Your tale elicited much interest in the Vatican. After I related it higher up, I was asked to institute additional inquiries, which I did – it doesn't matter how," he added, when von Stoffen tried to articulate a question, "I have channels and friends. The information is scarce, but one thing is clear: we are talking resurrection, at least in a sense. This is something that is solely in the hands of God. No mortal can presume to play with life and death. But here we have an organization seeking to prove that mere individuals hold the key to changing the time of your death. Can't you see why the Holy See would be concerned?"

"You know, I'm really flabbergasted. I have been a member of Easby's inner circle for years now. Still, my knowledge doesn't go particularly deeply into his activity. He's always secretive, I believe, because many of his so-called projects are crazy, stupid New Age ideas that don't have a leg to stand on, so he keeps them secret to avoid ridicule. On the other hand, he has the money, and if he wants to blow it on these half-witted propositions, that's his privilege. That's how it is, and you shouldn't be making more of his project than there is to it. I really had no idea that you would take it so seriously – I mean, I told you about it because I thought that it would be an interesting piece of information for the Church, simply as a good joke – but aren't you overreacting? After all, when Easby fails and makes a fool of himself, that will be the end of it, so why worry?"

Le Fevre got up. His countenance had turned severe and cold during von Stoffen's tirade, and he placed his hands on the table and leaned forward, gazing straight into his eyes. His following words were almost whispered: "And what if he succeeds?" he asked.

Von Stoffen felt an inexplicable chill running along his spine. He was tough and seasoned, but something in Le Fevre's reaction was scary. He got up and faced him, scanning his expression to try to understand what he was hiding behind it.

"You can't be serious!" he said, at last.

"Can't I?" retorted Le Fevre. "In the Vatican's archives, we have records of events dating back to the fifteenth and the sixteenth centuries, which seem to indicate otherwise. We keep those archives carefully sealed to the outside world. True, reports of witchcraft written during those centuries are not very reliable, but we can't take chances."

"I still don't get it. Why would this have any practical impact?"

"I'll explain. Assume that I was to set up an organization that proved its ability to lengthen life. I would then undertake to lengthen yours by setting up a project to be carried out in the future when we know what you would have died of. At that time, my organization would undertake to reverse the process and cure you of the illness that was supposed to kill you. I am sure that you would agree to give my organization all your possessions, at the time of your 'final' death, in return for its services, wouldn't you?"

"I assume so."

"That organization would become the most potent body on Earth – much more potent than the Church or any government."

"But why would I believe that you would really lengthen my life and save me from illness?"

"Easby would have the results of his current project to prove it and, besides, what would you have to lose? The organization would get your money only when you died and on conditions. For instance, there would have to be a serious illness in your past, of which you were cured. That description fits people worth billions today, who would donate their money under contractual obligation even if they were skeptical because it couldn't be proven that the whole thing was a fraud."

"So what are you saying?"

"I'm saying that we want this folly stopped, right now and for good. You seem to be best positioned to stop it, and if you deliver, your deal with the Vatican Bank will go through."

"Are you sure?" asked von Stoffen. "Can I count on that?"

"I have the authority to promise that to you. And you know that I always make good on my word."

"In that case, consider it stopped," said von Stoffen without hesitation.

Le Fevre's expression relaxed, and he smiled again. "I knew that we could count on you. But won't your associates give you trouble? I gathered from what you said in the past that Sir Easby is tough."

"Yes, but I know how to handle him. He trusts me," he said and laughed a little laugh.

"The poor sinner," said Le Fevre, smiling conspiratorially.

"It has happened in the past that people who worked against rightful interests got involved in an accident," said von Stoffen. He wanted Le Fevre to understand that he would do whatever it took. The Vatican Bank deal was too important to him.

"That's because, as I said, you're not a true believer. If, as you say, the person was working for the forces of darkness, it certainly was the Divine Providence that took care of it, not a mere chance accident. It was meant to be." He paused and nodded as if to emphasize the truth of his statement to himself. "You see," he added, "it's so much easier to understand the world when you have faith; and to come to terms with the results, no matter how sad."

"I understand," said von Stoffen. He found their conversation amusing. This man of the cloth was telling him that he didn't mind any dark deeds, as long as they suited his purpose, and had found an engaging way to let him know that. "Yes, the Divine Providence ... I can relate to that," he said at last. He had the habit of skirting religious issues. A Lutheran by birth, he wasn't a religious man, and theology meant little to him. He had always thought it wiser to keep that detail to himself when dealing with his associates at the Vatican, though; he had a feeling that it was better that way.

CHAPTER 12

London, England. June 2009

Franco picked up the telephone automatically without taking his attention away from the galleys of a paper that he was already late returning. His life had gone back almost to normal in the last few days; he hadn't heard from Easby and hoped not to hear from him again, and aside from a sporadic phone call to check on him, Kathia had thankfully left him alone.

"Good morning, Professor Lorenzi," said the voice in his ear. "This is James Easby. I hope I'm not disturbing you ..."

Franco's heart quickened its pace, and he sat up straight, dropping the galleys on the table. He had to breathe slowly and deeply to regain his composure.

"Oh, ah ... yes, of course. Good morning, Mr. Easby. Yes ... no, I'm doing routine work," he said finally. "You're not disturbing me at all," he added after a brief pause in a belated attempt at politeness.

"Good, good. I'd hate to intrude. As a matter of fact, I must apologize for taking off so hastily last time. I wanted to make amends for my rude behavior ..."

"You weren't rude ..." Franco tried to interject, but Easby went on without acknowledging the interruption.

"It was terribly rude of me to leave you all alone in that tea house, so I thought to myself, how can I make it up to Professor Lorenzi? Luckily, the opportunity presents itself. I am hosting a small party this weekend – Thursday through Sunday – at my country house in Yorkshire. It will be a very selective company, you know; intellectuals, scientists, and such like, and I'm sure you would enjoy it. I apologize for the short notice, but it was a spontaneous affair. A friend of mine suggested it only yesterday – she's a French actress, a charming young lady, you will like her – so I made a few phone calls. What do you say?"

"I ... I don't know what to say. I thank you, of course, but I don't know ... I'm not a party person, and I would probably bore your guests stiff."

"Nonsense, nonsense. A learned man like you can only add to the richness of the company and our weekend's enjoyment. Besides, that would allow us to talk and provide more details to you of the humanitarian project that I am chairing, which, as you recall, we discussed briefly. Time is running out on our attempts to help that relative of yours, so we need to step up our efforts. Of course, that includes making full disclosure to you and seeing whether you are willing to help. I would really take it as a personal favor if you were to accept my invitation."

"Well then ..."

"Capital. Capital. We look forward to seeing you on Thursday, then. I will send my driver to pick you up, say at noon?"

"Noon sounds right," Franco said feebly.

"From your home or from your office?"

"From my office. Yes, definitely." The last thing that Franco wanted was to give Easby the address of his apartment, but then he probably already had it, he thought bitterly.

"I look forward to seeing you," said Easby and hung up.

Franco replaced the receiver and then sat in his chair, feeling emptied of all strength. He didn't want to go anywhere near Easby but didn't know what else to do. What would happen to him if he refused? Would Easby have him kidnapped? And if he went, would he be in danger? He had to talk to Kathia. He went to the public phone down the hall and dialed the number that she had made him memorize. He thought that the precautions she had made him swear to take were silly, but on the other hand, he was growing paranoid on account of all her tales. The possibility that Easby could have bugged his phone made a chill run down his spine each time he thought of it. Kathia answered after the second ring. "What's the matter, Franco?" she asked.

Franco related his conversation with Easby and was annoyed to note the enthusiasm in Kathia's voice.

"That's great, Franco! That's a great opportunity. Probably at least some of the other guests, if not everybody, will be a member of the cult, and you'll be able to identify them to us."

"But I don't want to go. Do I have to spell that out for you?"

"You know that you don't have a choice," said Kathia flatly. "We've gone through it before, and we don't have time for petty arguments now."

"Can I make an excuse that won't raise suspicion? A touch of the flu or something?"

"No, you can't, and besides, this could be a one-time opportunity, and we can't waste it. But cheer up! Easby is well known for his great parties, and I'm sure that you'll have a good time. You have two days to get used to the idea, which is plenty. I'll stop by your apartment tonight to brief you, okay?"

"I guess so," said Franco moodily and hung up.

Kathia double-checked her cell phone to make sure that she was no longer connected, and then she turned to Richard Hawthorne.

"You were saying before your phone rang ..." he prompted her.

"I was saying, why didn't you tell me about this?"

"This" was a newspaper that Kathia had dropped on Hawthorne's desk, on which she had circled a headline.

"What am I, 'Information'? Am I supposed to help you read your newspapers? Is there anything else that you want me to do for you," he continued. "Perhaps I could pick up your laundry for you?"

"Don't you play dumb with me, Richard!" Kathia almost yelled. "I'm sure you know all about this 'Man's Body Found in Canal' incident. It says here, 'South Yorkshire Police today confirmed the body had been formally identified as Charles Brown.' You know who Charles Brown is," she stated accusingly.

"I'm sorry to disappoint you, but I don't. Do you care to check the United Kingdom's telephone guide and tell me how many Charles Browns you can find? Why should I know anything special about this particular Charles Brown?"

"Because that name is on the ECWC list of the known members of James Easby's cult, and because the newspaper says that he drowned at least three weeks ago and because that's when we stopped getting inside tips. I bet that Charles Brown was our anonymous informant."

"Your guess is as good as mine. Assuming that you're right though, which I don't think, what difference does that make?"

"It makes a hell of a lot of difference if you're withholding information from me. And it means that Easby is becoming more dangerous, that something is cooking that we don't know about."

"Come on, you know I'm not withholding anything from you."

"You better not, Richard. You better not," Kathia repeated dangerously quietly. She knew that she was in no position to force Hawthorne's hand and that her options were limited, but that wouldn't stop her from making a pest of herself if it served her purposes. She turned her back to Hawthorne and walked out, banging the door behind her.

Hawthorne eyed the door with dislike and addressed it in a futile attempt to have the last word. "Charles Brown, for God's sake. Who is Charles Brown? You're crazy!" he shouted, speaking to the door as a surrogate for Kathia, but he derived little relief from it.

CHAPTER 13

London, England. June 2009

Franco had no trouble finding Easby's driver. For one thing, he stood fully uniformed beside a silver Rolls-Royce that was parked conspicuously enough outside his office. And if he had any doubt that the Rolls was waiting for him, the curbside window was covered with a sign that said "Prof. Lorenzi." As soon as the driver spotted him, he hastened toward him, his outstretched hand ready to take Franco's suitcase.

"Professor Lorenzi?" he queried.

"Yes," Franco admitted, relinquishing the suitcase to the driver who opened the passenger's door for him.

Franco climbed into the car and sat down, looking around in awe. He had never been inside a Rolls-Royce and was surprised by the richness of the leather and wood and by the comfort of the seat. The driver sat behind the wheel, and before switching on the engine, he turned around and smiled at Franco.

"Are you comfortable, Sir? Please let me know if you need anything or if you want to stop at any time along the road."

"Thank you," said Franco, somewhat overwhelmed by the attention and the luxury. "How long a drive is it?"

"Barring any unusual traffic, we will be at Stanson Hall in a little more than three and a half hours. Please make yourself comfortable. You'll find mineral water and glasses in the case on your left, and also some snacks. I'll get going now," he said, and Franco relaxed in the backseat, determined to enjoy the ride.

Franco dozed off a little on the highway but woke up as soon as the car began making its way along narrow, tortuous country roads with their breathtaking view. The weather was glorious, and Franco, an open country enthusiast, took in the scenery with increasing pleasure.

"There you can see Stanson Hall, behind that tree line straight ahead," said the driver, who had kept silent for the whole trip.

"It looks like a big house," said Franco, who felt obliged to say something in response.

"It is surely big," said the driver with evident pride. "It's one of the finest homes in England. It dates back to the seventeen hundreds, but it was much altered in the early eighteen seventies by its owner, who added a fourth floor to the existing structure a west wing which included a conservatory, and an east wing containing a billiard room, fernery, and kitchens," he continued, sounding like a tour guide. "The house is late Elizabethan in style and built in grey stone with yellow stone dressings. The park comprises two hundred and thirty acres and is beautiful, with a small lake in the middle."

"That's very interesting," said Franco, who had given up hope of stopping the flood of information.

"Oh, it certainly is. I can give you many more details if you wish. It is sort of a hobby for me. I know by heart the history of many of the occupants of its twenty-two bedrooms, including who died in which room. Would you like to hear about it?" he asked hopefully.

"Maybe later," Franco mumbled, determined to keep silent for the rest of the drive.

Five minutes later, the Rolls-Royce stopped on the gravel before the main door of the Hall, which opened as if by magic. On the mat, waiting for him, stood a fat man of middle age, formally dressed and wearing white gloves. Franco stepped out of the car, thinking *he cannot be a butler; they don't have them anymore.*

"Welcome to Stanson Hall, Professor Lorenzi," said the man, making a broad, majestic gesture that encompassed the house and the grounds around it. "I am Watts, Sir James Easby's butler. Sir James is engaged elsewhere right now but will welcome you personally later. Meanwhile, may I show you your room?"

Franco was so overwhelmed by the whole setup that all he managed was a nod. Watts then turned around with a brief "Follow me, please," and led the way up the stairs to a bedroom. After a quick explanation of the house's topography, the dining arrangements and times, and the dressing code, which left Franco dizzy. Watts left asking him to ring if he needed anything and be down, ready for dinner, at seven o'clock sharp.

The time was only a little after four o'clock. Franco was too curious and excited to stay in his room until dinnertime, so after he freshened up quickly, he paced the floor, trying to decide what to do. His room, located on the third floor, had a large window that opened into a beautiful garden at the back of the house, and gazing out of it, he saw that it wasn't empty – a young woman was sitting on a stone bench, apparently intent on basking her face in the sun. She was too far away from his window to see precise details of her features, but she was obviously a fellow guest and probably like him, she didn't have much to do until dinnertime. Franco left the room, closing the door behind him, and headed for the gardens.

Franco was not timid. He knew that he was good-looking but had always viewed the fact that women seemed to be attracted to him as something not to be abused. Despite the many relationships he had had, he still did not fully understand women; he simply couldn't be bothered to get involved with them deeply enough to understand them and found it easier to be circumspect and approach them as if they were ticking bombs liable to go off unexpectedly. His approach to the young woman sitting on the stone bench was no different. She was in her late twenties and intimidatingly beautiful. She wore an airy white dress made of flimsy material and silver sandals that showed her well-manicured toenails. Her hair was dark chestnut and went down in ripples to her shoulders. He couldn't see the color of her eyes, which were shut against the sun, but he correctly guessed them to be deep green.

"Hello," he said, standing at a safe distance from her.

She leveled her gaze and opened her eyes, squinting and taking time to adjust her vision, and then she smiled. "And who would you be?" she asked.

"My name is Franco Lorenzi, and I'm a guest here. Just arrived," he added apologetically.

"Oh, you're the professor guy ..."

That was the first time that Franco had heard himself described as "the professor guy," and he couldn't help smiling. The unmistakable French accent of his interlocutor probably accounted for that.

"Yes, that's me," he said, smiling back.

She got up and gave him a hand to shake, saying earnestly, "My name is Eva Thibault, pleased to meet you."

"The pleasure is all mine, I'm sure," said Franco, shaking her hand without applying too much pressure.

"That's not really my surname, you know," she added, whispering conspiratorially. "That's my *nom d'art*. I'm an actress ... or rather, I'm trying to be."

"So, what's your real name?" Franco asked to keep the conversation going.

"I'm not saying. That's a secret ... well, not really a secret, but I'm much more interesting if I have a secret, right? And if you want to become a successful actress, you must be interesting, *n'est pas*?"

She sat down on the stone bench again. She motioned Franco to join her, and he sat beside her, amused; all the tension inherent to the occasion had been dissipated by her frank and extrovert personality.

"I'm good at keeping secrets, but I won't press you to tell me yours. So, what are you doing here?"

Her face was so animated that it seemed to change with every word she spoke, and Franco was held spellbound by it, enjoying its varying but always beautiful facets.

"Oh, I'm staying with James. He was a good friend of my father's, and since my father died, he's been so kind to me. He even invested in this movie so I could get a small part in it. It's just a beginning, but I know it'll get me noticed. That was so very kind of him, don't you think?"

Franco was amused and didn't want to curb her enthusiasm by telling her that he didn't have a clue what she was talking about.

"Very kind indeed," he admitted.

Eva got up and swiveled to face him. "It's getting late," she said. "I need to go and get ready for dinner. It takes me so-o-o long, you know."

Franco got up to face her and said, "I'll see you at dinner, then." She nodded and started to walk away, but after three steps, she turned back and came close to him. She gazed straight into his face for so long that Franco started to wonder whether something was wrong with it, and then she said, "Things may be different from what you think, you know?"

She turned away again and started walking toward the house. Franco called after her, "Wait! What do you mean? What is different?"

She stopped for a second, turned around, and said, "Just different. Things. They always are, aren't they?" and after that cryptic statement, she was swallowed by the green of the trees where the gravel path bent toward the house.

CHAPTER 14

Stanson Hall, South Yorkshire, England. July 2009

Franco stepped out through the drawing room's French windows into the quiet, cool evening. He leaned against the stone handrail that delimited the spacious veranda, trying to ignore the muffled sounds of conversation coming from within. If he was pensive, it was with cause. The dinner had been a formal event of the kind you only see in TV series, with all guests fully dressed – Watts had made sure to come by his room before dinner to vet Franco's attire. And although his host couldn't have been more genial, something in the atmosphere was out of order. Seated in front of him at the other side of the table was a tall gentleman with a slight German accent but with a marked Teutonic countenance, who had been introduced to him as Heinrich von Stoffen, an Austrian aristocrat. "So you teach Latin, they tell me," he had said while shaking Franco's hand. He had said so with a smile but somehow managed to make his words sound despicable. Franco hadn't liked him and had preferred to make conversation with the pleasant doctor who sat at the other side of the table beside von Stoffen. He politely spoke with Dr. Benini in English to avoid excluding the other guests from the conversation, but Benini's northern Italian accent was enough to make him feel at home.

But what really puzzled him was Eva, who sat to his left. More than once during dinner, her foot brushed against his leg, which could not have been accidental given the roomy seating arrangements. She also often intervened in the conversation, touching his arm to get his attention and kept it lingering unnecessarily in that position. Franco couldn't make sense of it; he wondered if this beautiful woman was hitting on him and then smiled at the absurd notion.

"A cigar?" a voice said behind him, and Franco turned to face Easby, who was carrying a box of Havanas.

"I don't smoke very often," said Franco.

"Well, I would say that this occasion calls for a smoke if one ever did. Take one," he prompted, and when Franco took a cigar, he continued, "How did you enjoy dinner?"

"Oh, it was excellent. And the conversation at the table was quite interesting."

"I'm happy that you're having a good time. Here," Easby said, lighting Franco's cigar.

Easby leaned on the stone rail beside Franco. The two men smoked in silence, peering into the garden's darkness until Easby spoke again.

"I promised to give you full disclosure of our project, and I will do so tomorrow, but before I do that, I want to ask you something. It may sound strange to you, but please be assured that I am speaking with all seriousness."

Easby pulled on his cigar in silence, and Franco felt compelled to say something. "That's okay; I'm open-minded," he said. He remembered Kathia's instructions well. Be open-minded but not too easy to get, she had said.

"Do you believe in the afterlife?" Easby asked point-blank.

"Do you mean, like heaven and hell? Well, I do believe that we have a soul and that there may be an afterlife like the Scripture says, but beyond that, I don't think I've ever given it much thought."

"No, I was meaning, do you believe that we may make contact with people who died? If you believe that there should be an afterlife, then believing that people that exist in the afterlife may contact us is not such a great leap of faith," said Easby, still gazing into the night as if to avoid looking at Franco.

"I don't know. I really don't," said Franco, searching his mind for answers to a question he had never really considered. "I've heard stories, and I've read reports of cases, but I've never had any firsthand experience, so I don't think I can form an educated opinion."

"You're talking like a professor," said Easby, smiling at Franco.

"Well ... I guess that's an occupational hazard," said Franco, smiling back.

"We have a powerful medium joining us here tomorrow. She's Italian like you and has given me and many other people convincing proof of her powers. Like you, I was skeptical until I met her, but now I'm fully convinced that we can make contact with people who died. Would you like me to ask her to show you?"

"A séance? Isn't that too creepy? I've never been to one ..." Franco was divided between his curiosity and the uneasy feeling that he might be dealing with things best left alone.

"It's crucial that you can convince yourself firsthand of the seriousness of the subject. This is no society game but a serious scientific endeavor. And you are an academic, so we value your opinion."

"If you put it like that ..."

"You'll find it most interesting, I promise. Well, I guess I have to go back to my other guests. Come in when you're through smoking; Eva has promised to sing to us, and she has a wonderful voice, not to be missed."

Franco followed his host's figure as it disappeared through the French windows into the house. Once again, he got the strange feeling of being an actor in a movie, only pretending to be on the grounds of a stately English home smoking an expensive cigar and playing the role of the pet guest of a millionaire. He might as well enjoy it while it lasted, though, he decided.

CHAPTER 15

Udine, Italy. July 1894

The Honorable L. stepped down from the carriage and joined the youth who had climbed down from the seat next to the driver. He waited while the young man knocked on the door three times in rapid succession, and the door opened to admit them into the Cecchi house. Without waiting for an invitation, the Honorable L. walked the short length to the sitting room door and let himself in. The Cecchi widow was seated in the same armchair in which she had received him on his first visit, but this time she jumped up when the door opened.

"What's the matter?" the Honorable L. asked curtly. "What was so important to get me out of bed in the middle of the night?"

"Please sit down," said the woman. She spoke humbly, without her customary smugness. She seemed frightened.

The Honorable L. unbuttoned his overcoat and took it off without taking his eyes off her. When he sat down, she let herself drop heavily back into her seat.

"I think that we may have started something that got out of hand," she said at last.

"What do you mean?" asked the Honorable L., suddenly attentive.

"You know that I'm a medium ... what people here call 'a witch'. I'm no witch, but I do speak with the dead, and they help me help other people – I know that you are skeptical, but that doesn't matter now. What matters is that you have enough faith to let me try to help you.

"Connecting with the dead is no easy task. It requires appropriate conditions – you can't do it in the street or in broad daylight – and needs much concentration and physical effort. After I make contact, I am always physically and emotionally drained. And sometimes I can't make contact, no matter how hard I try. The dead are disinclined to talk to living people. They don't trust us, and they don't like us and resent our intrusion into their world. You must convince them, and only after they feel confident enough about you do they manifest themselves. You see?"

"I hear you, but I don't see where all this is leading up to."

She lowered her gaze, avoiding his eyes, and continued to speak hesitantly, almost in a whisper. "I haven't slept a wink in the last three days. It started three days ago while I was cooking, and a face showed up in my frying pan. Then I started hearing voices at all hours, indistinct but growing in intensity and frequency until I had to admit that something unheard of was happening: the dead were trying to contact me.

"I was, and still am, scared. I couldn't understand what could be the reason for all this. Was I about to die? But then a name started to emerge from the mix of sounds that I was hearing, and you can imagine whose name that was: Evelyn."

The Honorable L. stirred in his armchair, obviously ill at ease. He was not used to hearing this kind of talk, and he felt that even only listening to it without deriding it made him an accomplice in some way.

"What does that mean?"

"I'm not sure yet. It could be, God forbid, forewarning that something bad is about to happen to her, or it may mean that your letter got into the right hands. Be that as it may, I can no longer resist the call, and I don't know what the consequence will be when I connect. Somehow, I was sure that you had to be here when I connected, I can't tell you why, but that was very clear in my mind. That's why I sent my son to you to beg you to come quickly."

"So what are you going to do now?"

"Now, I'll stop resisting the call. I'll open my mind to the spirits and let them connect with me. Whatever happens, please do not interfere, no matter how strange or frightening it may get. Are you ready?"

The Honorable L. nodded and sat back in his armchair, watching every movement that the widow made. She closed her eyes and leaned back, her hands open with palms up on her knees. For two or three minutes, nothing happened, and then the Honorable L. started to shiver as the temperature in the room became noticeably lower, despite the log that burned well in the hearth. The widow's eyes remained shut, but the eyelids betrayed their rapid, unnatural movement. Although she was a small woman, her body seemed to have swollen to a larger size with all its muscles in tension.

The Honorable L. was strong and courageous but could not help feeling a shiver running along his spine, nor could he ignore the goosebumps that showed on his arms. He had never felt so much at the mercy of fate, even when facing almost sure death in the most dangerous military campaigns. But he wouldn't run away from the blasphemous event, not if his presence was needed to help his daughter.

He lost track of time. He found himself helplessly suspended in a universe in which he didn't belong. He was condemned to watch the widow's body, now starting to twitch, without knowing what was happening and how it would impact his daughter's life. Suddenly the woman's mouth opened, and a shout came from it; it was an animal sound with a timbre of voice that didn't belong to the small woman from which it came or, indeed, to a human being. "Save Evelyn," she shouted, and then her body sank back into the armchair, releasing at once all its tension. The Honorable L. kept watching her, and after a few seconds, she opened her eyes.

"The letter got across. It worked. People on the other side are going to help us," she said, smiling a tired smile.

CHAPTER 16

Stanson Hall, South Yorkshire, England. July 2009

Franco woke up early the following day. He had felt tired and heavy after dinner, and not being used to drinking much, he would have liked to retire early to avoid his host, who kept refilling his glass with a port of vintage and price that Franco's finance couldn't even have allowed him to look at. But he couldn't leave without being impolite, so he kept himself awake until almost midnight when Easby announced that he was going to bed. As advertised, Eva had sat at the piano and sang old French songs for them. She indeed had a beautiful voice and accompanied herself harmoniously. Franco had enjoyed listening to her despite the effort needed to keep his eyes open.

It was past nine o'clock in the morning when he finished washing and dressing up and realized that he was hungry. He went downstairs toward the dining room, assuming that breakfast would be served there. The dining room was empty, but the French windows were open, and through those windows came a servant that Franco had not seen before. She carried a tray high above her shoulder, and as she saw Franco, she stopped and lowered it.

"Good morning, Sir. The weather is beautiful, and breakfast is served on the veranda. Please sit at any table, and I will be with you in a second."

Franco nodded and stepped outside. On the veranda, four round tables were set up for breakfast, and he picked the better-shaded one. The waitress came to take his order, and soon he was digging into a hearty breakfast. He was so busy eating that he didn't notice Eva's presence until she spoke.

"Good morning," she said near his left ear. "How was your night?"

Franco got up quickly and put down his fork, swallowing his last forkful hastily. "Oh, sorry, I didn't see you coming," he apologized.

"Of course. You were too busy stuffing your face," she laughed. "May I sit down or am I intruding on your *tête-à-tête* with your food?"

"How stupid of me! Of course, please do sit down."

Eva sat graciously at the table and gazed straight into his eyes. "So?" she said.

"I slept very well, thank you."

"That's not what I meant," she said without elaborating further.

"I enjoyed your concert yesterday. You have a beautiful voice," said Franco, hoping to be giving the right answer.

"Thank you," she said, seeming pleased.

The waitress came and went and then came back with Eva's order. They ate in silence for a while. "Where is everybody?" Franco asked when Eva pushed her plate away.

"Asleep or perhaps busy. Who knows? Who cares? They are dears but also boring old men. They always have important things to do, and I get bored easily. Let's go and take one of James's boats and cross the lake. It's beautiful there. Can you row at all?"

"Yes, but ..."

"No buts, please. You're the only reasonably young person around, and you can't leave me at the mercy of the house mummies. Have a heart! I'll get us a food basket, and we can have a picnic. Deal?"

"I'd love to, but Sir James has invited me here for a purpose, and he said yesterday that he will want to meet with me today, so I can't just take off and upset all his plans."

"Nonsense. I'll talk to James and bail you out. Meet me here in half an hour, okay?"

Franco had to remind himself that he was there on a mission. But on the other hand, socializing might help him get more information, he rationalized. And he couldn't deny that Eva was beautiful and that he was attracted by her. So what harm could a little innocent enjoyment do, he reasoned.

"I'll be here," he said. "I'll go and change into something more suitable for an oarsman," he added, smiling.

"Good," she said, speaking seriously, "don't be late. I hate to wait."

Forty-five minutes later, Franco was pacing the veranda impatiently, worrying that Eva might have changed her mind when he saw her approaching. She had changed into an airy dress and carried a tote bag in one hand and a basket in the other, which Franco hastened to take from her.

"I've got sandwiches, salad, and a chilled bottle of champagne. That should do. And I've spoken with James. He will be busy until late afternoon, so you won't be missed, but he asked that you let Watts know when you're back."

"What's in the bag?" asked Franco.

"A blanket to keep the ants away from the food while we eat."

They walked down the path that led to the lake and boarded one of the three white boats tied to a small pier. Franco took the oars and started rowing. The lake was small, but the vegetation around it changed very sharply and was much thicker on the other side, barely letting a little light through. When they reached the middle of the lake, Franco stopped rowing and pulled the oars in.

"Are you tired already?" Eva teased him.

"No, but it's nice here, and the sun is not too hot. Let's float around for a while. Meanwhile, you can tell me more about yourself."

"You start," she said.

"There isn't much to say about me," said Franco. When speaking with young women, he preferred to avoid talking about himself.

"How old are you?"

"I'll be thirty-two in November."

"And where does your family live?"

"My parents are both dead. My mother died when I was young and my father two years ago. I was born in Italy, in Milan, and lived with my father in London for five years. I went to school here."

"Do you have a girlfriend?"

"Not right now," said Franco. He hoped that he hadn't blushed, but his cheeks felt suddenly hot.

"Don't force me to use pincers to get your answers. Out with the dope. Give me the whole story."

"There isn't much more to say. I turned to classical studies, and I've been teaching Latin for years now. Not flashy as a profession, but I like it. Your turn now."

"Uhm, that wasn't much that you gave me. What do you want to know?"

"To begin with, I'm curious. You speak perfect English. At first, I thought you had a heavy French accent, but now it's barely noticed. You were faking it, right?"

"Ha, you caught me! Yes, I spent more time in England than in France, and my father was British. He met my mother in Paris and settled down there, but he spoke English with me since I was a baby. Stressing the French accent makes me more interesting, though; more out of the ordinary. I'm told that it's quite sexy."

"I shouldn't wonder. It also makes you sound frivolous, though, and I seem to detect that you are a bright young lady behind that mask. I meet many young people when I teach, and I can read characters."

"Is that a fact?" Eva taunted him.

"Let me try it on you. I would say that you wear that mask because it makes it easier for you to talk to people you don't know and to size them up when they're off their guard. How's my characterization?"

"I can't comment for fear to incriminate myself, Professor."

"That's as good as a confession," Franco smiled. "Now give me the goods, the real Eva, not the fake mask."

"All right. I was born twenty-seven years ago and grew up in Paris. My mother was a dancer, quite successful in her times. She left my father and me for another man when I was little, and I haven't seen her or spoken to her since. My father was a very good friend of James's; they had some business enterprise together, but they were also personally connected. Father used to work for James before I was born. I was thirteen when my father discovered that he was sick and was going to die soon. He never told me. He made James swear that he would take good care of me, which he has done in many ways, more than you would expect from anybody. Then he killed himself."

Eva had turned serious, showing a new, unexpected facet of her personality. Franco switched off the smile that he had kept until then, embarrassed to hear such private revelations.

"I'm sorry to hear that. It must've been tough for you," he said.

"It was a long time ago," she said, going back to smiling as before. "My father taught me to take the best from every situation, and that's what I always do. James was and is wonderful to me, almost like a father. I didn't know it, but just before he got sick, my father went bust. He never gave me any hint of it, and James kept it secret for years. He made sure that I got a good education in France and England, and I always thought he was using money left by my father. It was only recently that I discovered the truth."

"He must be a great man," said Franco. He had no trouble injecting admiration into his voice. Eva's tale had impressed him.

"You don't even start to imagine how great. Now get back to rowing, will you? You're getting me cooked here."

Franco took the oars and started rowing toward the far bank of the lake. He did so pensively. Too many things that he was learning here were not in character with what he had been told by Kathia, and that left him confused. He hoped that Kathia would be proven wrong, both for himself and for Easby, whom he was starting to like more every day.

The picnic basket that Eva had prepared turned out to be delicious. As soon as they reached the other side of the lake, they tied the boat to a tree and walked a short distance to a shaded flat patch of green, where they spread the blanket and sat down to eat. The champagne had heated up, and when the cork popped, the liquid burst out, wetting them both and drawing a good-humored laugh from Eva at Franco's contrite apology.

"So, how do you spend your time these days?" Franco asked.

"I used to stay in London, and here, a lot – as I told you, James is like a father to me, and his house is my house. He never married and didn't have children, you know. But now I have to stay in Paris most of the time for my career, you understand?"

"Do you live alone in Paris?"

"Yes, James bought me a nice flat for my twenty-first birthday, and that's where I live."

"Wow! An apartment in Paris as a birthday present ... is there anything he wouldn't do for you?"

"I don't know, but I know there is nothing I wouldn't do for him ..."

Franco hesitated, and then, on an impulse, he said, "I'm flattered that you feel able to share such personal thoughts with me."

"Don't be. It comes with a price," she said and smiled. "You'll have to match me. For instance, tell me about the woman you've been madly in love with and lost. Come on, how was she? Full details, please."

"That's easy," said Franco and smiled. "I don't fall in love."

"Yeah, sure!"

"No, I'm serious. I have a theory ..."

"You have a theory about love?"

"You could say that. My theory is that if you are careful never to fall in love, then whoever you're with won't break your heart when you lose her."

"That sounds completely dopey. You have no control over it."

"I do."

Eva glanced at him sideways and then picked up her glass and drank. After taking a sip, she poked him in the chest with two fingers.

"Ouch!"

She shrugged and said, "I'm just checking to see if you're human. Are you?"

"Let me tell you a story," said Franco. His voice had a serious ring to it, and Eva jerked her head up and gazed at him. "We have something in common, you and I. At least, I guess," he said. "My mother died when I was eleven years old of a misdiagnosed arrhythmia—a stupid, unnecessary death. My parents were like turtledoves, always together, always holding hands. When she died, my father's world ended. He kept going for a few years – for my sake – but I saw him die day after day. He never recovered and finally suffered a stroke that left him semi-paralyzed until his death. That taught me that love can kill. Luckily, I guess I'm immune."

"Boy, aren't you gloomy! What is it that you're doing, penance?"

"On the contrary. I'm enjoying life without complications."

"I think you're miserable, but that's your business. As you said, I've gone through rough times too, but I refuse to let the past ruin my life."

Eva had become all serious, and James moved his embarrassed gaze from her face to his sandwich into which he bit guardedly, not knowing what to expect.

"It's cream cheese and cucumbers," she said as if reading his thoughts. Then she took a bite of her own. Franco watched her eat. She did so gracefully and beautifully like she did everything else. Her bites were tiny, and she chewed slowly and delicately. When she chewed, a dimple showed up on her cheek and disappeared, only to show up immediately again.

"What?" she asked after she assimilated her latest bite as if by magic.

"Was I staring? Sorry," said Franco, blushing. "It's just that your face is so expressive when you eat that I could almost see on it what it was that you were tasting."

"They tell me that at the studios. They say that I would've been a great success at the time of the silent movies, but then they also say that the silent movies are dead and buried."

She laughed a brief, self-deprecating laugh and took another small bite of her sandwich. Franco put his own sandwich down and raised his glass. He had meant to toast "To the silent movies" but didn't get a chance. The clouds that were sparse when they had headed out on the boat had now built up, blocking the sun for quite some time, and as Franco touched his glass, a heavy shower started to fall without any warning. They jumped to their feet, looking around for shelter.

"Let's run over there, under that tree," Franco urged her. The tree in question was ancient, and thick vegetation had grown around it and intertwined with its branches, so the ground below it offered some shelter from the pouring rain. Incongruously, Eva started collecting the bottle and glasses. Rather than arguing the futility of that, Franco grabbed the basket and the blanket and then ran to the tree.

"We should've brought an umbrella," Eva said.

"Yes, we should," Franco admitted, "but it wouldn't have helped us any. Look, we're drenched already."

Eva burst out in a silvery laugh.

"What are you laughing at?" asked Franco.

"You're funny. Your hair is all sticking to your head."

"Well, you're not so hot either, you know," said Franco, but then on an impulse, he corrected himself. "Or, rather, you *are* quite hot."

He gazed openly at her. Her dress, now drenched, adhered to her curvy figure and did little to hide her breasts, revealing that she wasn't wearing a bra.

"Wow, Professor! You're loosening up," she said, smiling coquettishly at him. "But we have to go back before I catch pneumonia. Look," she said, turning practical, "the rain has gone down to a drizzle. Let's take the boat and go back."

They ran to the boat, which, luckily, hadn't filled up too much with rain and was light enough for them to lift and empty of the water puddles that had formed at the bottom. They jumped in, and Franco started rowing furiously, trying hard not to let his gaze rest too often on Eva, who sat across from him entirely uninhibited, without making an effort to hide any parts of her body that the wet dress was outlining. They reached the other side as the rain started to fall heavily again.

"Go ahead," said Franco. "I have to moor the boat first."

Without a word, Eva got out of the boat and started running toward the house. Franco tied the boat to the pier and then walked heavily back to the house. He was too wet to run.

CHAPTER 17

Stanson Hall, South Yorkshire, England. July 2009

Franco had just finished dressing after a long, hot shower when someone knocked on his door. He opened it to find Watts standing outside.

"Sir James asks you please to come to the library when you're ready," said Watts importantly, as if he were bearing news of momentous importance.

"Where is that?" Frank inquired.

"It's the third door after the drawing-room, Professor."

"Please tell him that I'll be there in ten minutes."

Watts left, and Franco put on his shoes and walked down the stairs to look for the library. The library door was closed, and Franco knocked on it before turning the handle and walking in.

The room left him speechless. It was much bigger than he had anticipated, with a high ceiling and walls entirely covered with books, thousands of them. A huge Louis XV desk, next to a far corner, looked tiny in the space. To his left, he saw a conference table that could sit twenty. At that table, Easby and Dr. Benini were seated together with a fat woman. The room was poorly lit, adding an impressive dimension to its already humbling setup. On seeing him come in, Easby got up and approached him.

"Good to see you," he said, good-humouredly. "I hear you got caught up in the storm. I hope you didn't catch a cold."

"Thanks, Sir James. It was nothing."

"Please drop the 'Sir,' will you? And I'd like to call you Franco if you don't object. No need to be formal here."

"Of course. I don't like being addressed as 'Professor' either."

Easby put a hand on Franco's shoulder and pushed lightly, urging him toward the others. "Let me introduce Maria to you," he said when they got close to the table.

"*Buongiorno,*" she said, without getting up or otherwise showing any enthusiasm at the meeting.

"*Buongiorno,*" Franco answered politely. "I'm sorry, I didn't catch your family name."

"No family name," she said curtly, "just Maria will do."

Easby smiled at Franco. "You shouldn't mind Maria's manners. Her strong suit is in other communication skills. Now to today's agenda. I have told Maria your name and nothing else. We don't know what will happen during the séance, but whatever manifestations you see, remember that they cannot hurt you and remain calm. Arturo and I have been through many of those, both with Maria and other mediums and are used to it, so watch us and follow what we do. But I don't want you to be disappointed if nothing happens; sometimes, no matter how hard we try, we simply can't make contact. Are you ready now?"

"I don't know if I'll ever be ready for this, but please proceed."

Maria was seated at the head of the table with Benini at her right and Easby at her left. Franco set next to Easby. Maria extended her hands on the table, palms up, and Benini and Easby held them. Easby offered his left hand to Franco, who took it, although he felt slightly silly as a result. Maria closed her eyes and leaned back in her chair, forcing Benini and Easby to lean forward to keep their grip on her hands. She started to breathe heavily, almost panting, and remained in that position for what felt to Franco like at least five minutes.

The room was perfectly silent but for Maria's breathing, but then Franco started to feel, and then hear, a vibration. It seemed to come from the table as if its surface had started to move relative to its legs with a quick vibrating motion. Franco felt that his back hair was standing straight on ends but didn't know whether to attribute it to the tension building in the room or to the temperature that seemed to have dropped. He gazed intensely at the other two men, trying to gauge their state of mind, but their faces remained inscrutable. Speaking was out of the question in that atmosphere, despite all the vibrations that seemed to become more intense as time passed.

Then everything stopped – the sound and the vibration and Maria loosened her grip on the others' hands and straightened up. She opened her eyes and smiled, looking serene.

"Well, I guess that didn't work too well," said Franco, relieved that nothing had happened.

"Shh ..." Easby admonished him. "Look!" he whispered, tilting his head toward Maria.

Maria had sat up. Her face was changing expression, with the muscles of her mouth twitching and relaxing in quick succession in different ways. The result resembled a slide show of expressions. A sound came from her throat, and everyone's attention was fixed on her. The table's vibration resumed and then subsided, and words came from Maria's mouth, but not with Maria's coarse and smoke-scorched voice; it was a pleasant, melodic voice.

"Baby," said the voice. "I'm proud. Of you, I am. Proud."

"Who are you?" Easby asked, addressing Maria. "Identify yourself, please."

"Remember Peschiera. The peach. I ... miss ... you. Remember. Remember."

Maria's body twitched, and she closed her mouth. A last strong vibration shook the table, and then Maria dropped her head on it and let go of the others' hands. Benini got up quickly and drew the curtains open, letting in light from outside. "Woof, that was intense," he said, speaking to nobody in particular.

Easby also got up and placed an apologetic hand on Franco's shoulder. "I don't know what happened; I'm sorry. That was quite disappointing. We usually keep the contact for much longer and can receive some detail of the spirit that we have evoked, but this time ..." he said to Franco, who sat petrified in his chair gazing fixedly at the books before him.

Maria slowly resumed a sitting position, shaking her head as if in disbelief. "That was a powerful spirit. Lots of emotions. It possessed me."

"We've never invoked her before, I think. I don't recall her," said Benini. His voice was firm, but his countenance betrayed that he was shaken.

"Pity she didn't identify herself," said Easby.

They had obviously engaged in small talk for Franco's benefit, to cushion the shock of the experience. It took Franco some strength to pull himself together and to say, "I know who she was."

"What!" said the others in unison.

"How do you know? What do you know?" asked Easby, who had sat down again and was now gazing closely at Franco.

"I was seven years old, on a weekend with my mother on Lake Garda, a place called Peschiera while my father was away on business. She gave me a sweet and juicy peach, and I ate it so quickly that I swallowed the pit, which got stuck in my throat and nearly choked me to death. I was lucky that one of the people around us was a physician. He saved me from suffocating by giving me the Heimlich Maneuver. I was so scared that I couldn't breathe, and they had to take me to a hospital and give me an inhalation. I was asthmatic for quite some time after that incident. I don't know if it was the shock or what, but it took me weeks to get back to normal. That was my mother's and my little secret; we never told my father what had happened because he was such an apprehensive person. My mother explained to me that it would sadden him to no purpose. He thought that a bad cold had caused my breathing problems. I never told anybody, and I almost forgot it myself."

Silence fell on the room, and everybody waited for him to say something more. "She said that she was proud of you," said Maria, breaking the silence that had followed Franco's revelation.

Franco got up. "If you don't mind, I would like to be alone now," he said, and without waiting for an answer, he walked out of the library.

CHAPTER 18

Stanson Hall, South Yorkshire, England, July 2009

Heinrich von Stoffen knew about patience but didn't like the notion. He was an imperious person, and he ran his microcosmos accordingly. His organization counted only a few heads, but he ran a tight ship and was used to getting results. Being unable to have his own way was an unnerving experience for him. He was nurturing a grudge against Easby for shutting him out of the project that he so sorely needed to wreck.

In his London residence – one of the three that he owned in Europe – a small but efficient and faithful team waited for his instructions, and he had no instructions to deliver. How more frustrating could that get? Meanwhile, his deal with the Vatican Bank was on the line. Under no circumstances would he allow it to fall through.

His thoughts turned to that irritating Lorenzi individual. He considered him ridiculous, with all his highbrowed academic mannerisms, and had been hard-pressed to conceal his contempt at the dinner table. Obviously, he was essential to the project, and von Stoffen wondered whether Easby could be stopped by getting rid of the inconvenient professor. He doubted it, though. From what he had understood from Easby, he was necessary but not essential, so if he disappeared, it might slow down the project but was unlikely to stop it; and as always, the process leading to it might entail complications. No, he concluded, it would have to be done in some other way. He needed information, and, much as it pained him, he was ready to do his best to charm Easby into giving it to him. And if it required being smooth and soft-spoken, and to beg for it as a favor, so be it.

He had joined the EHCS some five years before, not because he was overly interested in ghost hunting and in the related idiocies that were revered by its members, but because it allowed him to mingle with "Society." A friend of his, an old lady who had died soon after that, had introduced him to Easby, and he had understood immediately that becoming a member of Easby's inner circle meant being in contact with wealthy and influential people. He soon became the head of the Austrian chapter of the EHCS, which he hosted in his elegant Vienna home. The time he had put into the EHCS had proven a good investment; he had closed a couple of quite lucrative deals thanks to connections made there. In fact, knowing about what he had started to think of as "the resurrection project" might turn out to be the biggest coup of all and just what could tip the scales in favor of his Vatican Bank deal.

Yes, he concluded, he had to take a long breath, be nice to the old man, and try to get as much information out of him as possible.

CHAPTER 19

Stanson Hall, South Yorkshire, England. July 2009

James Easby sat in his studio, reading a long document. The curtains were drawn apart, but the afternoon light was too little and too diffused to make much difference to the brightly lit room. Heinrich von Stoffen walked up to Easby's desk, seated himself in one of the armchairs, and waited patiently for James to turn his attention to him.

"The séance went well," Easby said at last. "There was quite some commotion, though."

"So I heard," said von Stoffen. "Will he help us?" he asked after a brief pause.

"I'm sure he will. He's too shaken now, but I'll talk to him tomorrow."

"And what if he doesn't cooperate?" insisted von Stoffen.

"We have other options. Perhaps not as good, but viable. But he will cooperate, I'm sure."

Von Stoffen got up and stood for a long minute, studying Easby's expression. "What are you expecting him to do? How can he contribute?"

"Oh, we'll see," said Easby. He was good at being evasive.

"I understand from the little information that you gave me that you have a surrogate. Who is she?" von Stoffen asked, speaking casually.

"You know the rules, Heinrich. Only on a need-to-know, basis ... but I can confirm that we have a surrogate and that she's perfect for the job. Of course, she's the key factor in all of the project since we wouldn't have one without her. Therefore we are protecting her, hiding her in a safe place known only to a few until it's time for her to play her role."

Easby was uneasy. Von Stoffen was a relatively high-level member and had been helpful to the EHCS in the past, but he wondered whether it had been wise to invite him to Stanson Hall at this critical moment. He wished he hadn't told him about the project at all and avoided the embarrassment of having to fend off his curiosity.

"Damn, James! You know you can trust me. I'm all on edge, not knowing what's going on. I wish you'd tell me a little more about the process and the people involved. I feel excluded ..."

"You're better off not knowing, Heinrich. You know that. EHCS's rule. What's biting you, anyway? You know we are careful in everything we do."

"I don't know. Just a bad feeling, that's all. It feels like you don't trust me."

"You know that's not true. Nobody has been told more than you. You know what we aim to accomplish and what is at stake, and that's more than most members have heard. So go get a drink and chase your bad feelings away, Heinrich. Leave the rest to me, will you? There's no room for mistakes in this game, and I don't want to make any."

"I wish you'd let me in on this all the same," he murmured.

"If the need arises, you'll be the first to be asked to help, but right now, it's not the proper time. I need to know that you are at peace with that," Easby added, eyeing him closely. "Are you?"

"Of course," said von Stoffen. He got up and nodded, almost giving a hint of a bow, and walked out stiffly. Easby watched him with apprehension as he went. Everybody's nerves were breaking down, and he had to keep his own, but the burden was a heavy one indeed.

CHAPTER 20

London, England. July 2009

David Westmore gazed out of his window at the boats that droned along the Thames. Perfectly dressed in a gray suit and dark red tie, he could have been a businessman or a banker. Instead, he held the unassuming title of Undersecretary for Unplanned Research, which, as he used to explain to his collaborators, meant being responsible for all the jobs from which Downing Street would disassociate itself when they flopped.

"Pour it, will you?" he said, still facing the large window. Richard Hawthorne obliged by filling two cups out of the tray that a silent assistant had placed on the tea-table of the sitting area of Westmore's spacious office.

Richard Hawthorne waited patiently, sitting comfortably on a modern black leather sofa. Westmore finally abandoned whatever it was that had captured his attention twelve floors below and turned to him.

"I must confess that I haven't been entirely candid with you when I asked you to be my man at Scotland Yard, Richard. But you know the policy of this department as well as I do: we only disclose information on a need-to-know basis. However, the time has come that the operation demands that you have all the facts. By the way, what is Miss Ramirez doing these days? Is she giving you any more trouble?"

"Not much. I haven't heard from her lately."

"Does she suspect that we have an inside agent?"

"Very unlikely. She's convinced that we had an informant but that he is no longer viable."

"Good, good."

Hawthorne waited patiently for his boss to continue, and Westmore moved away from the window and came to sit in front of him. He added some milk to the tea, stirred it, took a sip, replaced the cup on the tray, and gazed straight at Hawthorne. His kind and calm demeanor hid his forceful personality well and always put his interlocutor at ease.

"What I meant by not being fully candid with you is that it is not true that we are only interested in keeping an eye on Easby to make sure that he stays out of mischief. We have a much greater interest in making sure that, within reason, his endeavor meets with success."

"What possible interest do we have in the black magic nonsense that his group is playing with?"

"First of all, don't hasten to label their project as 'nonsense.' You know that this department has had quite some success with projects involving ESP and other phenomena that are characterized by most as nonsense. Secondly, this department deals with the improbable, verging on the impossible, so we shouldn't be deterred by our own belief that this is very likely only poppycock."

"All right," said Hawthorne. "I'm keeping an open mind."

"Good for you," said Westmore. "Moreover, I know James Easby well, and I can tell you that he is by no means stupid or delusional."

"You worked together in the Service, right?"

"Actually, he was my boss. For a short while, before he came into money and left. I did envy him. Perhaps I still do."

"I'm sure you don't. You're not the retiring type."

"Maybe ... Be that as it may, how well are you versed in the history of the British Empire?"

"Pretty much like any other educated man."

"Then you will know how important, stronger, and far-reaching was the Empire until the nineteen-thirties. Then in September of nineteen thirty-nine, Britain declared war against Nazi Germany. Although Britain and the Empire emerged victorious from World War II, the effects of the conflict were profound. Britain was left virtually bankrupt, and the British Empire's days were numbered. So tell me, what do you think would have happened if the war never started?"

"I can only guess that Great Britain would be in much better shape today."

"You bet!" said Westmore, speaking emphatically for the first time. "We would still have India and the Colonies, and the British Empire would still be a strong and dominant world power. So, if I were to find a magic wand to change the past with so that World War II never happened, would it, or would it not be a tremendous achievement for our country?"

"Obviously, it would be huge," said Hawthorne, letting out a little laugh, "but unfortunately, the past cannot be changed."

"Don't be too sure about that, Richard. Given the right knowledge and the appropriate tools, it can perhaps be changed."

"What do you mean?"

"Let's recap. Easby is trying to develop a technique based on information passed on to him in an old document, which will allow him to change the past by curing a young woman who died of tuberculosis. If he succeeds, that's changing the past, isn't it?"

"Yes, assuming that he succeeds in his bizarre project, which of course is out of the question. But that would have a minimal impact on a single person's life and is nothing like changing world history."

"That's where you're wrong," said Westmore. He got up, took a heavy binder from his desk, and dropped it on the tea table. "It's all in there, the result of thorough and detailed research."

Hawthorne opened the thick file and flipped the pages. "Who is Alois Schicklgruber – gosh, what a name!"

"He was better known by his last name, which he changed when he was thirty-nine years old to become Alois Hitler. He was Adolf Hitler's father. As it turns out, he was a philanderer who married three times and had countless affairs and eight known children. Adolf Hitler was the fourth child born of his third marriage with Klara Pölzl. But what is not generally known is that for all his philandering, Alois Hitler loved a woman by the name of Anna Stupp, who was a waitress and twenty years old when they met, around eighteen hundred and seventy-seven. In that dossier, you will find rare evidence by a close friend of Alois of the depth of his love for Anna Stupp and of his desperation when she died of pneumonia in eighteen hundred and seventy-nine. There is little doubt that, but for her premature death, Alois Hitler would have married Anna Stupp, in which case he would not have married Klara Pölzl, and Adolf Hitler would have never been born. Without Hitler, there would not have been World War II – or in the worst case, it would have happened on a much smaller scale. Do you see it now?"

"This is a lot to digest ... so your plan would be, if we can learn from Easby how it is done, to save Anna Stupp so that Hitler would never be born. Am I getting my tenses right? I can't imagine what the world would look like a moment after you succeeded ... and who can guarantee that it wouldn't be worse than it is today?"

"Guarantee? There's no such thing in life, but we do have probability, instead. Our statisticians have been asked the question – of course without disclosing the reasons behind it. We asked them to extrapolate the world today based on the assumption that Hitler died young, and their results were extremely good for the Empire. I am almost certain that we would only stand to gain from it."

"But how would that work? Would all the books on my shelves that tell about the war change their content or simply disappear? The apartment where I live was built on the ruins of a building destroyed by a German V2, so would I wake up in a different place?"

"Those are all interesting questions, aren't they? I guess part of the excitement is that we don't know the answers and won't know them until we go through with it. But let's remain logical; can you envisage a situation in which the world would be a better place after going through World War II than if the war never happened?"

"If you put it that way ..."

"I can understand your confusion. You haven't had the advantage of the time needed to think about it and appreciate the potential as I did. Take your time to do that."

"So now that I know, is there anything that you want me to do?"

"Not right now," said Westmore, "but things may move quickly, and it was important to give you the whole picture and get you ready for any possible situation. Particularly, you need to keep an eye on our inside agent. Under no circumstances should we allow the agent to come to any harm. I wanted to emphasize that to you, and now that you know what's at stake, you can better appreciate the potential dangers and prepare to meet the challenges."

"I understand. I'm glad you gave me the heads up. I'll go back now if we're done here."

The two men shook hands, and Hawthorne turned to leave. As he was about to turn the handle, Westmore called to him, "Richard ..."

"Yes?"

"That Miss Ramirez of yours may have a point with this Charles Brown affair. It reminds me of something that happened fifteen years or so ago. I wouldn't rule out that she was right."

"She's not stupid. Not at all. But she's trouble."

"You know, one of the advantages of older age is that you get perspective. I was restless like you when I was your age, and I remember my boss – not Easby, the one who took his place – telling me that I would understand when I got older. Well, I did. I don't take things to heart as I used to, anymore."

"I still do. If I didn't, I wouldn't be able to do my job properly. In fact, I suspect that you keep me because I take things to heart."

"I keep you because you're the best, and I hope that someday you may replace me. And also because of the fire that burns in you. But it burns in your Kathia too, and that may get in the way. Keep her in check, will you?"

Hawthorn nodded in assent and walked out.

CHAPTER 21

South Yorkshire, England. June 1995

The blue Jaguar that turned right into the thick of the trees seemed out of place in the silent countryside; more so because it was followed by a Rolls-Royce, which did not turn into the sidetrack but, instead, stopped on the country road. Both cars turned their lights off, and the drivers sat behind the wheels for a few moments, adjusting their vision to the pitch-dark night. Then the door of the Rolls-Royce opened, and a man of middle age stepped out. He strode quickly and with powerful confidence toward the Jaguar and opened the rear door. The inner light revealed a man of about fifty or sixty, elegantly dressed in black-tie attire, slumped in the rear seat. The stench of alcohol left no doubt as to his condition.

"Mark," the man from the Rolls-Royce said softly, prodding the drunken man's shoulder gently.

The man named Mark snored but gave no sign of awakening. The other beckoned to the driver of the Jaguar, who got up swiftly and joined him. He was neatly dressed in a driver's uniform, complete with white gloves and cap, and stood respectfully beside the car's rear door.

"Let's help him out," said the Rolls-Royce man. He reached inside and pulled Mark halfway out. The driver hastened to take Mark's other arm, and they made him stand between the two of them. The fresh air apparently managed to penetrate the alcohol's fumes because Mark opened his eyes, blinked, and slurred a few words.

"Are we home?" he asked wistfully.

"Not yet, Mark," said the Rolls-Royce man. "You drank a bit too much and are unwell."

The two men started to walk Mark slowly away from the car, almost dragging him because his feet didn't seem to support him.

"He gave me thash ... that ... he made me drink it. I want to go home," he said.

"Soon, Mark, soon," said his companion, "but first we need you to take some fresh air so you'll feel better."

"I don't want fresh air," complained Mark, but the others ignored him.

The dirt road on which the Rolls-Royce had stopped ran parallel to a small river, and the men soon reached its bank and stopped.

"Sit down, Mark," the Rolls-Royce man ordered, but Mark had closed his eyes again, and if he heard him, he didn't respond.

"Put him down ... face down," ordered the man, and he and the driver slowly lowered Mark's body, so his head was above the water.

They remained silent for a few moments, and then the Rolls-Royce man pushed Mark's body a few inches forward, and then he pressed his head with his right hand into the water. Mark's head gave a sudden jerk, and he made a feeble attempt to struggle, which lasted only half a minute during which the driver held his hands and feet tight, and the Rolls-Royce man pushed his head harder into the water. All that Mark managed to produce were a few gurgling sounds that soon stopped. When Mark's body relaxed and remained perfectly still, the Rolls-Royce man signaled the driver. They lifted him a little, puffing under the effort, and pushed his lifeless body into the dark, murky water into which it immediately disappeared.

The two men walked back to the Rolls-Royce, and the man seated himself in the back. "Let's go home," he said simply, and the driver drove away, careful not to hit too many holes in the dirt road.

The Rolls was a precious car, and the driver was conscious of his duty to drive it home safely.

David Westmore strode decisively from the river bank to the black sedan with the dark windows, which had stopped on the dirt road. Behind him, a police team was bagging the body of an old friend, but if you didn't know Westmore, you would never have suspected that he was in any way upset. The door opened as he approached, and an old man in a black coat and hat emerged. He gazed at Westmore and waited.

"We lost Mark," Westmore said. He stated that simply and flatly.

"How?"

"Drowned. Made to look like a suicide."

The old man gazed down toward the river bank and the slow activity that was going on there. "Given the situation, keeping it as a suicide may be a good option," he said, speaking pensively.

"Sir!" said Westmore, showing emotion for the first time. "You're not planning to let this go unpunished?"

"What proof do we have that it was not suicide? And are we able to pin it on somebody?"

"We have a pretty good guess about the identity of the individuals involved, and with a thorough investigation ..."

"You don't *know* it. You suspect them, and you may well be right, but I won't allow an investigation that may jeopardize the safety of other agents and of other operations. When you're older, you'll understand."

"But ..."

"Suicide it remains, and that's final, Westmore," the old man ruled. He climbed inside the black car, which immediately drove away.

CHAPTER 22

Stanson Hall, South Yorkshire, England. July 2009

Franco watched the trees' shadows get longer at the edge of the garden, where he had found a secluded spot to sit and think. He had done much thinking since storming out of the séance room but had come up with few conclusions. He had played and replayed that afternoon's events in his head, which only increased his confusion every time. He had felt the need to be alone to digest the implications of what appeared – no matter how much it sounded crazy to him – like a message from his late mother, delivered from the other side. But what bothered him most was that, despite the encouraging message, at least as far as he could interpret it, he had not felt that the entity speaking to him was benevolent. He had felt distanced and even threatened by the contact and needed time alone with himself to reconcile the feeling with his sweet memory of his mother. Silence and solitude were what he really needed, but, of course, he hadn't budgeted for Eva.

"Hey!" a voice said behind him. Turning around, he saw that Eva was approaching from the tortuous path that led to Franco's hideaway from the house. Resigned to this invasion of his solitude, and also a little pleased by it, he slid on the bench on which he was sitting to make room for her. Eva didn't wait for another invitation to join him and sat beside him. "What's up?" she asked.

"Nothing. I'm just sitting here."

"You took off!" she said accusingly. "What are you, a hermit?"

"No," said Franco, smiling despite everything. "I needed to be alone for a while. Things have been happening ..."

"I heard," she said curtly. "Are you done being alone, or do you want me to go away?"

"No, no. Stay. I'm fine," he said, sounding everything but okay.

"Good. What about dinner?"

"Oh, I don't know. I don't feel like joining the others tonight. I think I'll skip dinner. I'll tell Watts to fetch me a tray with something."

"Perfect. I wasn't planning to attend myself. Do you like South American food?"

"I guess. Why?"

"Then take me out to dinner. I know a place in Sheffield with great food and good music. The *Caipirinha*."

"Sheffield?" said Franco, surprised. "That's quite far away."

"Not when I drive James's Jaguar," said Eva, laughing and dangling the car keys before his eyes.

The idea started to sound appealing to Franco; he wanted to get away for a while and take time to get over his disturbing experience, but he didn't want to offend Easby.

"But ... what will James think of me?" he mused. "Staying in my room with a headache is one thing, but going out to revel is another."

"We already have James's blessing – and Jaguar," she reminded him. "He told me that you needed distraction and suggested that I take you out for a change of atmosphere. After all, we're the only non-mummified people in the house. More importantly, I'm bored stiff, and I deserve some fun. Can you be ready in fifteen minutes?"

Franco got up and gazed at her with admiration. "You're amazing, you know? I feel better already."

"Yes, I know I am. I'll wait for you in the car in fifteen," she added and motioned to him to get going.

Eva was an able driver but perhaps a bit too overconfident for Franco's comfort. He held tight to his seat while she drove on the narrow country roads, perfectly relaxed at 70 mph. He suggested that perhaps she might slow down once or twice, but she merely smiled sweetly at him and kept going at the same speed. He was relieved when they stopped near a low building with the *"Caipirinha"* sign on it.

"Do you mind if I drive going back?" he asked.

"Not at all. That means that I can drink as much as I want. You can definitely drive," she said. She handed him the keys ceremoniously and walked in without looking back. Franco followed suit.

The restaurant was only half-full, and they got a nice table by the band, which played unfamiliar Latino music. A male and a female singer alternated singing songs in Spanish and Portuguese; the food was more than decent, and the atmosphere was intimate and relaxed. Franco found himself telling jokes he had long forgotten and relaxing, helped by Eva's silvery laugh that became more and more frequent as she drank more *caipirinhas* and champagne.

"I want to dance," said Eva. The dance floor was almost empty, with only two couples dancing.

She got up and pulled Franco after her. On the dance floor, she put her head on his shoulder, and he placed his hands on her waist. They danced in silence for two songs, and then she whispered in his ear, "Let's go back." Franco didn't know if she meant back to the table or to the house but was happy to stop dancing. The silent dance forced him to concentrate on her perfume and on her perfect, white skin, and that was making him dizzy.

At the table, they ordered coffee, and Franco paid the bill. "Ready?" he asked her, and she nodded. They got up, and he looked at her. Her cheeks were flushed because of the alcohol and the heat in the restaurant. They walked up the stairs that led to the exit, and she slid elegantly into the passenger's seat while Franco kept the door open for her.

"You'll have to show me the way, don't go to sleep," he said as soon as he fastened his seat belt.

"I'm not sleepy," she retorted.

"I thought you were. You've been silent ..."

"I've been thinking, Professor. We girls do that too, every now and then."

"Sorry," Franco said, speaking defensively. "I didn't mean—"

"That's all right," she said. She sounded annoyed.

"No, really ..."

"No problem. Turn right here and then straight until I tell you to turn left."

Following Eva's sporadic instructions, Franco drove slowly until they reached a narrow and winding country road that he didn't remember driving through before. There Eva ordered, "Pull over."

"What's the matter? Are you unwell?" asked Franco.

"Just pull over," she repeated.

Franco found a place where the road broadened next to a patch of trees and stopped. Eva opened the door and stood out, and Franco hastened to cut the engine and circle the car to check on her. She stood, leaning against the car, but the night was so dark that Franco had to get very close to see the expression on her face. Eva was smiling, and that surprised him. She reached for his waist and pulled him closer. Their lips met, and she kissed him gently. The thought of backing off or resisting didn't even cross Franco's mind, but when their lips parted, he took a small step back and said, "You're drunk."

"You bet I am. Drunk *and* hot." She put her hands around his neck and pulled him hard, so they both fell onto the passenger's seat, then she kissed him again, this time harder.

"Eva ..." Franco started to say when he got a chance to speak again.

Eva had started to unbutton his shirt and stopped for a second. "You're not taking advantage of drunken me if that's what you're worried about. I know what I'm doing."

"But here? People may come this way any second ..."

"Here!" she said, and there was no arguing with her about it.

CHAPTER 23

Ambri, Switzerland. July 2009

Sally gazed at Hans with dislike. It wasn't that he had done anything wrong; on the contrary, it was his precision that irked her. His thin hair was combed back and seemed glued to his scalp, always in perfect order, each hair seemingly perfectly aligned with its neighbors. His green and white striped jacket was always immaculate and reminded her of a Nazi waiter she had seen in a movie. Above all, he avoided small talk, and that maddened her. Sally loved small talk, and after the first two weeks of seclusion, she had tried to entice Hans and his wife into talking to her. Still, all she had got from her approaches were grunts, a few sparse *"Ja*-s," and short functional sentences when unavoidable.

"Your Tylenol, I have brought," said Hans, placing a small bag with a pharmacy symbol stamped on it on the dressing table of Sally's room. Having completed his task, he took no further interest in Sally. He turned around and marched heavily to the door. He was tall and meaty, and each step resounded on the wooden floor, giving the impression of shaking the whole chalet.

"Stop!" Sally ordered, and Hans obliged and turned around.

"*Ja?*" he inquired.

"I've been sick for more than a week now, and I've had a temperature during most of the last two days. I want you to call a doctor."

"Doctor Benini will come," he said, speaking with a toneless voice.

"Doctor Benini was here three days ago and is not expected back until next week. I need a doctor now," said Sally, working herself up while speaking.

"You have Tylenol. Those my instructions," Hans said stubbornly and walked out.

Sally didn't know whether to cry or to throw a shoe at him. She sat on her bed, feeling exhausted by the fever that had subsided only for short intervals. True, Dr. Benini had said that it was a simple flu, but it surely didn't feel like it. She felt different – sick in a different way. She worried that perhaps Dr. Benini was underestimating her illness, that she could get too sick by the time he came back and realized his mistake.

As a condition of her contract, she had relinquished her cellular phone and had agreed to a clause that prohibited contacts with persons outside the project. She guessed that the clause covered outside physicians, but of course, it was not meant to include emergencies. She now regretted her stupidity in not asking Dr. Benini for a way to contact him that didn't have to go through that ox, Hans. Sally had reached a point where she seethed with rebellion. She resolved that she wouldn't put up with their stupid rules, contract or no contract. After all, she only wanted to see a physician, which had nothing to do with the project. So if Hans wasn't going to get a doctor to her, she would get herself to a doctor.

She swallowed two Tylenols and lay down to rest for a while. Half an hour later, the fever had subsided, and she felt strong enough to get up. The afternoon was already advanced, so she took a light jacket in case it would get cold by the time she returned, and then she tiptoed out of the room and down the stairs. Neither Hans nor his wife were anywhere in sight, so she left by the front door. Instead of turning right toward the garden where she used to sit and read, she took the path to the left, which she knew led into town through the wood. She had gone a short distance into the wood when Hans's figure blocked the path.

"You must go back, *Ja*?" he said unceremoniously.

"I'm going to see a doctor," she answered, undeterred.

"*Nein, du nicht!* You go back to the house," he said, and this time he sounded threatening.

Sally stopped and gazed at him in disbelief. "Why! Where do you get off, treating me like a prisoner? If I want to go and see a doctor, I'll do it as I please," she said, now feeling really mad. "And I'll report your behavior, you know? The gall!"

Hans was a man of few words and did not respond. He simply approached her and put his hands on her shoulders, pushing her, so she turned around, then he said, "You walk, or I take?"

Sally started to shiver, but not because of the fever; she had just realized that she was a prisoner in a not-so-gilded cage.

CHAPTER 24

Stanson Hall, South Yorkshire, England. July 2009

"Good morning, Sir."

Franco opened his eyes and focused his gaze on the silhouette of the man who stood at the door holding a tray loaded with a pot, cups, and other accessories. He had heard a knock on the door, he vaguely recalled, and must've said "come in" because there was Watts.

"Good morning, Miss," Watts added politely when the bedsheets stirred further, and Eva emerged from them, smiling brightly, and then he turned to Franco again. "You have missed breakfast time downstairs, Sir, so I've brought you coffee and toast with butter and marmalade. I hope that it will be to your liking. Shall I put the tray on this table over here?"

Franco nodded weakly. All he wanted was for Watts to get out as quickly as possible.

"Sir Easby would like to see you in his study at ten o'clock, if that suits you, Professor," said Watts, clearly unruffled by the circumstances.

"Yes, yes. I'll be there, thank you," said Franco hastily.

"Do you need anything further, Sir? Miss?"

"No, thank you," said Franco. He spoke pointedly. It seemed that Watts was enjoying lingering, but a few seconds during which Franco stared at him in silence apparently drove the message home because he turned around majestically and left.

"Well, you *are* a stiff!" Eva said when the door closed behind Watts, "but I like you this way ..." She hugged him and kissed his chest, and then she pushed him back onto the cushions and rolled herself aside.

"What was I supposed to say?" asked Franco, who did not know whether to laugh or to be annoyed. "Did you want me to invite him to stay and have coffee with us?"

Franco gazed at Eva, still unable to believe that this beautiful woman was there in his bed with him.

"The poor old dear was dying of curiosity, and you've just been mean to him, but he'll get over it," she said, adding a little laugh. She kicked the bedsheets away and quickly wore her dress, passing it over her head without bothering to look for her underwear. "I'll go brush my teeth and wash my face, and I'll be back. Don't drink all the coffee while I'm gone," she admonished him. She took her shoes in her hands and disappeared down the corridor.

James Easby got up from behind his desk to greet his visitor. The study was elegantly furnished with a sizeable hand-painted desk, antique armchairs, chairs, and wood-paneled walls. He shook Franco's hand, placing his left hand on his shoulder and smiling warmly.

"How are you today? Did you enjoy yourself in Sheffield? Let's sit over here," he added without waiting for an answer, pointing to a round table that could sit four.

"It was good, thank you. I needed a diversion after yesterday afternoon's – how shall I put it – rather unsettling experience."

"I understand. I fully understand, and I'm sorry if I was instrumental in putting you through this, as you say, unsettling experience."

"You couldn't know ..."

"No, obviously I couldn't," said Easby, and then after a brief pause, he added, "I'm afraid that what I have to tell you – what I promised to disclose to you when we first met – is also rather out of the ordinary. But enough beating about the bush. Here's a short NDA for you to sign. Please read it and sign it so we can get down to business."

Franco took the document that was titled "Non-Disclosure Agreement" and read quickly through it. It was brief and essentially stated that all information conveyed to Franco by the EHCS and its officers was confidential and EHCS proprietary and that Franco undertook to keep it confidential and not to disclose it to any third party.

"Is this really necessary?" Franco asked. "This is the first time that I have seen this kind of document."

"I'm afraid that this is the rule of the EHCS," said Easby. He sounded embarrassed and spoke apologetically. "Personally, I wouldn't really need this from you. I trust you implicitly, but we are very protective of the fruits of our hard work ..."

"Oh, all right. I don't really have any reservations," said Franco. He was pretty sure that disclosing information received by a criminal organization to help prevent a crime would have been lawful. On the other hand, if the EHCS turned out to be a harmless, legal organization, then he certainly would keep their confidential information secret. And Franco was growing more and more convinced that Easby was no criminal; still, he was there to listen and learn and was determined to keep an open mind.

"Thank you very much. I apologize again," said Easby, taking the signed paper from Franco's hand and glancing at it quickly. "Now I can be open with you. I think that the best way to start is to let you read the appeal for help that we received," said Easby, handing a paper to Franco. "This is a facsimile of the original, which is kept in a safe place."

Easby watched as Franco read slowly through it.

"I don't understand," said Franco after he read and re-read the first sentences. "This letter bears a date of eighteen ninety-four ... and the writing is so old-fashioned and difficult to read."

"I know. Please bear with me and read to the end," said Easby.

Franco read slowly, at times going back to re-read a paragraph. Easby waited patiently for him to finish and only spoke when Franco put the letter down on the table. "Do you recognize the name and signature?" he asked.

Franco nodded. "It's my great-grandfather's, but how can it be?"

"We did research when we got that letter, so we're probably ahead of you and know more about your family's history than you do. Do you know who Evelyn was?"

"I've heard her mentioned. My father spoke about her often when he was in one of his moods. I know that my grandfather had a sister named Evelyn, who died young. I must even have a picture of her somewhere in an old family album that my father kept, but that's all I can remember off the cuff."

"That's quite accurate," said Easby. "She was your great-aunt. The poor young woman died of tuberculosis in the summer of eighteen ninety-four. At that time, there was no known cure for this illness. Antibiotics hadn't been discovered yet, and either your body was strong enough to recover from it, or you died. She died when she was only twenty-six years old."

"But ... but this letter doesn't make sense. Here it says that we will read it after his death, which was long after Evelyn died, and still, he is expecting us to save her. It must be a prank, a forgery."

"At first, we thought so too, but your great-grandfather was a very well-known figure, a war hero and a member of Parliament, so it wasn't difficult to find samples of his handwriting and compare them with that of this letter. There is no doubt whatsoever that he wrote it; three different graphology experts confirmed it. So now you see why we are taking this seriously."

"I've heard so much about my great-grandfather, who as you say was a hero and a personality in his time, and this letter is not in character with him. He was a rational person who didn't subscribe to any religious or other belief, except straightforward logic. He made a point of it throughout his life. But if this letter has been authenticated, perhaps we don't know everything about him."

"You should remember that he was in despair when he wrote it, and people in dire straits seek help in unusual places. Nevertheless, we would have probably not pursued this any further had it not been for Maria. You have already had a demonstration of her impressive powers. When she came to us with this letter, she also gave us precise information that was missing from the letter, such as the exact place where Evelyn died, the name of the physician who treated her, and plenty of other details that were confirmed as genuine one by one by our research, which made it clear to us that the knowledge she had was real. She is the great-granddaughter of the woman who helped your great-grandfather through this. She said that her great-grandmother came to her in her dream and told her where to find the letter she had hidden in her house a hundred and forty-five years earlier and provided all the other details. I must stress that, to the best of our knowledge, those details are not easily available and, in practice, they could be verified only because we had them beforehand."

Franco got up, no longer capable of staying still, and paced the room, trying to put order into his tumultuous thoughts. Coupled with his mother's unexpected message, this was much too much for him in such a short time. Easby sat in silence, respecting Franco's need for movement and waiting patiently for him to speak again.

"I ... I don't know what to think. The letter says that we should follow instructions to save Evelyn, but where are those instructions? They are not in the letter."

"The instructions have apparently been lost. They must have been originally kept together with the letter but were not there when

Maria found it. That's why we need her so much. She has flashes in which she sees things. By piecing the fragmentary information that she has given us so far together, we were able to reconstruct part of those instructions. Not all of it, but we believe that we know enough now to move forward, and Maria is confident that she will have the missing pieces of the jigsaw soon."

"You seem to be on top of it, so why do you need me?"

"If with God's help, this is going to work and we can bridge the centuries and bring healing to Evelyn, it will be by the concerted efforts of a group in which many good and dedicated people participate, and you are an essential member of that group. I should explain; without going into the many fine details right now, the process involves finding a young person infected with TB, bringing her to the same physical location where Evelyn died, at the same time of the year when she died and curing her. We have been able to locate a suitable young woman who's presently sick, but because she is no blood relative of Evelyn's, Maria says that our efforts will be futile unless we also have a blood relative of Evelyn's on the premises at the critical moment. Your presence is needed to help us make contact with Evelyn, which will give her the strength to heal. Your family ties will be our bridge to her. Do you understand now?"

"I understand, but you will forgive me, I hope, for being unconvinced. I find it hard – to put it extremely mildly – to believe in this convoluted trans-century theory. I must confess to being confused by yesterday's events, combined with this strange letter, but it will take more than this to convince me that it can all work."

"I can understand your perplexity," said Easby, gazing straight into Franco's eyes, which, now that he had seated himself, were again level with his, "because even I can't tell you in all honesty that we will succeed. I am putting a lot of work and no little money into this effort because of my faith that it will, but I can't promise it. But let me ask you this: given that neither you nor I can rule out that all this is true, and even though there is only a slight chance that what we have undertaken here may save Evelyn's life, do you think it would be right on your part to deny her the chance to be saved, no matter how remote?"

"Now that's a tough question ..."

"I don't think so. To me, it's a perfectly simple question with a straightforward answer. If a perfect stranger came to me and said, 'look here, James, there is a chance in one million that you are the only person who may be able to save another person's life, and you can do that at no cost to yourself simply by donating some of your time,' I wouldn't hesitate for a second."

"You're right, that's what everybody should do ... In theory. But this is really not the same thing. The scenario that you just pictured would work well with any established medical situation. But this is plain weird."

"Look here, Franco. I need to tell you something else. This is indeed one project that, if it succeeds, will have a limited effect resulting in your grand-aunt's life being saved – at least from the danger of dying from tuberculosis. We are not omniscient, and we don't know whether something else may kill her later on. But there is much more at stake than that. We're not doing it only because of your great-grandfather's appeal, although I must confess that, by itself, it got me emotionally hooked. The truth is that we can learn a lot from it."

"Like what?"

"Like ... I hesitate to say it. I don't want to raise any false hopes with you ..."

"Go ahead," Franco prodded him.

"How would you like to have a chance to save your mother's life? To change your past and that of your father?"

"How do you know about my mother?"

"As I told you, we did a lot of research on account of Evelyn. We had to look for her relatives – that's how we found you – and so we learned about your family history. Your mother's death was a case of medical malpractice, I understand. If we learned how to intervene where modern medicine has a cure, we could still save her. She could still be here with you now. Wouldn't you like that?"

"I don't dare think about it ..."

"But you should." Easby got up and put a fatherly hand on Franco's shoulder. "This project is bigger than Evelyn; bigger than us," he said.

Franco remained silent, searching for answers in his head. "If it weren't for you, who obviously are a serious person," he said at last, "I would probably get up and leave right now. But crazy as it may sound, I want to give it a chance. That doesn't mean that I am convinced that what you're trying is possible; it only means that I'm ready to reserve judgment and come on board to see what happens. Watching from the sideline, as it were, at least at first."

Easby got up and, clearly moved by Franco's words, he took his hand and shook it warmly. "You won't regret it," he said. "Thank you."

"So what's next?" asked Franco.

"We still wait to hear from Maria about the timing for the final stage of the process. It should be very soon, so please make yourself available at short notice. I assume that you are going back to London tomorrow? Of course, you're welcome to stay at Stanson Hall for as long as you want, but my own engagements force me to go back to the city."

"I appreciate your invitation, but I still have tests to grade and work to do in preparation for the next semester, so I, too, have to go back to work."

"You know, I think that I understand something, now, that eluded me yesterday," said Easby.

"What?"

"I understand why your mother said that she was proud of you. She well should!"

CHAPTER 25

Udine, Italy. July 2009

Franco drove the rented Fiat Punto slowly along the road that led from the Venice Airport to Udine through sleepy villages and sporadic commercial centers. The BA flight had landed on time, and he wasn't supposed to meet Easby's researcher until 3:00 PM, so he had the time to get reacquainted with the countryside that he hadn't seen for years.

He let his mind wander to the last few days, which had been confusing, to say the least. After breakfast on Monday, he had parted from his host, feeling that he had failed his mission during his weekend at the Hall. He had done little to gather the information that he was supposed to bring back. He realized with a pang of guilt that he had given little or no thought to Kathia's instructions most of the time. True, Easby had noted his cellular phone number and promised to be in touch soon, but nothing in his demeanor had justified Kathia's allegations that he was a criminal mastermind; to Franco, he had been nothing short of a genial host. He had to admit that James sounded a little potty at times, but as far as he could tell, those were the innocuous New Age ideas of an old man with too much money and free time on his hands. And besides, much as he hated admitting it to himself, the thought that there might be something in what he had heard kept nagging at him. No matter how hard he tried to suppress the thought, being able to do something toward saving his mother's life was not something he could ignore. And after all, the séance had proven to him that the notion of contacting people on the other side was not completely unacceptable.

And then there was Eva. They had shared a ride with Easby's driver, who had taken them back to London in the Rolls-Royce. He had dropped them at the St. Pancras train station where Eva had taken the 3:02 PM Eurostar to Paris. Franco had waited with her for a few minutes for the train to arrive, fantasizing that he might jump on it and go to Paris with her.

"When am I going to see you again?" he had asked.

"Oh, I don't know, *mon cheri*. I may be busy for a while with this movie, you know? I'll call you," she had said, and then she had kissed him on the tip of his nose, waved him goodbye, and left.

Her departure had left him unsatisfied, uncertain of where he stood with her. A non-committal relationship with a beautiful, uninhibited, and fun young woman was what he really needed at that juncture. That would have been a welcome change from the intellectual, darkly opinionated Zoe with whom he had spent his time during the last few months. Eva was the exact opposite; she was effervescent, full of life, and undemanding. He had repressed the wish to call her several times since they had parted ways but had managed it with difficulty and just barely.

Then there was Kathia. She was furious at him and wouldn't stop riding his back. He had put off calling her, from the phone booth near his apartment, until late on Monday evening, knowing that she wouldn't be calling him because of the danger of wiretapping and hoping that she would be satisfied with a quick phone report that he had nothing to report, but the moment she had heard his voice she had simply said, "I'll be at your place in a few minutes," and had hung up.

She was a woman of her word, and less than fifteen minutes later, she was banging on his door. Franco had let her in and had gone to sit on the sofa without a word.

"Why didn't you call me the moment you got back?" she had rebuked him.

"I had things to do," Franco had retorted, feeling and sounding annoyed. "I don't work for you, you know?"

"That's where you're wrong. That's where you're damn wrong!" she had said, working herself up visibly as she spoke. "I'm your chance to stay alive, remember? To keep you alive, I must get at Easby, and your job is to help me do just that. Now report," she had ordered.

Franco had rebelled at the thought that she was taking for granted that he would help her get at Easby. It was perhaps her arrogance or the fact that she was set to go after James no matter what that had made him realize there and then that his mind was made up not to cooperate. At least not yet.

"Listen," he had said, managing to keep his calm, "I have nothing to report. It was just a nice, relaxing, and pleasant weekend. Good food, beautiful countryside, pleasant company. That's it."

"That's it," Kathia had repeated, sounding dangerous.

"That's it: no hooded men, no sacrifices at the time of the full moon. No lycanthropes. Nothing. I'm sorry to disappoint you."

"What did they do to you, Franco?" Kathia had asked. "Did they threaten you? Are you too scared to talk? Did they brainwash you?"

"They didn't do anything to me. Easby is just a regular guy. His guests were regular people – a physician, a businessman, a starlet, and some other mixed persons I can't even remember; they were so commonplace and boring. You're barking under the wrong tree."

"Just a regular guy ... how nice," she had said, speaking acidly. "And what about the matter for which he contacted you in the first place? How do you explain that away?"

"I don't know what it was about," he had lied. He had realized there and then that he didn't want this woman to disrupt Easby's project, which – admittedly, with a chance of one in a trillion – could open the door for saving his own mother. "He said that it wasn't urgent ... or important. He said he would call me about it sometime. Really, Kathia, you scared me for nothing. I should be mad at you – in fact, I am."

Kathia had gazed at him with pursed lips. She was obviously furious and hadn't believed him, but there was little she could do at that point, and Franco had been counting on it.

"Look here," he had said, speaking soothingly, "I'm not trying to be difficult. If anything evolves, I'll get in touch with you immediately, okay? So may I have some privacy now? Please?"

"I hope you know what you're doing," she had said, speaking slowly. "You may be putting in danger not only your own life but also the lives of others. Remember that when someone dies because of you."

"Don't be ridiculous!" Franco had spurted.

She had turned around and had left without closing the door, so Franco had to get up and shut it. He knew that he hadn't seen the last of her, but at least he had bought himself some time to figure out how he really felt about Easby and his project.

In the next couple of days, he had thought on different occasions that someone was watching him and had wondered whether Kathia was having him followed, but hard as he tried, he had never spotted a tail, so he had decided that it probably was only his imagination playing tricks on him.

On Wednesday, the phone had rung, and Easby's unmistakable voice had come through the earpiece.

"Hello, it's James. Franco?" he had said.

"Yes, oh hello," Franco had said, taken by surprise.

"I promised to call you if I needed your help, and now I do. How would you like to take a quick trip to Udine?"

"Udine? How? When? Why?"

"Stupid me! I should have explained, but I'm too excited to think straight. We have a researcher looking for documents related to your great-grandfather. He has found a sealed document in the archives of the Udine municipality. It was kept sealed by order of Udine's major until a few years ago, but now the sealing order has expired. However, it can be delivered only to a living relative, which would be you, of course. You see now?"

"Actually, I don't. What is all the excitement about? It may be an interesting document, but I doubt that it's worth the trouble and the expense of taking a flight to Italy especially for it."

"It's worth much more than that. Maria told us that her great-grandmother had said that a second copy of your great-grandfather's letter and enclosed instructions had been kept in a safe place, but she hadn't told her where. So you see, it must be this document, and it must contain the full instructions that went missing from the copy that we got. It has to be the key to the whole project. Will you go and get it, please?"

Easby's enthusiasm was contagious, and Franco's heart had started to race. And with the enthusiasm, all the fears had come back as well. Still, going to Udine presented no danger, and anyway, he could see no way – or reason – to refuse to help.

"When?" he had asked.

"I have you booked on the 9:50 AM BA flight tomorrow morning, which will get you to Venice's Marco Polo airport by 1:00 PM. You can drive, right?" he had asked with sudden concern.

"Of course."

"Good, good. We have rented a car for you. All you need to do is go to the Avis counter and say your name. Everything is paid for, and you don't need to worry about that."

"Well, this is a bit sudden, but you seem to have taken care of everything," Franco had said with admiration.

"It's not me, really. My secretary. She's a gem. Anyway, she has booked a room for you at the Astoria Hotel in Udine. Our researcher,

Doctor Marchetti, will meet you there at 3:00 PM. The hotel is paid for too. Once you retrieve the document, he will take care of the rest. I hope I've covered everything."

"I think so."

"If you need anything please call me any time. You have my cellular number."

"I do."

"I want you to know that I really appreciate your help. I sincerely do," Easby had said. He had sounded soft and fatherly and grateful, and Franco couldn't help thinking how off the mark Kathia was with her conspiracy theory.

CHAPTER 26

Udine, Italy. July 2009

It was raining buckets when Franco reached the Astoria Hotel, a short, violent summer shower that had taken him by surprise. The lobby was empty except for a small man with a beaky nose, who wore a brown suit two sizes too large for him and sat sunken in a low, puffy armchair. He jumped up as Franco came in.

"Professor Lorenzi?" he inquired timidly, and only when Franco nodded and answered with "Doctor Marchetti?" did he come closer and shake his hand.

"You got wet, ah?" he said, stating the obvious. "Please take time to go up to your room and freshen up. We are not due at City Hall until four. I'll wait here."

When Franco came down a few minutes later, Marchetti handed him an umbrella he had borrowed from the hotel. "We can go when you're ready," he said. "It's only a short walk from here."

"Perhaps you could first tell me a little more about what we are supposed to do?" said Franco.

"Yes, of course. Let's sit over here," he said, pointing to one of the sitting areas of the lobby. They sat down, and then he asked, "What would you like to know?"

"Well, pretty much everything. I know virtually nothing about this document that I understand you have discovered."

"We don't know much either. At this point, it's all speculation. As I assume you are aware, I have been charged with carrying out historical research to locate documents written by your great-grandfather around the year eighteen ninety-four. Particularly, I am to locate documents that mention his daughter, Evelyn, who at the time was seriously ill. I searched several archives and have found many letters of a political nature and some personal correspondence – your great-grandfather was somewhat of a graphomaniac if you'll excuse my saying so, but then many people wrote a lot at the time. However, except for a passing mention of Evelyn in a couple of letters, no document really focuses on her."

"So why do you think that the document we are going to retrieve bears any relation to her?"

"I only have the dates to go by. I am told that the most important period for my research starts on June eighteen-ninety-four. The window is very narrow, perhaps only two or three months. The document we are going to obtain was sealed by decree of the Major of Udine on the thirtieth of June of that year. Of course, it may relate to something altogether different. We won't know until we read it. Shall we go?" he added, gazing at his watch.

The walk to City Hall only took five minutes, but they had to wait for an elderly secretary to guide them to a tiny office where an officer with an undecipherable job description invited them to sit down.

"So, you, ehr ... Professor Lorenzi, are the nephew of the son ... or rather, the great-grandson – is that correct?" he stopped in mid-sentence, clearly embarrassed by his confusion, and Marchetti came to his aid.

"Professor Lorenzi is the sole direct surviving relative, as documented by the chain of birth certificates and the Registry Office records that I have submitted with my petition on his behalf. I have here another copy for your convenience."

"Where did you get all those?" Franco whispered with surprise, but Marchetti merely shushed him, pointing to the officer as if to say, "Don't confuse him more than he already is."

"Yes, this is quite in order," the officer agreed after a while. He opened a drawer and took from it a square envelope sealed with an official-looking seal. "Please sign here," he added, and after Franco signed, he handed the envelope to him. Marchetti was quick to take it from Franco's hand and to put it in a plastic bag. "For protection," he said. They thanked the officer for his time and left.

The rain had stopped, and the air was fresh and clean. They stood outside City Hall, and Franco suddenly grew excited at the prospect of reading the document. "Let's go to the hotel and open it," he suggested.

"Nooo!" said Marchetti. "We must make sure not to damage it. We don't know under which conditions it has been kept, and opening it without caution may damage it irreparably. I'll have to put it under a nitrogen atmosphere for a few hours, at least before opening it. There may be other problems – fungi, for instance."

"So what do we do?" Franco asked. He was disappointed but understood the need for precautions.

"You're staying the night, right? Your flight back is tomorrow afternoon, if I'm correct? Yes? Then I suggest that I go and run some tests now, and maybe we can meet for dinner, and if my tests show that we can safely open the envelope by then, we'll do it together. What do you say?"

"It sounds like a plan to me," said Franco. "I'll walk around a bit, and then I'll go back to the hotel. When and where do we meet?"

"The Astoria has a good restaurant. Let's meet there at half past seven," said Marchetti, and with a quick handshake, he left, walking briskly.

CHAPTER 27

Udine, Italy. July 2009

Joseph Mead waited patiently outside City Hall for Franco to come out. He didn't mind waiting; he was a patient man – which was lucky because much of his work involved waiting. Waiting for people to be taken places or waiting for people to die. He never took anything personally and was never angry or upset because of a job he had to do. One of his many gifts was his anonymity. Despite his large body size, he was so unimpressive that people seldom remembered having seen him before. Going unnoticed was a great advantage for Joseph and one on which he capitalized often.

His official job was to drive Heinrich von Stoffen around in his beautiful cars. He preferred the Mercedes to the Rolls-Royce but took good care of both. Before entering into his employ, Joseph had served one of von Stoffen's associates, now sadly behind bars in an English jail where he was due to serve a long stretch. Left without an employer, Joseph had considered his options. He was no great thinker but appreciated that a prior acquaintance with his prospective employer would pave the way to getting a job. From the little he knew about his former employer's business with Heinrich von Stoffen, he was the person he wanted to work for. On the day that he knocked on his door, five years earlier, von Stoffen had had no idea how valuable Joseph would turn out to be to him, but he remembered his friend's praises of his services and many gifts and took him on without hesitation.

Joseph was a thief and a killer, but he mostly thought of himself as a professional. He was no sadist and found no pleasure in killing, but he accepted the need to terminate some individuals as a business necessity. He felt no excitement, no regrets, and no qualms while on a job or when it was done. On the few occasions in the past when killing had been a necessity, he had done it quietly and mechanically. He always thought about it as "a job," which was all there was to it for him. And he had his ethics; he never discussed a "job" with his employer explicitly, although they both knew what they were talking about when von Stoffen said that a person was "a business hazard," or an "obstacle" to a business deal. He was always pleased to be able to report to his employer that the obstacle had been removed.

He stood on the other side of the street, slightly diagonally placed to City Hall's entrance. A movement at the door got his attention. He watched as Franco and the other person that he couldn't identify stood on the sidewalk, talking. He pushed the "send" button of his cell phone, and as soon as he heard von Stoffen saying "Yes," he spoke fast.

"I have followed him, and he went to the hotel as he was told to do in that recording that we heard. He met with a man who must be the researcher that was mentioned when they spoke." Joseph was always careful to omit names when speaking over the phone. "They have come out and are talking. I think they're going to split. What do I do?"

"Keep following the professor," came the quick answer. "He's the important one. Don't lose him. Have you taken a picture of the other one?"

"Of course," Joseph answered, "I sent it to you already." Had he had feelings, he might have sounded as if he was hurt by the question. Instead, his response was a matter-of-fact one, as always.

"All right. Wait a second. Let me check." Silence followed, and then von Stoffen said, "Hmm ... I've never seen him. I've changed my mind. The professor is not likely to disappear since he just got there, and we know where he's staying. He's sure to spend the night in town. Try to follow the other one and to find out who he is, and then go back to the hotel and keep after the professor."

"Understood. They are leaving, I must go. I'll report."

Joseph pocketed his cell phone and started walking after Franco's companion – or, "the subject," as he liked to think of his target. Calling him that made him feel better as if he were a detective on an important job. Moreover, depersonalizing his potential victims was a necessity that made his life much easier, and it had become a habit.

He followed the subject from afar for a while until they reached a crowded shopping area. The subject was holding what looked like an old and battered briefcase in his right hand, and Joseph realized that the right thing to do was to take it from him. This person had been to City Hall with the professor, and if they had gotten something there, it had to be in that briefcase because the professor wasn't carrying anything. Joseph quickened his pace and soon caught up with the subject, who was hindered by the heavy shopping crowd and by what appeared to be a timid disposition, judging by how he allowed every child who walked by to push him aside without complaining or pushing back.

Joseph got ready for the snatch. He had done this many times before and knew the drill. You approach your victim from behind, grab the bag from a corner or a strap, and then you pull with all your strength; and if you're strong and heavy like Joseph and your victim is taken by surprise, it's the work of a moment to wring it off his hand and to disappear with it in the crowd before he knows what happened to him or recovers from the blow enough to cry out loud.

Joseph followed the familiar routine, but to his surprise, instead of letting go of the bag, the subject simply followed his pull and fell flat on the floor with a loud "Ahh!" still holding it tight. In a flash,

Joseph realized what was wrong: the subject had handcuffed himself to the briefcase. The realization that he had been right and that the briefcase contents must be valuable brought no satisfaction to Joseph. Passersby had begun to take notice, and many were pointing to him. Others were helping the subject and creating an effective barrier between Joseph and the briefcase. At that junction, Joseph took the only sensible course of action: he turned around and ran without looking back, followed by angry shouts.

CHAPTER 28

Udine, Italy. July 2009

Franco came down from his room at seven-thirty, refreshed from the brief nap that he had taken after walking around the picturesque streets of ancient Udine, with its antique buildings, cobblestoned pavements, and dark porticos. A melancholic waiter seated him at a small table. The restaurant was empty but for a big man who occupied a table in a far corner and seemed to be giving his full attention to his food. Franco felt unusually good-humored, perhaps because his trip to retrieve an old document was more like a homecoming vacation than a quest. To while away the time, he ordered a Campari soda and sipped on it while he waited for Marchetti.

It was already a quarter to eight when a waiter approached him. "Sir, I have a message for you from Doctor Marchetti," he said. "He regrets that he won't be able to come and says that the package is not to be opened under any circumstances and that you'll understand. Will you be ordering now, sir?"

Franco was astonished by Marchetti's behavior. It wasn't only that he hadn't shown up, but he hadn't even told him what he would be doing with the document. He now realized that Marchetti hadn't given him a phone number where he could be reached, so there was nothing he could do. However, he had to let James know, so he dialed his cellular phone number, but all he got was his voice mail.

He left a message, reporting the retrieval of the document and complaining about Marchetti. "Unless I hear from you, I'll be coming back tomorrow as planned," he concluded his message and hung up. Kathia would certainly have attached some sinister meaning to Marchetti's behavior, and Franco wondered whether there could be more to it than met the eye. Even in the unlikely event that foul play was involved, he concluded that he had nothing to worry about. He didn't really care about the old document, and if that was what Easby was after, he was welcome to it. He couldn't help feeling uncomfortable, though, not having all the pieces of the puzzle. He was fed up with the whole story and resolved to go back to London and tell everybody – Kathia, Easby, and all the others – to get lost and leave him alone.

After a moody and solitary dinner, Franco took a walk around the block, killing time by gazing into the closed shops' windows. As he turned the corner near a cinema house, he saw two men standing on the sidewalk and talking animatedly. The man with the back to him looked very much like Marchetti, with the same too large and wrinkled brown suit. He couldn't be sure because of the distance and because he couldn't see his face, but he felt sure enough that it was him and called out "Marchetti!" The man in the brown suit turned quickly toward him and back – too quickly for Franco to see his face clearly – and then he walked away at a fast pace. Franco debated whether to run after him, but then, he thought, the man might simply be a passerby understandably alarmed at being addressed by a stranger in the street at that time of night. Still, his way of walking was so similar to Marchetti's ...

Franco's indecision lasted long enough for the man to disappear around a corner. His interlocutor also was gone, and Franco hadn't even noticed which direction he had taken. The street suddenly felt like an unsafe place to be – too silent and yet obviously populated by people who felt more at ease in the dark than he did. With a shiver, he turned back toward the hotel, walking fast, barely short of running.

CHAPTER 29

Ambri, Switzerland. July 1894

The Honorable L. sat upright in the wooden chair, gazing into his daughter's pale face. She looked like a china doll, and her pallor was enhanced by lightly rose-powdered cheeks. Her nurse always insisted on light makeup, and the Honorable L. was grateful that she did because it helped to hide the signs of her illness.

He never tired of looking at her, and, as much as he tried to chase away the thought, he wondered what would happen when he would no longer be able to do it. He had been sitting beside her bed for over an hour now, yearning to take her hand and feel her but resisting the urge to avoid waking her from her much-needed sleep.

Evelyn stirred slightly – almost only a shiver – and then opened her eyes. "Father, dear ..." she said, smiling with pleasure when she saw him.

"I'm here, Ev," he said, now taking the hand that she offered naturally.

"Have you been here for long?" she inquired.

"Just a while ... I didn't want to wake you up."

"You must always wake me up when you arrive. Seeing you is a much better medicine than sleeping."

They sat in silence, contented with being with each other. Everything that had to be said had been spoken many times before – or at least most of it – and silence was not something unnatural or a burden to them. After a while, Evelyn propped herself up against the pillows, coming to a half-sitting position. "You know, Father, I've had the strangest dream."

"Yes?" he prompted her gently. He was proud that his daughter felt close enough to him to tell him of her dreams. Girls, he knew, usually only revealed them to their closest female friends, or at most to their mother or sister.

"I was here, in this room, but I was wearing strange clothes – more like a boy's outfit. And the smell was different; I could actually smell it in my dream. Then I walked around and felt strong as I haven't been for a long time. A voice said – I couldn't see the man who spoke – 'You're getting better, you'll soon be cured,' and then I don't remember much, but I think I woke up for a moment before going back to sleep. What do you think it means, this dream?"

The Honorable L. felt a large lump in his throat that almost choked him, but he had to speak. As many times before, he was grateful for his beard and mustache that covered much of his face and made it easy for him to hide his emotions. At last, he mastered his voice and spoke as naturally as he could. "It means that your body is building up the strength to fight and is telling you that it's up to you to win the battle. That you can do it and will do it," he said, hoping that his voice carried conviction.

"Dear Father ... you always see wars and battles everywhere." She remained silent for a few moments and then added, "I wish I knew how to win mine ..."

Evelyn closed her eyes and brought her hand quickly to her face, but not quickly enough to hide the tear that was rolling down her cheek, marking an uneven trail in her makeup.

CHAPTER 30

London, England. July 2009

It wasn't the first time that von Stoffen's spacious Wimbledon residence had been turned into headquarters for an operation, but he still disliked the presence of so many people in the house. Von Stoffen liked to work alone or with Joseph when really needed, and to him, three were a crowd. Nevertheless, there was no choice; too much was at stake, and he could leave no room for mistakes. He walked into the basement and approached the man who sat at the table near the door with headphones on his ears. The man courteously removed them and turned his attention to von Stoffen.

"Nothing yet," he said.

"Is it functioning properly now?"

"Yes, it seems to be working without a hitch. I don't know what the problem was before. Probably a disturbance due to some electric equipment at their end."

"Keep listening," von Stoffen ordered. He looked around the room. At a farther table, von Stoffen's secretary and *factotum*, Janet, sat next to a switchboard reading a book. In the farthest corner of the basement, two men were smoking and playing cards. The room was still, and the atmosphere was heavy with expectation.

Von Stoffen turned back and climbed the short flight of stairs that led to the kitchen. He was too nervous to sit still and poured himself a drink from a bottle on the kitchen table and drank from the glass, standing. He wasn't a heavy drinker, but today he definitely needed a stimulant to calm his nerves. He was a man of action and was not good at waiting. Waiting unnerved him, particularly now that he didn't have enough facts to go by when planning his strategy. Too many questions were open: who was the man with whom the professor had met in Udine, and what was his role? Joseph's report had made it clear that he and Lorenzi had gone together to City Hall to retrieve the document – but why was it so important to Easby that it justified making a special trip to get it? It was important since the man had treated it as such, you don't handcuff yourself to unimportant items.

The bug in Easby's office had malfunctioned, and all that had been recorded of his conversation with Lorenzi were the details of a BA flight and of a hotel in Udine – enough to send Joseph after him on the same flight, but not enough to explain what it was all about.

And above all, the question remained of the whereabouts of the surrogate. He hadn't been able to extract even a hint from Easby, and he knew how obstinate he was; not a chance of getting anything out of him if he considered it a secret. For perhaps the tenth time, von Stoffen cursed the Vatican Bank and its officials. They were so damn shortsighted that they couldn't see that his housing deal was a winner. Why did they have to link it to this stupid resurrection quest? But then he only had himself to blame for telling them about it – although, without that incentive on the table, they might have simply refused to fund his deal. There were wheels within wheels, and probably they weren't telling him all there was to know; that's how it worked with the Vatican. Secretiveness was a second religion to them. No point tormenting himself, though. It was too late for recrimination anyway ...

The sound of a buzzer jerked him from his deep thoughts. The buzzer meant that something was stirring, so he ran down the stairs and into the basement. The man near the door was waiting for him, standing.

"He got a phone call. Here, listen to the recording," he said, handing von Stoffen the headset. As soon as he nodded to signal that he was ready, the man pushed a button, and von Stoffen heard a whirring sound, followed by a click and then voices.

"Sir James?" a voice that von Stoffen didn't recognize said.

"Yes, Marchetti?" Easby's voice responded.

"I just got off the plane. There were complications, I ..."

"Not now!" Easby interrupted him. "Come to my office."

"I'll be there as soon as I can," said Marchetti.

"Fine. I'll be waiting for you." said Easby and, after a brief pause, asked, "Is Lorenzi all right?"

"I think so," said Marchetti.

"Good," said Easby, sounding reassured. "I'll see you soon."

Von Stoffen took off the headphones and called to one of the men who were playing cards. "Peter, come here!"

The man called Peter dropped his cards and approached.

"Take this picture," von Stoffen said, handing him a printout of the photograph that Joseph had sent him via MMS. "This man should be arriving at Easby's offices soon. I want to talk to him before Easby does. Bring him here."

"And if he doesn't want to come?" Peter asked.

"I'm sure he doesn't. You'll need to be convincing. You know how to, right?"

"I'll take Dave and the van. Dave!" he called to the man who had been playing cards with him, who got up, extinguished his cigarette, and joined them.

"Good. I'm counting on you. Get going," said von Stoffen, and then he went back to the kitchen to finish his drink. This time he drank smiling; the waiting was over, and he was feeling much better now that the action had started.

CHAPTER 31

Udine, Italy. July 2009

The excellent breakfast served at the Astoria hotel did little to restore Franco's equanimity. He was sitting moodily, drinking his third cup of coffee, when his cell phone rang.

"Latin lover," he heard Eva's cheerful voice from the other end of the line.

"Hey," said Franco. He wasn't expecting a call from her, and it instantly lifted his mood. "What's up?"

"A little bird told me that you are in Udine, just a stone's throw away from me. So how would you like to behave like a real Italian hotheaded Valentino, jump on your stallion and ride to see me? I have a whole free weekend."

"Well, Paris is not really a stone's throw from Udine, but of course ..."

"Who's talking about Paris? I'm in Venice. We had some shooting to do here – for the movie, you know – and finished early, so everybody went back, but I have a friend who's got her aunt's apartment to herself for the summer, so I'm staying with her. Come join us; it's free."

"I'll have to call the airline and reschedule my flight back," Franco said, turning practical.

"Don't worry, James's secretary already did. You have a seat on the flight from Venice that leaves Monday morning."

"You knew I would come ..." Said Franco, who still needed to decide whether to feel manipulated or be flattered.

"I thought so. Why? Was I wrong?"

Franco hesitated for a second, but he knew he couldn't win the argument, so he conceded, "You know you weren't. I'll check out in half an hour. How do I find you in Venice?"

"Call me when you're near, and I'll tell you where to meet me. See you soon, Latin lover."

"I wish you wouldn't call me that."

"Why?"

"Because it sounds like you're making fun of me and of my work," Franco said, speaking gravely.

"Oh, lighten up!" she said. "And get your sexy ass over here."

Franco couldn't help laughing. "We'll talk about it," he said.

"I'm waiting," Eva said and hung up.

Franco couldn't know that the man who sat at a nearby table got up in the middle of his breakfast and left as soon as he saw Franco passing through the door.

Franco drove to Venice in good humor and even sang along with the radio. The expectation of a long weekend in romantic Venice alone with Eva made him push hard on the accelerator. Since the car would be of no use to him in Venice, he decided to return it at Venice's Marco Polo airport. To go from the airport to central Venice, he had to take the boat, which meant competing with angry and sweaty tourists for a seat in the next one leaving. Luckily, the tourists didn't appreciate the power of a tip and got left behind to wait for the next boat. Having secured a place on the boat, he could let his mind wander thinking of Eva.

As soon as the familiar shape of central Venice started to appear, he dialed Eva's number. "I'm on the boat from the airport. I should be there in fifteen minutes or so," he said.

"I'm out shopping. In fifteen minutes I should be ... Let me think. No, meet me in Piazza San Marco. In the arcade to your left. I'll wait for you at the second café, the one with the gorgeous cakes in the window. *Ça va?*"

"I'm on my way," said Franco.

As he pocketed his cell phone, Franco wondered why the man sitting next to him had gotten so close. He looked vaguely familiar, and he must've seen him before, perhaps at the airport. The boat was crowded, but that didn't justify listening to other people's conversations. *People have no manners, nowadays,* he thought bitterly, but then maybe this tourist didn't speak English, he reassured himself.

Eva was waiting for him all right. She looked radiant in what had to be a designer outfit – or maybe everything looked beautiful on her, he thought. Remembering her sisterly goodbye kiss at the station, Franco wasn't quite sure how to behave but decided that a hug was a safe bet. Eva jumped up as he came in, and as soon as he stopped hugging her, she looked him square in the eyes and then kissed him, a long, wet, and sensuous kiss. A few young couples sitting at the other tables, obviously on their honeymoons, looked on with overt appreciation. Someone sitting in the back of the café clapped.

"Welcome," Eva said simply.

"Wow," was all that Franco managed to say.

"Let's get out of here," she whispered, and Franco knew that she meant it.

Franco's suitcase was small and light, but it felt weird to wheel it around the streets of Venice, so he was relieved when after ten minutes, they stopped before an antique wooden door, and Eva said, "This is it." The door opened into an inner court with a grand stairway that led to a second floor.

"This used to be a nobleman's palace, but it has been turned into an apartment building. Christine's apartment is on the second floor – the one in the middle with the brass plate on the door," she explained.

They climbed up the stairs, and Eva pushed a bell. The bell produced Christine, a hearty redhead with the most freckled nose that Franco had ever seen. She smiled warmly at them and said, "Hi, Franco ... I presume. Welcome!"

Franco liked her instantly. She moved aside, and Eva dragged him in.

"You must be tired from the trip," said Christine. "Would you like a drink or something? Are you hungry? I can fix you a toast. Eva, dear, take Franco to your room while I put something together."

"I'm really okay," Franco tried to protest, "I'm not hungry."

"You're wasting your breath," said Eva, smiling. "Chris is going to feed you whether you like it or not ... and you'd better like it."

The apartment was spacious, and the bedroom to which Eva took him was huge, at least by his standards, with an antique parquet floor and a large king-size bed complete with a canopy. A French window opened to a balcony that hung above a small canal, and Eva showed it proudly to Franco as if she were the owner.

"The mattress is not really comfortable," said Eva, obviously noting that Franco was looking at the bed, "but it'll do. I don't mean to let you sleep a lot anyway," she added, jokingly.

"This is a luxury apartment. Christine's aunt must be wealthy," said Franco.

"I don't know about her aunt, but Chris is very well off. Her father is a Hong Kong banker, and you know what that means ..."

"Actually, I don't, but never mind. How did you two come to know each other?"

"Chris and I were best friends in junior high school until her father had to relocate, but we've kept in touch all these years. I really love her, and she adores me, which makes it unanimous."

"She looks very kind," said Franco.

"Wait until she starts stuffing you," Eva said with a silvery laugh, "and then tell me how delicate she is. She can be really dangerous if you refuse to eat your calories. She's a chef at heart. Now let's go before she gets too jittery."

CHAPTER 32

Venice, Italy. July 2009

As soon as the apartment's door closed behind Franco and Eva, Joseph emerged from behind the sheltering shape of the stairway and walked quickly out of the inner court and into the street. He receded until he reached the next building, and then he stopped and dialed a number he knew well.

"I'm in Venice," he said.

"Report quickly, I'm busy," said von Stoffen's voice from the other end of the line.

"The professor met up with Miss Thibault. They went together to a house not far from the center. A young woman opened the door for them, and they went in. I came out to report."

There was silence at the other end, and Joseph waited patiently for his boss to speak.

"That's interesting. So here's where they've been hiding the surrogate. Hmm ... I need to think what to do about her."

"Instructions?" Joseph inquired.

"Not yet. Get a new phone and call the other number in an hour," said von Stoffen and hung up.

Joseph was never really excited – excitement was simply not part of his makeup – but now he felt that his heartbeat was quickening, slightly. "The other number" meant that the action was about to start and that his boss wanted to give him instructions over a channel that was not traceable. It meant that he could be instructed to kill. He didn't look forward to killing because he never experienced pleasure, anger, or any other passion when on a job; emotions were for the weaklings and got in the way of performance. He simply found satisfaction in a job well done and welcomed new challenges.

He walked purposefully toward the narrow streets behind Piazza San Marco, where busy restaurants and cafés were packed with tourists. He knew by experience that those were the best places to collect stray cellular phones negligently placed on tables by misguidedly trusting diners. Forty-five minutes later, he had three different cell phones in his pockets and had located a quiet, isolated spot near a secondary canal from which to call his boss. He leaned against the wall enjoying the view, and waited for exactly one hour to pass. Joseph was precise and punctual, not because von Stoffen appreciated it but because he didn't know how to behave otherwise. When exactly one hour had passed, he flipped the first stolen cell phone open and dialed a number he knew by heart.

"I'm here," he said when he heard von Stoffen's voice saying, "Hello."

Von Stoffen started without a preamble. "We got information that the item they retrieved yesterday is an old document. It is hidden behind the lining of the professor's suitcase. You must get it for me and bring it here, but don't open it."

"What kind of document is it, if I may ask? It may help me identify it."

"Our informant either didn't know or wouldn't say. Right now, he's in no condition to tell us, and we can't wait any longer, so you'll have to use your judgment."

"All right, I'll manage. Is that all?"

"No. We have a problem with the woman in the apartment." Von Stoffen paused for a second and then specified, "The surrogate, the one who opened the door. She's an obstacle; a very bad one for business."

"Does that mean that she has to be removed?" Joseph asked quietly.

"Yes. It does."

"Any particular method?"

Von Stoffen seemed to be hesitating for a moment, weighing the question, and then he said, "Any method you choose, but try not to draw too much attention to it."

"Understood. I'll report when I'm done with both items."

"Good luck," said von Stoffen.

"Thanks," said Joseph and hung up. Without a second thought, he dropped the cell phone into the canal and turned back. He was hungry and had put his eye on a nice restaurant where he planned to do himself good. He always felt hungry before removing obstacles.

CHAPTER 33

Venice, Italy. July 2009

"Have mercy, Chris," Franco begged, "I'm going to explode soon. I'm a bachelor, and I never eat this much at lunch."

"All right. Just a tiny little bit of this cake, and you're done," said Chris, cutting a king-sized slice off the cheesecake. "I made it especially for you when Eva told me that you would be arriving."

"No use in fighting it, Franco. I've warned you."

"You didn't eat half as much as I did!" Franco said, pointing at Eva's plate accusingly.

"Leave her alone," Chris rebuked him, "she's an actress, and it's her job to starve. You're a macho pig; you don't have to be thin."

Franco gazed at Chris. She was slender and good-looking. She wasn't beautiful – not in the sense that Eva was – but still quite attractive. In a way, she was her exact opposite: homely, even motherly despite her young age. He liked her and her ability to make him feel like an old friend after only a few minutes.

"You're not fat either. How do you do it, the way you cook?"

"It's simple: I cook for other people, not for myself. That's why you have to eat everything, so it doesn't go wasted."

"I hear you," said Franco, "but I'm done here. I'll go and take a nap if you don't mind."

"Go ahead," said Eva. "I'll do the dishes, and then I'll join you."

Franco took off his shoes and lay on the bed. It was sort of bumpy and uncomfortable, but he didn't mind. Everything was too perfect for an old bed to spoil it for him. A few minutes later, Eva joined him with a coffee tray. "Let's have coffee on the balcony," she said.

"How Venetian," Franco joked.

The balcony was furnished with a small, round iron table painted white and two matching chairs. The canal below it was a small one and small boats passed by only sporadically. The air was cooling down thanks to a light breeze that blew in the narrow, elongated space between the buildings.

"It's perfect!" Franco said, sounding and feeling ecstatic.

"It can get better," said Eva, and pushing the table aside, she climbed on Franco's lap and kissed him.

"It doesn't get any better than this," Franco said when she let him breathe again.

"It doesn't, does it?" Eva said. She started to unbutton his shirt and kiss his chest as she did.

"It does, it does! I'm sorry. You're tickling me ..." Franco guffawed.

"You ain't seen nofin' yet, as they say in those old American movies," said Eva and started to unbutton his pants.

"Wait!" Franco urged her.

"What for?"

"We can be seen here. Look there, that gondola is coming our way."

"So what? A gondolier's life is drab. Let him have some fun," said Eva, and she continued to unbutton him.

"You're crazy, you know?" said Franco. He grabbed her hands, and then he lifted her up and carried her inside and to the bed.

The shadows of the houses outside were already long when Franco woke up from a satiated sleep. He looked at Eva, who slept at his side, only partially covered by a thin sheet. She was serene and smiling. He caressed her shoulder, and she opened her eyes.

"Hey, there," she said.

"We fell asleep."

"Yes. That was ... nice," she said.

"And wild. Are you always like that?"

"Like what?"

"Like ... wild."

"No. That was special treatment for you."

"You're kidding me," said Franco.

"No, I'm not," she said, lifting herself up and supporting her body on an elbow to bring her eyes level with Franco's.

"I don't understand ..."

"That's because you're thick, Professor. Tell me, what do you think about us?"

Franco lowered his gaze and considered the question. He knew that he was treading on thin ice and had to be careful how he reacted. "I think we're having a great time together."

"That's not what I meant. Do you think that there is something special – some special connection between us?"

"I'm not so good at definitions. I know I like you a lot, and I think you're exceptional." Franco shifted uncomfortably, knowing that he was too obviously cautious with his statements, but she had him in a dangerous corner.

"I see ..." she said and looked away.

"I mean ... don't take that the wrong way. In the short time that I've known you, my feelings for you have grown stronger than for any other woman I have met before. It's just that I don't like to put tags to relationships."

"Ah, yes, your so-called theory about love."

"You can mock me if you like, but that's how I think that life should be lived."

"Let me ask it this way. Assume for a moment that you meet a woman that makes you happy, that you want to go on living with her, and that, at least for the foreseeable future, you are not prepared to give her up."

"Yes ..."

"Wouldn't you tell her, 'I love you'?"

"I don't use the 'L' word. I thought we had that covered."

"Well, then you could avoid using the 'L' word. You could say *je t'aime*. In French, it sounds even better."

Franco kept silent for a long pause. He turned his face to the open window and let the cool breeze play on his skin for a moment, and then he turned back to her. "What are you trying to say, Eva?"

"I'm not trying to say anything. Forget it."

She kicked the bedsheet away and collected her clothes from the floor.

"I'm sorry if anything I said angered you. I didn't mean to. I really like you and ..."

"Forget it, I said!" Eva spurted angrily. Then she approached him and said more softly, "Let's not spoil our weekend. We're here to have fun." She kissed him lightly, and then she disappeared in the direction of the bathroom.

CHAPTER 34

Venice, Italy. July 2009

"Hurry up, or we'll miss the Spring," said Franco.

The local producer of the movie that Eva was shooting had given her tickets to a gala dinner, preceded by the performance of Vivaldi's Four Seasons, which would be played in a beautiful ancient church. The concert was about to start in fifteen minutes, at half past seven, and they had left early to be there in time. Walking beside Eva, Franco felt misplaced in his simple business suit, however embellished by the pricey Brioni tie that she had bought as a present for him. She had surprised him with it while they were dressing; the last thing that he had expected was for her to go to the trouble to buy him a present, and that simple gesture had left him speechless.

Eva wore a black evening dress in which she looked simply stunning and velvet high-heeled shoes dotted with tiny brilliants. Those very shoes were at the root of the trouble that now threatened to make them run late. A ten-minute walk had been too much for one of the delicate heels, which had come off; Eva was lucky that Franco had been quick to grab her, or she would have taken a nasty fall.

"Oh *merde!*" she cried. She supported herself on a wall with one hand and took off her shoes with the other. "I've had enough. I'll walk the rest of the way barefooted."

"Your feet will get dirty," Franco cautioned.

"I don't care. I'll wash them. At least I can walk, and we have a chance to pick up my other shoes and get back in time."

At the apartment door, they rang the bell, but there was no answer. "I have a key," said Eva, reaching into her tiny Christian Dior evening purse and producing it. "Chris must've gone out."

"She said that she had to stay home and study for her exams," said Franco.

"Well, then she changed her mind, or perhaps she doesn't like Vivaldi and was just making excuses for not coming with us."

They got in, and Eva headed for the bedroom. Franco remained in the hallway and used the time to tie his shoelaces again. He liked them to achieve a perfect butterfly effect – the only quirk he had acquired from his father – and was so engrossed in them that the muffled cry coming from the bedroom failed to register at first. But the sound of something crashing on the floor and a strange, low-key moan drew his attention. He went into the bedroom to inquire about their origin, and the picture that presented itself left him petrified for a second. A man struggled with Eva, his left hand on her mouth and his right arm around her neck. They were half turned from the door so that the man couldn't see him. Franco's suitcase was open on the bed, and all his clothes had been tossed around on it and on the floor.

Almost instinctively, mechanically and without planning, Franco picked up a small bronze figurine of a Moore, which was on display on a table by the door. Without hesitation took a step forward and brought it down on the back of the man's head. The man released his grip on Eva at once and fell forward, carrying her down with him in his fall. Franco rushed to help her to her feet as she gasped for air. He folded her in his arms where she remained, sobbing.

"It's okay, it's all right. The damn burglar ..." he said, stroking the back of her neck.

"Did you ... Did you ... is he dead?"

Franco gazed in the direction of the man, who lay on the floor. Blood was oozing from an ugly-looking laceration on his scalp, but he was breathing.

"I think not. He would deserve to be dead," said Franco with anger.

His gaze fell on something familiar on the bed; he pushed Eva gently away from him and went to pick it up.

"I'll be damned!" he said. "How on earth did this get here? I gave it to Marchetti."

"What is that? Why are you so excited about it?"

"Because it shouldn't be here. And because this is no ordinary burglar, I think, if he was looking for this. And I don't know what it is; it's sealed, and I was cautioned not to open it because I may damage it. This is so confusing ..."

Eva had regained some of her composure, although she was still sniffing, and her eyes were red and puffy. Even with her hair thoroughly ruffled, Franco couldn't help pausing to think that she was the most beautiful woman in the world, perhaps more adorable now that she had lost some of her outer crust of self-confidence and looked vulnerable.

"We need to find a rope or something to tie him up before he wakes up," said Franco, turning practical.

"Go and look in the kitchen," said Eva, "I'll search Chris's bedroom. She may have some lace or something there."

Franco nodded and left the room after Eva, taking the envelope with him. He didn't like the idea of letting it out of his sight. He had only managed to walk into the kitchen and open a drawer before a loud cry came from the direction of Chris's bedroom. "Ahhh!" it went, and then there was silence. Franco ran out of the kitchen and got to the foyer just as Eva came out of the bedroom. As she saw him, she dropped on the floor and sat there, weeping.

"What's the matter? What happened?" Franco asked, stooping and taking her hand.

Eva kept her gaze fixed to the wall and shook her head, swallowing quickly. At last, she turned to him and said, "In there," and then she started weeping again.

Christine's head was turned back and to one side in an unnatural position that made her look like a broken puppet. All it took Franco to understand that she was dead was a quick glance, and the realization froze him on the spot. He couldn't bring himself to go near her, but at the same time, he was unable to avert his gaze from her. He started to shake but immediately realized that he had to take control of the shock, for himself and for Eva. He had to figure out what to do next. Slowly, almost on tiptoes as if not to disturb Christine, he backed off into the foyer and sat down on the floor beside Eva, who was now crying silently, tormenting her upper lip with her teeth.

"We can't stay here," he said, speaking gently. "We have things to do."

"Like what?" She said, speaking almost inaudibly and still looking straight ahead.

"We must tie that murderer up and call the police."

Eva did not respond but put her hand on Franco's knee and pushed herself up. Franco put his arm around her shoulders and guided her gently toward their bedroom. Everything in the bedroom was as they had left it, except that the burglar had disappeared, leaving a small pool of blood on the parquet.

"He's gone," gasped Eva.

"He must've sneaked out while we were searching for rope. I thought I had stunned him, but he must've been faking it," said Franco. "I don't know what to do now. Nobody's going to believe us that there has been a burglary. They will think we're making up a story to cover for Christine's death and will suspect that we killed her."

Eva sat on the bed. Her back was bent, and she had lowered her head almost down to her knees. Franco realized that she was too much in shock to help figure out their next steps. He was dismayed to find himself in such an impossible situation, which he didn't fully understand. One thing he knew for sure, however: this had something to do with Easby's business. Yes, he thought Easby was responsible for their being in trouble, and he would have to find a way to get them out of it. His cell phone had fallen on the floor when he struggled with the burglar, but he found it under the bed and dialed Easby's number.

"James!" he cried with relief when he heard his voice. "We're in trouble, Eva and I. Someone followed me to Venice to take the envelope away from me – and I didn't even know that I had it. And he killed Eva's friend, and I hit him, but he got away; I thought he had passed out, but he didn't. I don't know if I'm making sense ..."

"Franco, my boy, where are you right now?"

"We are in the apartment. That's where Eva was staying with her friend Christine. Christine is dead now. She's in the other room."

"Slowly, my boy. Listen to me. You must get out of there immediately, you understand? Immediately!"

"But ... Why? We must call the police," said Franco.

"I don't exactly know what's going on, but I know that you're in grave danger. Take all your belongings, yours and Eva's, and leave immediately. Don't tell me where you're going. You can call the police anonymously from a public phone, later."

"I don't understand. Why do you say that we're in danger?"

"I'll tell you quickly. We can't waste time. You can't waste time. We'll think and talk more about this when you're in a safe place. But I'll tell you quickly what I know. The person you met in Udine, Marchetti, was attacked in the street after you two separated. He was worried that they might take the document that you had retrieved away from him – do you still have it?" Easby asked, sounding apprehensive.

"Yes, yes. I have it with me."

"Keep it safe any way you can. It may be the key to everything."

"The key to what?" asked Franco.

"I can't explain right now. No time. You'll have to trust me. Do you trust me?"

Franco mulled over the question. He wasn't sure whom he could trust anymore, but he didn't have much choice. He needed someone on his side who understood what was going on and could give him some advice.

"I trust you," he said at last.

"Good, good. So while you were at dinner, Marchetti got into your room and looked for a place to hide the document. He saw that your suitcase was lined, so he opened the zipper and stuffed the document between the lining and the shell. In that way, he was confident that if whoever was trying to steal his briefcase from him succeeded, the document would still get back to me safely with you."

"I still don't understand. If they thought that Marchetti had the document, how come they came to look for it here?"

"Marchetti called me from the airport this morning and said that he would take a cab and come immediately to me. He never arrived. Apparently, whoever stopped him also made him tell where the document was."

"Come on! You're talking kidnapping ... I can't believe it."

"Not anymore. We're talking murder now. Eva's friend had the bad luck of being at home when they came for the document, and, as you see, they are stopping at nothing. You understand now why I'm saying that you must leave immediately? We don't know who else is around. You must be very careful not to be followed and not to give away your location when you call me or anybody else."

"I see," said Franco.

"How's Eva?" Easby asked.

Franco gazed at her. She hadn't moved since the beginning of his phone call.

"She's in shock but physically okay."

"Go now. Waste no more time," said Easby.

"I'll phone you when I can," said Franco and switched off.

He was quickly becoming resigned to his new reality. He started to collect his clothes and stuffed them quickly into his bag, and then he took off his tie, put it in the bag, and zipped it. Next, he took Eva gently by the arm and pulled her up. She turned wet eyes to him and, again, fell sobbing into his arms.

"What do we do now? What do we do?" she asked, sobbing.

"We need to go away, quickly. Where's your suitcase?"

"But ... What about Chris? We can't leave her like this."

"They will take care of Chris. We'll ask someone to do it when we are in a safe place."

Franco finally managed to collect Eva's things with little help from her. A few minutes later, they left the building with Franco dragging Eva's big suitcase, on top of which his own looked tiny. The document was safely stuffed in the inner pocket of his jacket.

The Santa Lucia railroad station was quiet. Eva and Franco waited by a public telephone for the time to pass. They had second-class tickets for the 10:17 PM, which was the last train to Padua, and Franco had decided to call the police at 10:05 PM. That wouldn't give any zealous officer a chance to come to the station and try to stop them. They stood in silence, sipping coffee from Styrofoam cups. It was the first refreshment they had had since everything had begun.

Getting to the train station hadn't been easy either. The hour was late, and the public transportation, the famous *Vaporetto*, was seldom and far between. At first, they waited by a canal for a water taxi to come by, but apparently, the Venetian taxi drivers were not out looking for clients. Franco had to bribe the doorman of one of the hotels to have him call a water taxi, but at last, one arrived, charged them an outrageous fee, and took them to the station in time for the last train out.

Franco picked up the phone and dialed 118. He couldn't remember the general emergency number, and that was the one that appeared on a torn-out sticker that was glued to the public phone. A sleepy voice answered.

"Nature of the call, please," he said.

"I need to report a burglary," Franco said.

"This is a health emergency number, not the police," the voice complained.

"Yes, but someone got hurt really badly during the burglary. This is also a health emergency. Hurry up, please!"

"Oh, all right," said the voice sounding annoyed, "give me the address and your name."

Franco gave him the address and a fake name and said, "Please come quickly; we are waiting for you."

The operator hung up without responding, and Franco turned to Eva.

"Come," he said, speaking gently and taking her by the elbow, "we have a train to catch."

CHAPTER 35

Padua, Italy. July 2009

The receptionist at the *Cavalieri Hotel* unwillingly shifted his attention from the comics in which he was immersed and sized up the customers who had just wriggled through the narrow door into the tiny and shabby lobby. In truth, calling it "a lobby" was pretentious since it barely afforded room for four people to stand between the door and the reception desk. It was not unusual for customers to walk in past midnight – or at all hours, for that matter. The train station area attracted all kinds of people and not the best members of society; still, the pimpled receptionist had hoped for some quiet at that time of night and resented the interruption. He eyed the couple with distaste; he'd seen too many of those, and the story was almost always the same. She obviously was a runaway girl, fleeing an abusive husband or stepfather, and was carrying her home in that big suitcase. The creep must've picked her up at the train station and was going to take advantage of her for the price of a meal, a warm bed, and a few Euros. Well, he thought, that was no skin off his nose; he wasn't out there to save the world like those characters in his comics.

"Yes?" he said. His body language was openly unwelcoming.

"Do you have vacancies?" the man inquired.

"For how many hours?" he asked. He spoke dryly, making sure that his customers understood how little enthusiasm he was putting into it.

The man hesitated. He was probably calculating how much it was going to cost him, and then he said, "For one night."

"A full night?" The creep was surely planning to take a long ride on that poor girl.

"Yes," said the man.

"It'll cost you twenty-seven Euros, paid upfront."

"That's fine," said the man and put the money on the counter.

The girl hadn't said a word, and the pimpled receptionist gave her a quick glance. She looked nice and clean. *What a shame,* he thought. He took a key from the pigeon holes behind him and put it next to the money. "Number thirteen," he said. The man picked the key up and nodded.

"It's up the stairs there," the receptionist added and pointing to a narrow stairway half-hidden behind a dirty curtain, "and we have no elevator," he added with satisfaction. At least the creep would have to schlep her suitcase, which looked heavy, up the stairs. "There is a sink in the room, but you don't want to drink from it. I can sell you a bottle of mineral water for two Euros."

"I'll take two bottles," said the man, putting more money on the counter. He picked up the bottles and handed them to the girl. Before he had time to move, the receptionist spoke again.

"Two more things. We don't serve breakfast here, but you can go to the bar at the corner. It opens at eight, but remember that you have to be out of here tomorrow morning by ten. There is a shower at the end of the corridor. Towels are on a rack inside the door next to the shower to your right. You're allowed one towel each, and it's forbidden to take showers together. Have a good night," he concluded, and then he picked up his comics and started reading again as if they didn't exist.

Number 13 was on the left, close to the stairway, and Franco stood still facing its door for a moment while he fumbled with the key. He had to catch his breath after the heavy lifting of Eva's suitcase on the stairs. The corridor was poorly lit, and Franco had trouble finding the keyhole. He finally turned the key in the lock and pushed the door inside. The room was in complete darkness, and when he threw the switch by the door, a single light bulb in the middle of the room flickered and lit up. He dragged the suitcases in, and Eva followed in silence. The room was small and bare, with a battered old chair and a tiny table as the only furniture to keep company to a queen-size bed that left almost no standing room beside it. A soiled sink with a single, cold water faucet protruded from the wall in a corner, as advertised. Eva seated herself on the edge of the bed, and Franco moved the chair so he could sit in front of her.

"What are we going to do?" Eva asked. Franco understood how lost she felt and how much she needed reassurance. He also realized that no matter how lost he felt, nobody else was around to give her strength. The task was his. He took her hand in his and gazed straight into her eyes. He ordered his vocal cords to make his voice sound strong and secure and prayed that he would come across as the self-assured, strong man he needed to be.

"We need to rest. Tomorrow we'll plan what to do." He was as clueless as she, but he wasn't going to let her know that. "Give me your cell phone," he ordered.

"What for?"

"Just give it to me. Please."

Eva shrugged, fished into her bag, and handed Franco the cell phone. He took it, turned it off, and removed the battery, and then he did the same to his own phone.

"What are you doing that for?" Eva asked.

"I remember reading somewhere that your cell phone can be used to trace you even when it's turned off, and the only way to prevent that is to remove the battery."

Eva made a nervous gesture with her hand. "So we are fugitives now ..." she said.

"We don't know what's going on, so we must be careful. I only put two and two together on the train coming here; the burglar ... the murderer, I've seen him before. He was on the taxi boat that took me from the airport in Venice to meet you. He must've been following me; I don't know since when."

"Don't say that; you're freaking me out!"

Franco moved from the chair to the bed, sat next to her, and hugged her. "Don't worry, we'll figure this out. It's just that I want to be cautious. You heard what James said."

"I don't understand how James is involved in all this. I mean, Chris was my friend, and she had nothing to do with James. And why did he tell us not to tell him where we are?"

"I don't know. I can only guess that he thinks that someone is eavesdropping on his phone calls. You read in the papers that this is done all the time. Even newspaper reporters do it. Maybe someone listens to mine as well. You see, I went to Udine to retrieve this document," Franco patted his jacket and felt the reassuring crackling sound of old paper, "and it seems that this is what the burglar was after."

"Well, open it. Let's see what it is," said Eva.

"I've been told not to. It seems that I may damage it irreparably if I open it without appropriate caution."

"You and your caution!" Eva exploded, pushing Franco aside and making him lose his grip on her shoulders. "Because of your caution and your damn document, Chris is dead, and we are hiding in a whorehouse. I don't mind it if it blows up in flames. I want to see what it is."

"Eva, darling, please calm down," Franco said soothingly. "We are in no shape to make good decisions right now. Let's wait until tomorrow before we do something that we could regret later on, okay?"

Eva's fury extinguished itself against Franco's disarming attitude, and she put her head on his shoulder. "I'm so scared," she whispered.

Franco hugged her gently and whispered back, "Let's try to get some sleep now," he said.

"There is a long, black hair on the pillow. How are we going to sleep in this bed? This place is filthy," she complained.

"Let's turn the pillow around and go to sleep with our clothes on. We'll find a better place tomorrow, and I'll make it up to you, I promise."

Eva nodded, and they lay back on the bed, still holding one another. The emotions of that day had been so exhausting that Franco fell asleep without taking off his shoes.

CHAPTER 36

Udine, Italy. July 1894

The Honorable L. eyed the Cecchi widow with his usual measure of loathing, which was now heightened by the presence of her daughter – to his mind an utterly repugnant youth.

"Is Evelyn making progress?" asked the widow.

"It is difficult to say," the Honorable L. answered stiffly. "She has better days and worse days. We are yet to see the improvements we are hoping for."

"That's why I asked my daughter to join us," said the widow, looking unfazed.

"Please explain," said the Honorable L., who couldn't help raising an eyebrow at the thought that this common girl would be getting involved in his Evelyn's fate.

"I told you that you must place two copies of the instructions in places where they have a good chance of being found at the appropriate moment ..."

"I know," he interrupted her, "and that's why I have told my friend, the major, that I would bring him a document to be sealed in the city's archives. He has already agreed to take it, and I'm waiting for you to tell me to go ahead and do it."

"The reason why I asked you to come," said the widow, "is that I had a dream – I can barely remember it, and I can't interpret it, but I'm sure that it had to do with the right place for the letter. We need to interrogate the spirits more, and, as you can imagine, my daughter is also psychic. My son is not, but she's a powerful medium; perhaps she will be stronger than I in time. Together with her and with you, we will come up with a better answer."

"With me? What do you mean 'with me'?"

"We need you to participate in the séance. It's your flesh and blood who's involved, and your presence is necessary."

The Honorable L. was left speechless – an unusual condition for him. This dreadful woman actually wanted him to take an active role in a Satanic procedure. What's more, she wanted him to do it before this little girl. His whole conscience revolted against it, and he almost haughtily refused; but as he opened his mouth to speak, Evelyn's angelic face came before his eyes, and he realized, as before, that there were no lengths to which he would refuse to go for her. No matter how black a deed he might undertake, he knew it would turn into a holy one if undertaken on Evelyn's behalf.

"Shall we move to the round table?" said the widow.

They sat around the table holding hands. The Honorable L. sat stiffly as if to indicate his discontent. He held the widow's hand with his right hand and with the left her daughter's. To his surprise, the daughter's hand felt soft and pleasant to the touch; he could not identify anything evil in it. On the contrary, she emanated a feeling of right-doing, quite different from the one he got from her mother, and he felt happy that she had joined them. She hadn't spoken a word yet and limited her participation to following her mother's instructions docilely.

They had been sitting around the table for a short time when the widow, who had closed her eyes at the outset, opened them, released the Honorable L.'s hand, and asked, "Who is Camillo Golgi?"

"How do you know his name?" the Honorable L. asked with surprise.

"I don't. It just came to me as I made contact. The contact is gone now, and all I've got is that name."

"He's a friend. A good friend of mine. He's a physician, the rector of the University of Pavia. What does that mean?"

The Honorable L. felt for the first time that he was being drawn into something bigger than he, something he could not understand. He realized with embarrassment that the widow's daughter was still holding his left hand and that he was finding it reassuring. That this little girl could instill confidence in a hardened veteran like him was, in itself, something close to a miracle.

"It means that that's where you must place your copy of the letter, along with the instructions for the cure."

"You mean that I should not give it to the mayor as planned?"

His attention was drawn to the widow's daughter, who applied slight pressure to his hand and spoke for the first time. "I've heard it too," she said. "Split it, it said. The letter here and the instructions there." Having said that, she let go of his hand.

The Honorable L. felt weak, emptied of his strength without warning. He had just witnessed something he wasn't equipped to understand but which was giving him hope.

"I'll do as you say," he said.

"Good," said the widow, and then she motioned to her daughter to leave.

As soon as the door closed behind her, the Honorable L. said, speaking gently for the first time, "She's a good child. I'm glad that she'll be introduced to society as you wanted her to."

"Yes, I am very proud of her, but now let's not waste time. We need to make a small change to the letter, and then you must be on your way."

CHAPTER 37

London, England. July 2009

Heinrich von Stoffen's right pocket became suddenly animated as the small cell phone it contained started to vibrate. It was the phone with the prepaid SIM card he had bought in Budapest under an assumed name. He had been waiting for it to ring for hours now. He flipped it open quickly and barked into it.

"Where have you been, for God's sake?"

"I've run into some problems," Joseph answered in his usual flat and expressionless voice.

"That's not what I meant when I told you to avoid drawing attention to yourself. It's all over the news. CNN plays it in repeat with full details. It's a God-sent item for the press, with the dead girl in one room and blood all over the place in the other. What were you thinking?"

"The blood is mine," said Joseph, speaking tonelessly and unemotionally, as if he weren't talking about himself but rather about some stranger. "The professor dealt me a good one on the head, and I barely managed to get away. I had to break into an empty apartment next door and take care of myself, but I was out for a few hours, and that's why I didn't call you."

"I see," said von Stoffen, now calmer. "Do you have the document?"

A brief silence on the line was followed by Joseph's voice, which for the first time sounded embarrassed. "I had it, but the professor took it after he knocked me out."

"So now he has it ... I take it that you don't know where he is."

"I don't. He's probably on his way back to London or hiding somewhere around here."

"That's a very useful observation," said von Stoffen, forgetting that his sarcasm was wasted on Joseph, who always took every statement literally. "Where are you now?"

"I'm in a small hotel far from the city center. I have retrieved my bag from the locker where I'd left it, and I'm ready to follow instructions." He sounded apologetic, and von Stoffen almost felt sorry for him. Screwing up so badly was a new experience for Joseph, who had always been entirely dependable until then.

"How's your head?" he asked.

"Aside from the headache, I'm okay. I think I ought to have it stitched, though, because it still bleeds on and off, but nothing major. I'll find a doctor someplace far from Venice, and I'll have it done. It's too dangerous here, on account of my blood being in the hands of the police and all that on the news."

"All right. Take yourself out of the city and settle down someplace not too far. I bet that our friends are no longer in Venice, but they may still be around. I'll see what I can find out. Call me when you're settled in."

Von Stoffen pocketed the cell phone and dropped himself into the comfortable armchair of his study. He had a lot of thinking to do.

CHAPTER 38

Padua, Italy. July 2009

Franco and Eva were having their first relaxed moments since the burglary of Christina's apartment turned their world upside down. They were seated in the restaurant of a gas station on the A13 motorway, which at lunchtime on a Saturday was packed. It was bustling with activity and noisy with requests and questions were thrown at the self-service counter in different languages. The noise was made worse by the TV screen that hung on the wall next to their table, which screamed newsflashes in Italian.

Renting a car had been easier than Franco had thought it would be on the weekend. He had got up early, feeling still tired; sleeping with his clothes on hadn't been restful. He had drunk a hurried coffee at the bar on the corner and walked back to the train station shortly after 8 AM. He had come back with a midsize rented FIAT car in half an hour. Eva had been still asleep on his return. He had opened the door quietly and tiptoed to the bed. Then he had sat beside her and had caressed her hair gently for a while.

"Hi," she had said, at last, opening her eyes, but she hadn't smiled. She had dressed amazingly quickly, without asking questions, replacing her elegant dress with blue jeans and a simple T-shirt. Franco had brought back with him from the station a large take-away coffee. It was lukewarm by then, but Eva had drunk avidly from it while he was busy lugging the suitcases down the stairs.

There was no one at reception to say goodbye to, except a cleaning woman who was mopping the floor, so Franco had put the key on the counter, and they had left.

They had got into the car, and Franco had switched on the engine.

"Where are we going?" Eva had asked.

The answer to that was that Franco didn't know. He didn't want to get too far away from Venice because his flight back to London was due to leave from there. But on the other hand, he felt safer putting some distance between them and Venice and the homicidal maniac it contained.

"Let's drive away from here for a while," he had said. "We'll get a proper meal and find a nice place to stay, and then we can figure out what to do next. Unless you have a better suggestion."

Eva was out of suggestions, so Franco had picked the A13 at random and had driven on it until the signs to the restaurant had reminded them that they hadn't had any food for a long time.

With a good meal now in him, Franco was again able to look at the future more brightly. After all, now that they were warned of the danger, all they had to do was to be careful and get back home safely. They would look now for a nice place to stay, and despite the shock and the tragedy, they would try to make the most of what was left of their weekend together. In bright daylight, the outlook was not as bleak as it had seemed last night; surely James had had the time to figure out what they should do, and he looked forward to calling him. He sipped his coffee and smiled at Eva. Despite the rough conditions of last night, she was radiantly beautiful. She looked like she had come straight from a beauty parlor. Eva smiled back at him.

"You behaved very honorably toward a poor girl last night," she said. "I didn't like it."

"I was wasted," Franco said apologetically.

Eva looked more relaxed, and Franco was glad to see that her sense of humor, which to him was one of her sexiest features, was resurfacing.

The words "Venice" and "murder," filtering through the noise, got his attention and Franco turned his head toward the TV screen. He was confronted by a fuzzy black and white picture of himself and Eva, each holding a Styrofoam cup. Four different but very similar pictures were shown in a loop on the screen as a slideshow. The text that ran at the bottom of the screen read, "Police has issued a warrant for the arrest of two unidentified individuals, believed to be material witnesses in the murder."

Franco felt a chill running along his spine. He gazed at Eva and saw from the expression on her face that she was feeling the same. The pictures had obviously been taken by a security camera at the Venice train station. The police must have made a connection between the emergency phone call he had placed and the pictures. From the angle at which the pictures had been taken, Franco's face was not very clear and, if at all, he was barely recognizable, but the woman in the pictures was unequivocally Eva. Mercifully the newsflash moved on to the next item, and after a few seconds, they got up and left hastily. Franco put his arm around Eva's waist, and she buried her face in his chest, which made it awkward to walk but hid her features. As they reached the car and Franco unlocked the doors, Eva said, "Wait!" She opened the trunk, took a small bag from her suitcase, closed the trunk without bothering to zip the suitcase, and climbed inside. "Let's go," she said, speaking with urgency. She sat low in her seat, making herself inconspicuous. Franco drove out of the gas station and onto the motorway.

Eva opened the bag that she had taken from her suitcase, lowered her head almost into it and to Franco's surprise, she emerged from the exercise as a blonde. "I wear this wig in the movie," she explained.

Franco gave her a sideways glance without taking his eyes off the road. "You don't look like you," he said with appreciation. "That'll help," he added.

"What are we going to do?" Eva asked.

Franco tightened his grip on the wheel and said nothing. He had no answer.

CHAPTER 39

Este, Italy. July 2009

Franco left the motorway at the first exit. They had seen several highway patrol vehicles, and although they would obviously not stop them on the motorway, he felt unsafe and exposed there. A sign at the motorway's exit pointed to many directions, and he chose the one that led to "Este." He had never heard of the place and hoped to find a small, sleepy village where nobody paid much attention to the news.

"Where are we going?" asked Eva.

"We need to find a quiet place to be, where we can hide while we figure out what to do."

Eva didn't protest, and as they reached Este, Franco realized that he had made a good choice. It was a small town, nice and clean and very sleepy under the summer sun. He drove around until he saw a "Bed and Breakfast" sign. He inspected the house from the street and decided that it was just what he was looking for. It had a narrow driveway that a sign invited visitors to enter, which disappeared behind the house. A small sign, mounted on the main one, said *"Camere / Zimmer,"* which meant that they had vacancies. Franco drove into the gravel path, proceeding slowly to avoid making too much noise, but the sound of the tires on the gravel had apparently been enough to announce their arrival. As he turned left where the path bent, he saw a woman coming from the house toward a small gravel esplanade where two other cars were parked.

"We are on our honeymoon, smile!" Franco ordered, turning on his own radiant smile. He parked next to one of the other cars, switched off the engine, and got out quickly, smiling all the while.

The woman who waited for them was also smiling invitingly. She was about 60 years old and wore a gardener's hat. From that and from the garden gloves and clippers, Franco assumed that she had to be the owner.

"Good morning," she said.

"Good morning," Franco echoed. "I hope it was okay that I drove in ..."

"Yes, yes. No problem."

"Would you have a room? A matrimonial?"

"For how many nights? We normally take advanced bookings. We're on the Internet, you know?"

"I'm sorry. I didn't know that. I'm not sure how long we would stay. You see, my wife and I," Franco said, pointing to Eva who was standing by the car, smiling brightly and looking gorgeous in her blonde wig, "we are on our honeymoon –"

"Oh, how wonderful," the woman cooed.

"Yes. My wife is French, so I'm showing her the country. We wanted to be spontaneous, and I have made no advance reservations. We stop when we see a place we like and move on when we feel we are ready. I think we would like to stay here for one or two nights. Is that possible?"

"I can guarantee up to three nights, but the matrimonial room is booked after that."

"That would be perfect, thank you. Come Dear!" he called, and Eva approached them. "We can stay here between one and three nights," he said when she reached them. "Can we see the room?" he added, turning to the landlady.

"Of course. I'm Luisa," she said, putting out a hand for Eva to shake.

"Eva," she said, shaking it.

"Franco," he added, shaking it too.

The room was beautiful, with French windows opening into a gorgeous garden, which allowed them complete privacy, including a private entrance. Franco paid for one night in advance and then fetched the luggage. From the small bar in the hall, Luisa sold them diet Cokes and then went back to her gardening. They sat in the small private garden, sipping their Cokes.

"*Lune de miel*, ah?" Eva sighed. "It hardly feels like a honeymoon ..."

"You were great. Nobody would have thought that you weren't a happy bride intent on discovering Italy."

"I'm an actress, did you forget?"

A thought hit Franco. "Have you been acting with me too?"

"No, silly! What an idea ..." Eva laughed, and Franco felt relieved. He got up, grabbed the arms of Eva's chair as he leaned forward, and rubbed the tip of his nose against hers.

"I wasn't acting either," he whispered, suddenly speaking seriously. He remained silent for a moment. Eva had almost made him forget the fix they were in, but now he had to deal with it. Later there would be time to unravel the beautiful mystery called Eva. He sank back into his chair, conscious that he was not at liberty to enjoy and behave as if he really was having a peaceful honeymoon.

"I have to call James. I'll take the car and go looking for a public phone. I'll be back soon."

"Why don't you use your cell phone?"

"I can't. Someone may be listening, and we must be careful not to give away where we are. Cellular phones can be located when you make a call. But I won't be long, I promise."

"I'll come with you, then."

Franco shook his head. "Not a good idea. That newsflash is too recent, and someone may recognize you even with the wig."

Eva said nothing more. Franco squeezed her arm and left.

Easby didn't answer the phone. Franco waited and redialed three times in the following half-hour, but then he gave up and resolved to try again later. He drove back quickly, eager to take up his talk with Eva where he had left off, but she was nowhere in sight, and the door of their bedroom was locked. Franco knocked on the door but got no answer. He peered through the window and saw that the room was empty. His pulse accelerated for a moment, but then he managed to regain his composure. Eva was not stupid, so she surely was not taking risks walking outside. She must be in the main garden or somewhere around the house. Reassured by this thought, he walked back to the gravel parking area and knocked on the door from which their host had appeared on their arrival. Through the glass panels, he saw Luisa approaching from inside the house. She unlocked the door and stood before him. She seemed embarrassed.

"Hi!" Franco greeted her with a friendly smile. "I'm looking for Eva."

"I'm so sorry," said Luisa, without looking him in the eyes.

"Sorry for what?" Franco's heart started racing again. Obviously, something was amiss.

"She gave me the key here. Before she left."

"Left! What do you mean, left?"

"She took a small handbag and walked away. She walked away, just like that." Luisa was obviously distressed. She kept wringing her hands and gazing at the floor.

"But ... Didn't she say anything? Did she say where she was going, when she would come back?"

"No. I don't speak French very well. She said something that I'm not sure what it meant. I asked her if she was coming back, but she just said 'No, no' and went. Is there anything I can do?"

Franco took the key that Luisa had been trying for a while to hand him. He shrugged and turned away from her. He walked into the room and looked around. Eva's suitcase was still there, but it was open, and the little bag from which she had taken the wig was gone. Franco sat heavily on the bed, trying to make some sense of his last two days and failing miserably. He felt that he was on the verge of crying and knew that he had to pull himself together before going to pieces, so he went to the bathroom and washed his face with cold water. He was drying himself when he heard the door opening and saw Eva coming in.

"You're back," she said. "Did you speak with James?"

"Where have you been?" Franco asked without responding.

"I went for a walk. I was starting to feel claustrophobic in here."

"I expressly told you to stay in the room." Franco made no effort to hide his annoyance.

"Hey, you're not my father, okay? You don't get to tell me what to do."

"Why did you tell Luisa that you were leaving, ah?" Franco insisted.

"That stupid woman! I told her that I was going out for a walk, and I left her the key for you in case you came back before me."

"What's in the bag?" Franco asked point-blank.

"The bag? Why, the usual." Eva answered in a low voice.

"Let me see," Franco ordered.

Eva handed it to him, looking unhappy, and he unzipped it and went quickly through its contents.

"You took your toothbrush and a change of underwear. You weren't coming back!" he said accusingly.

"Oh, cut it out, okay? I took it without thinking because walking around without a bag felt unnatural. I'm here, right? So what's the fuss?" She gazed at him, and he held her gaze without responding. "I don't know about you, but I'm sweaty, and I'm going to take a shower. You can either join me or stay here and sulk. Suit yourself," she added and strode to the bathroom.

Franco sat on the bed and listened to the water running in the shower. He didn't know what to think. She had come back, true, but the way she had left to begin with didn't make sense to him. He sat with a bent head, and a blinking coming from the bag that he still held open in his hand attracted his attention. He fished into the bag, and his hand found the familiar shape of a cellular phone. He took it out and saw that it was on. He remembered turning it off for Eva and taking out the battery, so she clearly had connected the battery and turned it on at some point, and she could have only done it to make a phone call.

He flipped it open and pushed the "dial" button to return to the last number dialed. The number appearing on the screen had a London prefix he didn't recognize. Instinctively he pushed the button again and waited. The click of a receiver being lifted came almost immediately, and then a voice that he had heard before said, "Hawthorne."

CHAPTER 40

Este, Italy. July 2009

Eva came out of the bathroom with a towel wrapped around her. She was smiling, but as she saw Franco standing with her cellular phone in his hand, the smile disappeared from her face, and she stared at him in silence.

"You called Scotland Yard," Franco said. "Are you a cop? Are you working with Kathia? Were you planning to take off and leave me alone in this mess?"

Eva took a few steps toward Franco, but he backed away, keeping his distance from her. She sat heavily on the bed and took her head in her hands. After a few seconds, she straightened herself up and gazed at Franco. Her eyes were wet with tears, and the towel had dropped on her lap, leaving her still moist skin exposed. Even in his antagonistic frame of mind, Franco couldn't help noticing how beautiful she was.

"Please sit down. It's not what you think," Eva pleaded.

"Go ahead," Franco said without moving.

"I'm not a cop, and I don't know who this Kathia that you mentioned is. I know Richard Hawthorne."

"How? Why?"

"They approached me—the Secret Service. Richard is Secret Service. He only poses as Scotland Yard. They said ... they say that

James is not what he seems; that he's evil, and they wanted me to help them find out what he's really up to."

"And you believed them?"

"At first, I didn't. I loved James. I still find it difficult to hate him ..."

"Hate him? You told me that he had been like a father to you. How could you hate him?"

"They say that he holds great power over people and that he is responsible for my father's death." Eva sighed, and two large tears running down her cheek marked her statement, but she didn't seem to notice them and didn't wipe them away.

"How?" Franco asked, still acting distant.

"They arranged for me to meet someone – a defector from James's organization, who was close to him and to my father. He's been hiding since my father's death. We met briefly, and he told me that my father was murdered. That James drugged him, and then his men took him to the river and drowned him, making it look like a suicide. The Service knew about James's involvement in my father's death from the start. They didn't have evidence to prove it, and the head of the Service decided to let it pass for suicide to safeguard other agents. So that's why I hate James. Wouldn't you hate him if you were in my place?"

Eva was now crying openly, and tears were flowing down her cheeks. Franco was no longer able to keep the distance, and he sat beside her, passed a hand behind her shoulder, and hugged her gently.

"And what if those are all lies? They may be using you to get at him. These people have no conscience. I told you that I am a good judge of character, and I can't see any evil in James. Sure, he's a little dotty, but evil ... I don't think so. Perhaps he's being framed."

"I wanted to believe it. I still do. But now I don't know what to think. The man I met – perhaps he was an actor, and they made up the whole story. But if the story is true ... then he must be stopped, and he must pay for what he's done to me." Eva was sobbing now, and she put her head on Franco's shoulder. "Oh, Franco, I'm so confused!" she whimpered.

Franco held her, stroking the back of her neck until the sobs subsided, and then she got up, letting the towel drop to the floor. "I need to blow my nose," said Eva and went into the bathroom again, closing the door behind her. When she came back, the tears had stopped, and she was wearing a flimsy little dress. Franco was sitting on the bed, his back propped against the pillows, and she went to him to cuddle.

"I've been thinking," said Franco. He spoke as if nothing wrong had passed between them. He felt strangely embarrassed for lashing out at her.

"What?"

"I'll tell you in a moment, but first, what did you say to Hawthorne?"

"I told him everything, including where we are. He instructed me to sit tight and wait while he figured out how to safely get us out of here. It seems that we are quite popular in the news back in England, and that might be a problem," she added with a bitter smile.

Franco kept silent for a minute, absorbing the meaning of the news, and then he turned his head toward Eva, which immediately brought a wave of scent to his nostrils. She smelled of cleanliness and innocence – a fragrance that had become to him more addictive than a drug.

"Everyone is manipulating us. We have been used from the very beginning, and we can't trust anybody. We must assume that everyone is lying – James, Hawthorne, Kathia – I'll tell you about her later." He hesitated and then said, without looking at her, "The question is, can I trust you?"

"Franco ..." Eva said, pushing herself away from him a little. Her lower lip was quivering, and large tears had again formed at the corner of her eyes.

"I meant ..." Franco started to say.

"I love you," Eva said, simply stating a fact, and the tears that until then had hung at the corners of her eyes came rolling down her cheeks.

"Oh, my God!" said Franco. He hadn't seen that coming. "I'm sorry. I'm sorry," he whispered, holding her tight.

Speaking was out of the question. They were both overwhelmed with emotion and made love furiously at first and then tenderly. When they finally rested in each other's arms Franco whispered in her ear, "I trust you, now," and she hit him with a mock slap.

It was dark outside when they woke up. "I'm hungry," Eva complained.

"Me too. Let's go and find a pizza somewhere, then we'll have to make some decisions. I've been thinking."

"Liar. You've been snoring."

"I can snore *and* think at the same time. I'm endowed with many gifts. I'll show you when we come back."

CHAPTER 41

Este, Italy. July 2009

The pizza house was almost empty, which gave Eva and Franco comfort and a feeling of safety; they didn't need to worry lest the next customer might recognize them. Playing the role of the newlyweds came naturally to them, and so for one hour, they managed to forget their troubles and to enjoy each other's company in the pleasant, warm atmosphere of the *pizzeria*. They returned to the house and walked to their room, hugging and laughing. Luisa's head popped out of the main door, evidently drawn by the noise, but she simply shook her head as if in disbelief and retreated into the darkness of the house. Franco and Eva walked around the corner into their private garden and their room.

"I enjoyed it," Eva said.

"So did I," Franco admitted. His face was flushed, partly because he had drunk one glass of wine too many and partly because he was just starting to realize that Eva had unleashed his masculine instincts to a level that he hadn't experienced before. She had managed to make him forget their predicament for a while. He was worried by her declaration of love, though, but decided not to let it ruin their moments of intimacy; he would simply evade the question if the topic came up again. He grabbed her and threw himself on the bed, dragging her above him and kissing her. She kissed him back, but then, suddenly, she turned serious and sat up.

"This is not real, you know," she said.

"What do you mean?"

"We're not on vacation. We're fugitives from the law and from a homicidal maniac. We shouldn't be happy, laughing and enjoying ourselves."

"No? Do you feel bad being happy? I don't," said Franco, speaking earnestly.

"I don't feel bad – I can't explain. We should be *doing* something about it, not just hiding and doing nothing."

"You're right. I told you that I've been thinking."

"And?"

"And it's time we opened this envelope," Franco said, showing the old document that he had taken from his inner pocket. He let his body slide down to the foot of the bed, and Eva followed, sitting on the floor beside him.

"But ... you said that James asked you not to open it. You said it might become damaged."

"Yes, but you also said that we can't trust James, so maybe he doesn't want us to know what's in the envelope, from which it follows that we must open it."

"But how's that going to help us? I don't understand."

"I don't know if it's going to help us, but I know one thing: everybody is after us because of this document, so it must mean something, and I want to find out what it is."

A fruit plate had been placed on a small, round table by the window, and Franco took the knife that was meant to be used to slice the fruit and inserted its tip in the corner of the envelope. Then, he carefully and slowly slit the envelope open. He hesitated for a moment before spreading it wide open, and then he pulled out an old paper document. He scrutinized the first page and read as quickly as he could. The handwriting was old-fashioned, very thin and small so that the letters looked all the same and every word had to be more guessed than read.

"I've seen this letter before," he said at last. "James had a facsimile, and he gave it to me to read. It bears my great-grandfather's signature. It's in Italian; I'll translate it for you. But wait! It looks different; it has a part that I haven't seen before. Let me read it first."

Franco read slowly, careful to understand every word and the process took a long time. Eva watched him with concern but kept silent and didn't disturb him until she saw an expression on his face that frightened her.

"What is it? What does it say?" she demanded to know.

"I'll read it to you," Franco said, speaking gravely. Then he picked up the first page and started to read, translating simultaneously.

"*Sir, when you read these words, I will be long dead. However, it is in your power to save a life if you can bring yourself to believe what I know is true – that the present and the past are interconnected and that your actions can mend the trouble of the past. I beg you, sir, to keep reading to the end, with an open mind and heart, and to enjoy the power of life over death, of defeating death and donating life, and to rejoice in the incomparable power that you will acquire.*

"*This I beg you to hear. My daughter, Evelyn, my beautiful, lovely daughter, a kind and pure soul, is only 26 years old and is dying. She is suffering from consumption – tuberculosis is the term they use – and I have been given no hope by the doctors. Modern medicine is powerless against this monstrous illness, and without your help, she will die. But how can you help, you will ask, when more than 100 years have passed since the day I put my hand to pen to write this letter to you? You can and you must, but to do so, you must open your mind and heart to what follows.*

"*Sir, I don't know your name, but you know mine. You are my flesh and blood. I know that in the same way that I know that you can save my Evelyn. I have been told. And the simple fact that you, my future and distant relative, are reading this letter proves that what I am telling you is true and correct.*"

"It's giving me goose bumps," said Eva, getting closer to Franco and shivering. "What does that mean?"

"Wait," said Franco, "it gets weirder. *I am not gifted with far sight, but those who are can see you right now reading my letter. They know that the past and the future are one and are interconnected. And the knowledge that the future holds for you can be linked to the past and used for a good deed.*

"Perhaps I am asking much of you, but what I stand to lose is infinitely more than the little time and trouble that I ask you to take ... "

"Yeah, he calls this 'a little trouble'," said Eva acidly. "We almost got killed on account of this piece of paper."

"That's not what he means. He's referring to what awaits us ahead ... *the little time and trouble that I ask you to take to bridge the gap between our times and save my baby Evelyn.*

"But I understand that more than my mere prayer may be needed, so I am telling you this: by answering my supplication for help, you will not only save an innocent life – and God knows that whoever saves one life has saved a whole world – but you will be gaining a knowledge that will give you great power, the power to bring both ends together – the present and the past – and to change them at your will. That is my payment to you, if payment is required, or my gift of thanks to you if you follow willingly, as I believe you will, because no flesh and blood of mine have ever remained deaf to a rightful quest.

"This part is different from the letter that James showed me. There he said that practical instructions were included, but they apparently had gone lost. Listen to what he says here. *The acts that must be undertaken to bring a cure to my Evelyn are not difficult to understand, but they must be undertaken with great precision. I have placed full instructions in the trust of my learned friend, Professor Camillo Golgi, Rector of the University of Pavia, with whom I consulted from time to time during Evelyn's illness. I never told him what was in the sealed envelope with which I entrusted him, and he, as a gentleman, didn't force me to reveal why I insisted on his keeping it in Evelyn's file. I personally saw him place it in there.*

"So now I beg you: go and retrieve it and follow its dictates. Do not fail me because if you do and Evelyn dies, there is no telling what the consequences will be, in this and in your times, to you and the world that matters to you. Yours sincerely,"

"He's threatening you. I don't believe it!" Eva stood up, an indignant look on her face.

"He's desperate. He's doing his best."

"He's nuts! Bridging the past and the present, what idiocy."

"I'm not so sure," said Franco, speaking calmly. "There are things that we don't understand. You've heard about my mother and the séance ..."

"So now you believe this nonsense ... well, what's next?"

Franco folded the letter and placed it back in the envelope and in his inner pocket. "We're going to Pavia," he said.

CHAPTER 42

London, England. July 2009

Von Stoffen's face was growing redder as he listened to his Italian contact's apologetic speech over the telephone.

"So you're saying that you don't know where they are," he said, making each word sound like a pointed knife dropping on a wooden surface.

"Not yet, but we will."

"When, pray?"

"Soon. My contact said, soon."

"You said you had good contacts with the police."

"I do, I do! But you see, my contact is in Sicily, and this is happening up north, so he has to go through his own contacts there, and it takes time."

"Listen carefully," said von Stoffen, sounding venomous. "I am giving you a lot of money all year round to get results when I need them, not to buy excuses. If that's the best you can do, I can dispense with your services from now on."

A long silence followed these words until von Stoffen asked, "Are you there?"

"Yes, yes. Look here, Sir, I have given my contact the names of the persons you gave me and he said that the man rented a car in Padua yesterday. He's still checking this information because – you understand that he must be cautious – it was just preliminary. But he cannot put out a general call to locate this car unless he has a plausible reason for it."

"Then tell him to make up one."

"That's not so simple ..." von Stoffen could almost hear his interlocutor wriggle in his chair, "and it may also be costly because using police resources for personal purposes is a serious matter."

"Money is no object here. Tell him to go ahead and find them."

"And if he's not successful, what do we do then?"

"Then I'll give him a good reason to issue a formal arrest warrant for them, but let's try his way first."

"I'll talk to him right away, Sir."

"Do that," von Stoffen hissed into the receiver and hung up. "Idiot!" he added, speaking to the empty room.

CHAPTER 43

London, England. July 2009

Kathia was exasperated. She didn't seem to be getting cooperation from anybody. Franco had come back from his weekend with Easby, a changed person, and for all practical purposes was cutting her out. In the past, Richard Hawthorne had done his best simply to avoid her and had turned openly hostile during her last visit to his office. "I'm really busy here, Kathia," he had said, waving a hand in the direction of the many dossiers sitting on his desk, "so please be so kind as not to come barging into my office unless someone is about to be murdered because short of that all the other stuff I have here is of higher priority." Kathia had been left uncharacteristically speechless, and Hawthorne had added, "And please don't phone either, unless it's a life-or-death matter. Remember, I don't work for you." Kathia had left without a word, banging the door behind her. Hawthorne's rudeness had stung, and for the first time, she was questioning whether her hard work was at all worthwhile.

Two more phone calls, one to Franco's apartment, which got no answer, and the other to his cell phone, which got her his voice mail, increased her dismay. It was time for some good advice. Sitting in her small office, she picked up the phone and called her boss in Geneva. "Good morning, Gilbert," she said, feeling better merely at hearing his friendly voice.

"Kathia ... You haven't reported for a while. How're things at our London shop?"

"Not so good, in fact. That's why I'm calling you. We seem to be losing Scotland Yard's cooperation – or at least, my contact there isn't being cooperative."

"I know. They complained about the excessive time they have to spend on your behalf. They seem to think that you are engaging in a wild goose chase."

"They called you to complain? The skunks!"

"Yes, that was inappropriate, but I had to listen all the same ... we depend on them, as you know."

"Believe me, Gilbert, mine is no wild goose chase. Something's terribly fishy. They're throwing a spanner into my investigation. Either someone is trying to protect somebody, or they're simply plain stupid. Either way, I need help; I can't do everything by myself."

"I understand, and I'm sure that you're doing a great job as always," Gilbert said, speaking soothingly, "but without the support of the local police, you have your work cut out for you. I can don't do much at this juncture other than advise you to sit tight and try to get some more positive information. Surely if you can prove to them that the threat is real, Scotland Yard will come around. You must be patient."

"I'll do what I can," said Kathia. Even to her own ears, she sounded resigned, and that annoyed her exceedingly.

"I'm sure. I have to go now. Take care," said Gilbert and hung up.

Five hours wasted sitting outside Easby's office, watching people coming and leaving the building, had left Kathia angry, tired, and hungry. In her apartment, she dropped herself onto the sofa and started to unpack the take-away that she had bought from a seedy Chinese restaurant on her way home. She turned on her TV set and went to wash her hands. When she returned to the sofa, she started digging her chopsticks into the crispy duck but had barely taken the first bite when an item on Sky News got her attention.

"... These are pictures of persons that the Venice police believe are connected with the murder of a young Hong Kong student. The police are not releasing details, but hints are being dropped that the murder may be a crime of passion and that a triangle of lovers may be at the roots of this grisly homicide."

Kathia put the crispy duck box down on the table and stared at the pictures streamed in a slideshow on the TV screen. The woman looked familiar to her, and she was sure that she had seen her before but couldn't place her. The face of the man, on the other hand, was out of focus and blurred. In two of the pictures, it had been taken from an angle that made positive recognition impossible. However, something in the man's overall appearance rang a bell; she could have bet that it was Franco. That was utterly improbable, though – what would he be doing in Venice with a young woman who looked like a pop star? And Franco was a dreamy professor type who wouldn't hurt a fly, let alone be involved in a murder. But she had pushed the "freeze" button, and the more she gazed at the picture on the screen, the more she felt convinced that it was him. And the fact remained that for the past three days, she had tried to reach him without success. He must have gotten himself into some mess orchestrated by Easby. She should have expected it.

She picked up the phone and dialed his office and then his apartment, and when she got no response from either, she dialed his cellular phone, where again she reached his voice mail. Kathia hung up and sat, thinking and staring at the TV screen. The Chinese food went cold, completely forgotten. Then she redialed Franco's cellular phone.

"Franco, this is Kathia," she said after going through the voicemail routine. "I know the trouble you're in, and I may be able to help you. I'm your friend, please believe that. Please call me when you hear this message. I'll be waiting for your call any time. I think you're in grave danger, so don't wait too long to call me. No matter where you are – in which country, I mean – I can help you." If he didn't take the hint that she knew he was the man from the Venice pictures, he was dumber than she thought him.

The question now was whether he would be getting her message. She couldn't count on that, and if he didn't, she would have to find him before somebody else did. She mused over the situation for a moment, and then she brightened as she realized what she had to do. She pulled Dan Botti's name from the address book of her cell phone. Dan was her counterpart in Italy; he was a friend – well, actually more than a friend. They had met as cadets at the basic instruction course of the ECWC and had clicked immediately. But while Kathia had approached their relationship lightly and had no intention of getting involved in anything "heavy," Dan had made it clear that his feelings for her were much more profound. They had parted as friends and still saw each other on occasion. Dan's recurring declarations of love, and Kathia's repartees with vows of friendship, had become something of a ritual at which they both laughed.

She found his number and pushed the "dial" button. Dan's voice came quickly.

"Hey, *amore*! What's up?"

"Hey, *scemo*," she answered.

"Don't call me 'stupid' every time I call you 'love,' Ice Queen. You're breaking my heart."

"Yeah, yeah. I'm sure." She paused for a second and then asked, "How's ECWC business in Italy? Are you very busy?"

"Never too busy for you."

"Good. Can you meet me in Venice tomorrow?"

"You're kidding, right? You're in London or what?"

"Yes, I am, and I can take the next flight to Venice and meet you there by noon tomorrow."

"I told you that this would happen," said Dan. "You finally realized that you can't live without me, and now you need to see me without delay. I'm in."

"You wish ... this is official ECWC business."

"Did you have to spoil it for me right away? So what's the problem?"

"I'll tell you when we meet. Can you get away for a few days?"

"What do you think? We don't slave like you guys here in Italy. We take it easy. Judging from my activity level, I'm sure that Geneva thinks that I quit my job months ago. Nobody will notice if I'm away from the office. Are we staying in Venice? Do we need to get a hotel?"

"I think at least for one night. Yes."

"All right. I'll make a reservation and will send you a text message with the details. Separate rooms, of course ..."

"Don't be stupid," said Kathia and hung up. She was smiling.

CHAPTER 44

Pavia, Italy. July 2009

Franco faced a middle-aged secretary, who seemed to be an integral part of the old desk that blocked the entrance to the main hall of the San Tommaso Palace. This building housed the vast archive of the University of Pavia. He felt much less confident than he had given Eva to understand during his pep talk in the car outside. On their way there, they had stopped at an Internet café to gather as much information as possible about the archive, and what they had seen was not encouraging. As was to be expected of an Italian institute, the university was highly bureaucratic and made conditions to permit researchers to access the archive. An application form had to be sent in beforehand, which needed to be approved by the archive director. Franco paid the extravagant sum of five euros to be allowed to print out the form, which he filled in by falsifying the signature of the head of his department beside his own. Now with it ready in his pocket, he smiled at the secretary.

"Good morning," he said, "I am professor Lorenzi from the King's College in London. I'm here for that research ..."

Franco placed on the desk the King's College card that identified him as a visiting professor. The secretary looked at it, consulted a list on her table, and then gazed straight at Franco. "I'm sorry, but I don't have you on my list. Please show me the form."

"Oh, I'm glad that I have taken a copy with me," said Franco, fishing in the inner pocket of his jacket, "I'm so hopeless with formalities and papers, you know ..." he added, with a professorially helpless smile, handing it to her.

"But this form doesn't have the director's approval on it. You should have one signed by him."

"Really? My secretary never said that. She takes care of all formalities, and she mailed this already a month ago. She never mentioned that I needed anything else."

"That's a problem. I can't let you in without the director's approval."

"But that's terrible! I have come all the way from London especially for this, and Miss Peabody here is a graduate student. Her thesis hangs on completing this research. This is a catastrophe! Miss Peabody," he added, switching to English and addressing Eva, "I fear that I have bad news for you. We have come all the way for nothing; they won't let us in."

"Oh, what a disaster! What shall I do?" Eva gasped. She acted the distressed student masterfully, and Franco had to make an effort to suppress a smile.

"Wait a minute," said the secretary, who was obviously not accustomed to this kind of disturbance taking place in the august building. "This is highly irregular, but I'll ask the director what to do."

She got up and went into a narrow corridor behind her desk, taking Franco's fake application form with her.

"Miss Peabody?" Eva whispered. "What am I, an old spinster?"

"That's the first name that occurred to me, sorry. It lends you seriousness, though," Franco whispered back.

The archive was empty but for an old man who sat at a nearby table and a young student who was going through some material at the end of the hall. Franco engaged in idle thoughts about forcing his way in but knew it wasn't a real option. Five very tense minutes passed before the secretary came back accompanied by a middle-aged man whose demeanor held all the signs of authority.

"I'm the director, Professor Lorenzi," said the man, politely shaking hands with Franco. "I understand the problem, but we have rules here. And if we break the rules ... I wanted to ask you – your application form says that you're researching 'the use of Latin in medical documentation at the end of the nineteenth century.' That's an unusual topic, isn't it?"

"You're right. This is a very original subject that Miss Peabody here selected for her Ph.D. thesis. This research in Pavia is the last step in completing her work. This is so important because, as I'm sure you know, Pavia was at the forefront of medical research in that period."

"They're not letting us in, right? What shall I do? I don't have the money to come back again," said Eva, twitching her hands and actually producing a tear out of nowhere.

Eva's carefully timed tear seemed to work like magic on the director who, throughout these exchanges, hadn't taken his eyes off her. He turned to her and addressed her in macaronic English. "Misse Peabody," he said, "we are bureaucrats, not barbarians. We will not be between you and your thesis. I will sign this permission now, and you can make your research. But don't tell nobody that I did it, okay?"

He handed Franco the signed form, and Eva rewarded him with a smile that could have melted any bureaucrat. "*Grazie,*" she said, and gave him her hand, which he held for an unnecessarily long time, then he addressed the secretary and said, "Professor Lorenzi has come a long way to do this research. Give him all the assistance he needs." Then, with a last glance at Eva's generous cleavage, he waved goodbye and was swallowed by the same corridor from which he had come.

Franco felt obliged to be nice to the secretary who had helped them and smiled warmly at her. "The director is a very nice person, but we really owe everything to you," he said. "I don't know how to thank you."

"Oh, that was nothing," said the secretary, blushing. "Now, you will want to start your research. The medical files are in the basement; I'll unlock the door for you. If you need to make copies, you can use the basement Xerox machine, but please stop by me when you're finished to pay for the copies. We close at a quarter to one, and it's now ten o'clock, so I hope you'll have enough time, but you can come back tomorrow if you need to. Tomorrow we are open."

Franco nodded dutifully, and they followed her down the stairs and into the basement, where she turned on the lights and left them.

"What now?" Eva whispered.

"Now we need to go through all the shelves and look for the material belonging to this Professor Golgi. Let's start from opposite ends."

They scanned the shelves in what promised to become an endless endeavor because thousands of files had been shelved in no apparent order. Franco was starting to despair when Eva called out to him, "Come over here! Check this out."

She pointed to a sign by a door, which said:

NO ENTRANCE
This is a precise reconstruction of the study of
Bartolomeo Camillo Emilio Golgi
1906 Nobel Prize for Medicine
Admittance by prior arrangement only

"Bingo!" she said. "I didn't know that this guy was a Nobel Prize laureate."

"He wasn't yet when my great-grandfather wrote his letter. What we're looking for must be here. Let's see how we can get in."

The door was an antique piece, finely chiseled and with a handcrafted iron and copper handle, but the lock was solid, and no matter how hard Franco pulled, it wouldn't budge.

"We're sunk," he said, feeling and sounding disheartened. "We can't get in, and we don't have a good excuse to ask for access. And besides, we don't know who may be on our trail, but I'm pretty sure that we are running out of time."

"Don't give up," said Eva, speaking resolutely. "Let's look around for something to force the lock with."

"So now we are going to be guilty of breaking and entering, in addition to being suspected murderers," said Franco bitterly.

"Do you have a better idea?"

"No, but what if it triggers an alarm?"

"Have you looked around? There is no alarm in this place; they barely installed a few smoke detectors. I bet that they count on the bars in the windows and the locked door on the stairs. And who would want to burgle this place? It only contains worthless, smelly old paper."

Franco looked around and saw that she was right. No motion detectors could be seen anywhere, and the few small windows were blocked by heavy bars. He found a stool near one of the shelves, dragged it to one of the windows, and stepped on it to examine it more closely. Through the dirty glass, he saw what appeared to be the sidewalk at the back of the building, in a narrow street paved with cobblestones. His eyes were at street level, and he could tell that the place was deserted.

"You're right," he said, stepping down from the stool. "The windows are barred, and it looks like they haven't been opened for ages. I can't see any sensors except for smoke detectors. Let's look around for something to help us open that door, and let's hope that they don't have an alarm attached to it from the inside."

Franco searched under the shelves and in every corner of the basement but found nothing.

"Did you find anything?" he asked when Eva rejoined him empty-handed.

"Nothing. There is a small room in that corner – a janitor's room or something – but it's only full of brooms and cleaning stuff. Nothing useful."

"Let me see it," said Franco.

It was a tiny room indeed, and other than a bucket and a couple of wooden brooms that had seen better days, it was empty. They were about to leave when Franco looked up and stopped. "Here's the answer!" he said. The room had a small, square window, different from the ones in the basement. Franco turned the bucket upside down and stepped on it. "Look!" he said with excitement. "This window has bars that lock into the wall, but it opens from the inside."

He had to apply all his strength to turn the handle, which actuated a sprocket that bolted the window, but at last, it budged, and the bars moved back. He pulled, and the window opened.

"This window has no bars on the outside. I could lift myself up now and leave through it. That's the solution!"

"How? How are we going to do it?"

"I'll leave the window unlocked, and we'll come back tonight with equipment."

"You know that we'll be in big trouble if they catch us ..."

"We're in trouble already, baby. A little bit more won't make a big difference."

"This is exciting, you know?" Eva pressed her body against Franco, who almost lost his balance. "Have you ever made love in a janitor's closet?"

"No, and I don't think that I could perform now. I'm too freaked out, and it's too dangerous."

"You used to be more fun to have around," said Eva, faking a complaint.

"I'll be fun again when we manage to pull ourselves out of this mess. Now let's go and photocopy some stuff. We need to show that we've been researching."

CHAPTER 45

Ambri, Switzerland. July 2009

Sally lay in bed, her eyes closed and her breath so light that Benini had to double-check to make sure she was actually breathing. She slept in an almost sitting position, and her nightgown showed dark brown stains that were unmistakably blood.

"Sally," he called in a low voice.

Sally opened her eyes and blinked. They were dark brown, almost black, and stood out in the sweaty pallor of her face. "Doctor Benini," she whispered feebly, "I'm feeling terrible. It's hard to breathe, and I'm coughing blood."

"You've got a nasty flu. Hans should have called me sooner."

"I told him ..."

"Doesn't matter," said Benini, who had taken a syringe from his bag and now stuck a needle into Sally's arm. "I'm giving you something that will make you feel better. All you need now is rest. Make sure not to exert yourself."

"Thank you, Doctor Benini. But I wanted to tell you ..." Sally stopped and let her eyes wander on the ceiling as if to look there for what she had wanted to say.

"Yes?" Benini prompted her gently.

"I can't remember. I know that Hans has been mean to me, but I can't remember what it was that he did."

Sally's expression was one of puzzlement. She was obviously drifting away, whether because she was so weak or because of the drug that Benini had just given her.

"Don't worry," said Benini. "It'll come back to you."

But Sally's eyes had closed again, and she gave no sign of having heard him.

London, England.

von Stoffen's secretary buzzed him from the basement. "You have a call from Italy, and after you're finished, you may want to come down. John has recorded a conversation for you."

"Put him on," he said, and after a second, he heard the voice of his Italian contact.

"We know where they are," he said, sounding triumphant.

"Where?"

"In Pavia. The information is being double-checked, but a man with your subject's name has made a credit card purchase in a shop there. This is just a preliminary heads-up, but I'll have full details very soon."

"I need those details the moment you have them," said von Stoffen.

"You will have them," said the voice, and von Stoffen hung up. The thought of commending his interlocutor for an excellent job done never crossed his mind. People he paid were supposed to get results.

He walked down the stairs and into the basement, where the operator at the eavesdropping position handed him a pair of headphones. Von Stoffen put them on, and after he nodded, the man pushed a button. The voice of Arturo Benini came through loud and clear.

"James, we have a problem," he said. "I've just visited the surrogate, and she's in terrible shape. If I don't start treatment immediately, she will die soon. I've given her palliatives, but she may have less than a week ..."

"Don't call me on this line," Easby's obviously annoyed voice cut him short.

"Oh, all right. I'll call you on the other one," said Benini, and the line went dead.

"Damn!" said von Stoffen to himself. He removed the headphones and asked the operator, "Where did the call come from?"

"It was a number in Italy."

"Uhm," grunted von Stoffen. He handed the headphones back to the operator and left.

CHAPTER 46

Pavia, Italy. July 2009

Franco had checked in at the Astoria Hotel, overruling Eva's objection that checking in at a five-star hotel might make them conspicuous.

"We must go to a big hotel where I can book a room for myself and sneak you in," he had said. "If we go to a small one, they will ask for your passport and will take a good look at your picture without a wig. It's too big a chance to take."

Now they were having dinner in the room, and the excellent food had made Eva forget her discomfort at having to hide in the bathroom each time someone knocked on the door.

"This is so romantic!" she said. "I'm having a clandestine dinner with the Dark Knight who's going to burgle a palace to save the world."

"I'm glad that you are enjoying this," said Franco bitterly. "Personally, I've been waiting for someone to arrest me at any moment while I was buying the crowbar and the screwdriver. I must've had it written on my forehead that I was planning a burglary."

"I think that all those masculine tools make you look even sexier." Eva dropped from her left hand the piece of bread that she was eating and caressed Franco's knee, while with the other hand, she kept eating her soup.

"Well, I don't feel sexy. I'm scared out of my wits, and I don't know if I'll be able to pull this off."

"I'm sure you will."

"And it didn't help to see your face pasted all over town on the front page of every newspaper. I don't know how come we haven't been spotted yet. I worry about the way that archive director was studying you."

"He wasn't looking at my face, believe me. Far below it."

"Let's hope ..."

"Eat your dinner, my Dark Knight. You'll need the strength," Eva concluded.

Franco ate sparingly and without pleasure. He envied Eva's appetite, but the prospect of what he had to do that night was keeping him off his food.

Eva had insisted that she should be a part of the burglary operation. After much argument, they had decided that she would sit in the car at the corner of the building in the back street and signal by turning on the headlights if she saw anybody coming, to alert Franco if he was about to emerge from the basement.

Getting into the basement had been easy, and Franco now stood by the door of the Golgi study. He examined the lock with the flashlight and then inserted the screwdriver between the wing and the frame and pushed it aside. To his surprise, the wing moved, the lock unlatched, and the door opened without effort. Franco held his breath, waiting to see if the alarm sounded, and when nothing happened, he wanted to kick himself for not trying to push the wing aside in the morning.

Inside, old wooden shelves were stuffed with files neatly arranged alongside some books and old, thick and heavy bound notebooks. The files on the shelves were ordered alphabetically, and Franco went straight to the shelf marked with the letter "L." It took him a while to find what he was looking for because he carefully put back each file he examined. But after a few minutes, he pulled out a file marked "Evelina Lorenzi." It was thick and contained many notes, but also held a sealed envelope on which the words "Material Received from Hon. L." were written in clear handwriting. This had to be what he was looking for, but he couldn't be absolutely sure that there wasn't anything else in there that he needed, so he placed the whole file in the plastic briefcase that he had bought together with the tools. He took a last look at the room to make sure that he had left no traces of his visit and then retreated into the basement. When he pulled the handle, the door closed behind him, returning to its original locked state. It was perfect; nobody would suspect that it had been opened.

Franco almost ran to the janitor's room. He was relieved that his work had been completed without a hitch and was in a hurry to get out. He stepped on the bucket and prepared to heave himself through the window up to the street level when a flash of light warned him, and he let himself drop back down. He gazed cautiously through the window. Three young men were walking in the street from the far end of the building toward Eva's parked car. Franco remained hidden until they passed the basement window and moved on, and then he cautiously opened the window again. The three had reached the car and were peering into it.

"Hey!" said one of them to Eva, who had opened a crack in the window. "Can we help you?"

"Je ne parle pas Italien," came Eva's muffled voice from within.

"A tourist, cool!" said one of the bullies. "Come on out, and we'll help you."

"Yes, help you, ha ha!" guffawed another.

Eva didn't respond, and the three bullies leaned on the side of the car and started rocking it. Franco pulled himself up quickly from the basement and approached the car.

"Stop that!" he ordered.

The three stopped and turned toward him. One of them took a step forward, placing his face near Franco's, and asked, speaking with a belligerent tone, "Says who?"

Franco acted without thinking. "Says this!" he answered, swaying the crowbar that he held in his right hand, which came home on the bully's thigh, tearing away a piece of his trousers along with some skin. The bully stepped back with a cry of pain and looked incredulously at the blood that had started to stain the fabric of his trousers. "Why did you do that?" he whined.

Franco used the time to raise the crowbar above his head in a menacing gesture.

"He's crazy!" cried one of the bullies. The three of them exchanged glances and then turned around and ran away.

Franco climbed into the car and let himself drop onto the passenger's seat. He felt exhausted.

"Did you find it?" Eva asked urgently.

Franco nodded. "Let's go," he urged, and Eva, without a word, stepped on the accelerator and drove away.

CHAPTER 47

Pavia, Italy. July 2009

Back at the hotel and in the safety of their room, Franco and Eva let their exhilaration at the success of their plan take over.

"You rule!" said Eva, hugging him. "You're an absolute king! Let me see the loot."

"Careful, it's old, and you don't want to damage it ..." Franco cautioned, handing her the plastic briefcase. He sat on the edge of the bed and watched Eva's display of childish enthusiasm with the satisfaction of the grown-up who has brought home a rich gift for his kids.

Eva unlatched the briefcase and took the file out. She opened it and skimmed through the papers.

"There is a lot of stuff in here, and it's all written in Italian. Which one is the paper we are looking for?"

"I'm not sure. I haven't had the time to go through it, but I think it should be in there," he said, pointing at the envelope with the neat handwriting. "Still, as you say, this is a thick file, and I need to read it all to make sure."

"You're not going to touch it with your filthy hands ... or me," she said, smiling coquettishly. "Look at you; you're as dirty as a coal miner. Go take a shower. We need to celebrate. Be quick; I want you to order some champagne."

"Yes, it was a dirty job going through that window. And I can use a shower to clean my head also. It has been quite an evening ..."

"Very true, my Dark Knight," said Eva. She touched his cheek lightly and gently moved a lock of hair that had stuck to his forehead. "I was quite impressed. I didn't know that Latin professors were trained for combat."

"They aren't. I don't know what got into me," Franco said, speaking apologetically.

"Animal instinct? Saving a damsel in distress? I like that."

Franco got up heavily. "I'll take a quick shower," he said.

Eva nodded, and Franco kicked his shoes away.

"Wait a moment!" Eva cried.

"What?"

"This," said Eva. She approached him and, without touching him, she stood on the tip of her toes and gave him a long, warm kiss.

"I'm only going to the shower," Franco said, "what was that in honor of?"

"You earned it," Eva said simply.

Franco nodded, pleased, and walked into the spacious, marbled bathroom. It was richly furnished, and the shower had been fitted with a huge head that turned showering into a real treat. As the hot water caressed his body, Franco felt his muscles relax. He only then understood how tense he had been since the beginning of the evening. He lingered in the steamy cubicle, emptying his mind of all thoughts and feeling the energy return to his body.

Torn between the pleasures of the shower and the knowledge that Eva was waiting for him, he toweled himself, donned the elegant bathrobe with the A-H monogram that the hotel had hung on the bathroom door, combed his hair with his fingers, and opened the communicating door to the room. Cold air from the room hit his face and made him stop on the threshold for a moment. It took Franco only a second to realize that something was amiss; the room was empty, and his eyes raced around, seeking Eva, although he knew that she was gone.

And so were Evelyn's medical file and his car keys.

CHAPTER 48

Venice, Italy. July 2009

Dan and Kathia's day had been a chain of one frustration after the other. The local police didn't have a working relationship with the ECWC, and a police inspector, who had, at last, agreed to talk to them, made it plain that he doubted that any such organization existed. However, if it did exist, he would be happy to cooperate with them after a proper request was submitted in triplicate through the proper channels and approved. Would they like to come back in two weeks?

"This idiot is making fun of us!" Kathia erupted.

"Shh. Certain words sound the same in Italian," Dan admonished her. "Calm down, okay? Thank you very much for your time, Inspector," he added over his shoulder as he dragged Kathia out. "Do you want to get us arrested?" he asked her.

"I want to kick his ass!" said Kathia.

"Well, you can't. Let's go and take a look at the scene."

The apartment was guarded by a bored policeman who was happy to have someone to make conversation with. He barely glanced at Dan's credentials and accepted them at face value. He then let them into the apartment. A thorough search of the rooms didn't reveal anything that might help them find out what had become of Franco, and they left after a few minutes, much to the policeman's regret.

Having run into a dead end, there was little left for them to do.

"How about an aperitif at the Hotel Danieli?" Dan asked.

"We're not on vacation; you're aware of that, right? And besides, the Danieli is awfully expensive," Kathia objected.

"I'm paying."

"In that case, it would be a shame to refuse," said Kathia. She was glad of the opportunity to relax a little and, besides, there was nothing more for them to do there.

They sat in the elegant lobby of the Danieli Hotel, and Kathia drank her Kir Royale thoughtfully.

"One Euro for your thoughts," said Dan.

"That's all my thoughts are worth for you?"

"Name your price."

"I'm stymied. I have charged into this like a wild beast, jumped on a flight, and dragged you here to accomplish absolutely nothing. I feel like an idiot. By the way, I'm giving you these thoughts for free."

"I might be offended, you know, when you say that meeting me in Venice accomplishes nothing. To me, it means a lot. And besides, you need to be where the action is, so when your protégée calls, you can jump in and save the day."

"You're a dear, Dan," said Kathia. She smiled and put her hand on his arm in a gesture of endearment. "That doesn't make me a greater success, though."

"Girl, you need a distraction! I know a great restaurant – with music, dancing, and everything. You'll like it."

Dan was right. A good meal, accompanied by a great bottle of Italian wine, had done wonders, and Kathia had almost forgotten her frustration.

"Let's dance," she said when the band started to play a lively South American tune. Her face was flushed, and she felt a little dizzy.

The hell with Easby and everybody, she thought as she walked toward the dance floor with Dan in tow.

Dan was a good dancer, and they pirouetted harmoniously, followed by the diners' admiring glances.

"I'm glad that you talked me into going out tonight," said Kathia. "I really needed it."

"Daddy knows," said Dan.

The band was now playing a slow tune, and Kathia put her head on Dan's shoulder. "I may need some more distraction, later on," she said, breathing down Dan's neck.

"I'm ready to go right now," Dan answered, hopefully.

"Let's go," said Kathia.

Then the phone rang.

"Kathia ..." said Franco's voice and ruined what was promising to become a lovely night.

Franco turned down the lights and sat in the semi-darkness, trying to make sense of the situation. Eva had deceived him all along, that was clear now, and perhaps all her stories were lies. *Probably her father was living happily in Paris,* he thought bitterly. Perhaps – and the thought made him wince – she had never cared for him at all. He found it hard to believe that she had faked her feelings for him, but there he was, abandoned, deceived, and extremely depressed. But who was she working for? And what was her purpose in stealing the file when she knew that she could talk him pretty much into doing anything she wanted? It didn't make sense.

And now he had to decide what to do. He couldn't stay at the hotel much longer, and there was nothing more for him to do in Pavia. Besides, he wondered whether it was dangerous for him to stay there; Eva could give away his location, but he rejected the thought that she would willfully put him in danger. Running after Eva was out of the question; she had taken the car and had probably left town already. But he could call her. Yes, she would have to explain, and maybe he could talk her into coming back. He reached into the pockets of his jacket from which he took his cell phone and its battery, reassembled the cell phone, and turned it on. It came to life with a long beep, and the screen showed an alert that two voice mails were waiting. He ignored it and furiously dialed Eva's number. He heard the rings – all 14 of them – and then his cell phone announced with a quick "tut-tut" that it had given up trying. Franco sat in the one armchair provided by the hotel, closed his eyes, and let his body slump. He felt drained of all energy, and his body simply refused to move. He let his mind wander between different flashbacks of his time with Eva until he felt that thinking about the past hurt too much. Besides, he had the present to take care of. *Here's the proof that my theory about love works,* he thought. Had I let myself fall in love with Eva, I would be devastated by her betrayal now.

He was honest enough with himself to admit that he was devastated anyway. Reluctantly, he pushed the voicemail button of his cell phone and listened to the messages. The first one was from Easby and had been left the day before. "My boy, this is James," it said. "I know that you're in trouble. Please call me as soon as you can. This is extremely urgent, so please call me the moment you hear this message. I'm waiting for your call."

Franco wasn't given the time to consider Easby's appeal because the voicemail system immediately played the second one.

"Franco, this is Kathia," said Kathia's voice. "I know the trouble you're in, and I may be able to help you. I'm your friend, please believe that. Please call me when you hear this message. I'll be waiting for your call any time. I think you're in grave danger, so don't wait too long to call me. No matter where you are – in which country, I mean – I can help you."

So the one thing about which everybody was in agreement was that Franco was in trouble. He found little comfort in that. He clearly had to call someone, but whom? He no longer automatically believed Eva's story about Easby. He'd found it hard to believe that he was evil from the start.

But on the other hand, Kathia had connections with the police and might be able to help him better than James. Calling them both was a contradiction in terms and out of the question. After a brief hesitation, he dialed Kathia's number.

"Kathia ... It's Franco," he said when she took the call after only two rings, and he heard her "Hello."

"Thank God! Are you okay? Where are you?"

"I'm in Italy."

"I know that. I've seen the pictures. But where in Italy?"

"So you know ...," said Franco, actually feeling relieved that she knew about the Venice murder. "I had nothing to do with it."

"I didn't think for a moment that you were involved. Still, it looks like you're in a big mess. But tell me where you are so we can discuss what to do."

"I'm in Pavia, and I'm in trouble. I can't give you the details over the phone ..."

"Don't even think of it. Look, I'm in Venice. Can you come and meet me?"

"No, no! I'm not going anywhere near Venice. There's a murderous maniac there who's after me. And besides, I'd better stay away until this affair is solved."

"All right, I'll come to you. Where are you staying?"

Franco gave her the name of the hotel and added, "Please come soon."

"I don't have a car, and the trains don't run at this hour. I'll rent a car and leave as soon as I can tomorrow morning. I'll try to be there by noon. Keep your cell phone on but don't answer any calls except mine."

"Just come quickly, okay?"

Kathia's calm voice and practical approach had restored some of Franco's confidence. Perhaps he wouldn't have to go through this alone.

"Click," he heard the sound of Kathia signing off.

He was alone again.

CHAPTER 49

Pavia, Italy. July 2009

Joseph Mead was puzzled. It wasn't often that his employer made unreasonable requests – Joseph considered very few chores to be unsuitable – but this time, he was being capricious.

"Where in Pavia?" Joseph had asked when von Stoffen had issued his orders to "go and find them."

"They're staying in a hotel."

"Do you have a hotel name? Something?"

"No. I hope to have it soon, but I don't want you to wait for it. Pavia is a small town. There won't be that many hotels. Get going. The sooner you start, the sooner you find them."

So Joseph had driven to Pavia, arriving early in the morning. He had walked into a telephone booth at the train station and had torn out the Yellow Pages, which listed 14 hotels. He was now seated in the train station's bar, drinking coffee and thinking what to do. His head hurt – a pulsating pain that reached down to his shoulders. The bleeding had stopped, so he hadn't sought medical help; you never know who may be nosy and report a suspicious wound to the police, but now he worried that the wound was perhaps infected. That pulsating pain was worrisome, but he had to forget it and concentrate on his job.

He ordered a beer and studied the Yellow Pages. He would start with the more sordid hotels, the one- or two-star hotels where the subjects were more likely to hide.

Eva woke up in the car. She felt cramped, and her mouth was pasty. She checked her watch and saw that it was only a little after 6 AM. She surveyed the area around the car through the windows and was relieved to see that she was alone. When she had stopped at the rest area the night before, an 18-wheeler had stood in the parking zone, and it was gone now. She had parked there with mixed feelings; on the one hand, the semitrailer hid her from the road, but if that driver saw a woman alone in the car and got ideas into his head, she would be in danger. At last, she had decided that sleeping with the doors locked and the key in the ignition was safe enough. She had been too tired to keep looking for an alternative sleeping place anyway.

She opened the door and washed her face with mineral water, and then she drank the little water left in the bottle. She took a stick of spearmint gum from her bag, and the fresher feeling in her mouth made her feel better. She sat up, debating what to do. She was dying for a cup of coffee and wondered whether stopping at a gas station to buy some could be dangerous. But the wig had protected her well so far, and she needed gas anyway ...

She let her mind go back to the evening before and to Franco. She hoped he hadn't taken her departure too hard, but who was she kidding? He was probably devastated. It couldn't be helped, though. The alternative was too dangerous for her and for Franco. By taking the documents, she had turned herself into prey. She had made sure of that by leaving a message on Easby's office machine. "I did as you said. I have the original documents," she had said in the message. "I have taken them from Franco, and I have left him."

"That was a dumb thing to do," Richard Hawthorne had told her when she had called him again and reported. "Whoever is after those documents will now come after you."

"I know, and that was the idea. You said that you would get me out of here, and you wanted the documents. Now you can kill two birds with one stone. Besides, now that you know that you're in a race for the documents, you'll get moving quickly, or you may be too late; and I want out of here post haste."

Hawthorne had sighed and proceeded to give her detailed instructions. Eva ran them in her head again to make sure that she hadn't forgotten any detail and was reassured that she had everything well memorized.

The gum had lost its freshening power, and Eva spat it out, and then she resolutely closed the door and turned the ignition key. She had to have coffee.

James Easby hadn't slept a wink on the previous night. People seemed to be falling out of his sight continuously. Marchetti had disappeared off the face of the earth, and so had Franco. With them gone, both the documents that they had been sent to retrieve were lost, at least temporarily, and Maria insisted that they were critical. Eva, who was supposed to meet with Franco, wasn't returning his phone calls and had left a cryptic message on his answering machine. He hadn't asked her to do anything about the documents that Franco had retrieved in Udine, so her message didn't make sense. On top of it all, Benini was about to crack because the surrogate was dying.

Something bigger than he and his organization was on the move, that was clear, and he wasn't seeing all the sides of the equation. Easby was logical and pragmatic and understood that he was no longer in full command of the situation. The time had come to take extreme measures. He lifted the receiver and dialed a number that he knew by heart.

"Office of Undersecretary David Westmore," said a voice at the other end.

"This is James Easby."

"Yes, Sir James. Mr. Westmore is in his office. I'll put you through to him immediately."

"So what brings you here, James?" asked Westmore, gazing out the window at the Thames, which was his preferred way to start a conversation.

"You known damn well what, David. My operation is in trouble, and I don't know how much of my trouble I owe to you."

Westmore moved away from the window and came to sit in the armchair in front of Easby. He had poured tea for his visitor, but his own cup remained empty. His principles included not drinking with some people.

"None at all, really," he said. "In fact, since the moment that you told me about your project and asked me to avoid interfering with it, I've done my very best to help you – not as a favor, mind you. I really believed you when you explained to me how The Kingdom could benefit from it. I have kept the ferrets away from you as much as I could manage, and I have tried to facilitate you, but you will understand that there is a limit to what I can do officially. After all, yours is a rather odd project, don't you agree?"

"I know that at first sight, it may look like I'm acting a bit eccentric, but I've put solid research behind it."

"So did we, so did we."

"Then you know that it presents possibilities ..."

"Indeed. But you see, you've been too vague. All you were prepared to tell me is that you are working on developing a technique that could save the lives of individuals who died in the past. But I don't know if you are talking of a time machine or of an alliance with the devil – and I don't know which of the two is the crazier idea. If it weren't for our old acquaintance, I would have had you thrown out on your ear or committed to a loony bin. You must give me something more if you need my help."

"The problem is, some of the stages in the project may seem a little ... you may consider them to be somewhat unorthodox, so I don't know how much you want to know."

"Do you worry that I may find that what you are about to tell me is objectionable?"

"Yes, and perhaps a purist might say that not every step that we have had to take can be viewed as being strictly legal."

"But my dear James, virtually everything we do here is strictly illegal. That's why, formally, my department doesn't exist. I don't think that anything you'll say can scandalize me."

"May I assume then that you're willing to listen and to help?"

"To listen, yes. To help, within reason, dear James. Within reason."

Easby took a sip of his tea, taking time to think. He had few options left. He had come this far, and now he had to cross this bridge. He put the tea cup down, sighed, and gazed straight at Westmore.

"Get ready for an interesting tale, then," he said. "I have located an old document that contains instructions that we believe will allow us to do what we're talking about. I have sent a professor – someone who's helping me – to fetch it, together with the researcher who discovered it. My researcher has disappeared in thin air, somewhere between Heathrow and my office. The professor was attacked by unidentified persons in Venice and now has disappeared too. I need to know if you have any information about who might be behind all this."

"You surprise me, James. I know nothing about it at all, but I'll see what I can find out."

There was little doubt in Easby's mind that Westmore was lying and had more information than he cared to admit. He knew how things worked in the Service, and his only hope was that helping him would match Westmore's interests. He had to keep the communication channel between them open until something came through it, in one form or another.

"I really need your help on this, David. Please call me when you find out who is involved."

"I will, as soon as I can," said Westmore, not meaning a word of it.

Monsignor Le Fevre leaned forward. He was seated at his ornate Louis XV desk, which occupied a corner of his vast study next to the large windows that allowed a generous amount of sun to come in. He studied the document that his secretary had placed on the desk before him. He read it at length, and then he signed it and looked up.

"Sometimes, the weight of responsibility is heavy. Very heavy, indeed. One wonders, Martin if one is doing the proper thing."

Monsignor Le Fevre was having a bout of the jitters. Recalling his conversation with von Stoffen, he had to admit that he had been somewhat economical with the truth. The Holy See did not know his activities in the matter, and only a handful of people in the Vatican were in on this unauthorized process – and even they had been given only scant details. He didn't want to think of the consequences that could ensue if anything went wrong, and he was held responsible for the failure and the instigation of illegal activities.

His assistant, who had waited patiently while Le Fevre read through the document, took one step forward, lifted it from the desktop, and placed it neatly in a brown folder. He was a young priest, but Le Fevre appreciated his acumen and often made him the recipient of his monologues. He had a way of developing complex ideas by proposing them to his interlocutor and then challenging them with scathing arguments. Martin knew better than to interfere with the process or voice an unsolicited opinion. He kept silent, waiting for the question that, sooner or later, was sure to come.

"What do you know about resurrection?" Le Fevre asked.

"I know that when our Lord Jesus Christ returns to earth, he will physically raise all those who have died, giving them back the bodies they lost at death," Martin recited.

"And ..." Le Fevre prompted him.

"And I believe in the true resurrection of this flesh that we now possess. We sow a corruptible body in the tomb, but he rises up an incorruptible body, a 'spiritual body.'" Martin glanced quickly at Le Fevre as if to gauge the correctness of his response.

"You declaim well," said Le Fevre, putting down the gilded pen that he had used to sign the papers, "and, no doubt, your faith is strong and your knowledge broad. But let me ask you this: do you believe that resurrection of the flesh may be brought about by a mere mortal? And if that happened, what repercussions would it have on your faith?"

"Oh, that ... You mean the tale that you mentioned in the memo to the private file ... I don't believe it for a moment, of course. Obviously, it's a troubling heresy, but I thought that you indicated that it was being taken care of."

"You haven't answered my question. What would happen to your faith if it were proven to you that a mere mortal could resurrect long-dead people? What effect would that have on you?"

Martin's expression darkened, and he narrowed his eyes to mere slits. He was obviously engaged in deep thought. After a while, he opened his mouth to speak, but his speech was impeded by a stammer – a clear sign, Le Fevre knew from his association with this young man, that he was deeply troubled.

"But ... bu-bu-but ... It ca-ca-can't be."

Le Fevre fixed his gaze on a point at the far end of the room. "I haven't slept well lately, Martin. I have a feeling that this may be more dangerous than we estimated. And it troubles me that I have heard about it by mere chance. That was remiss of me."

"You can't be everywhere," Martin offered by way of consolation.

"I can't afford not to," Le Fevre answered curtly.

"So, what can be done, Monsignor?"

"I am dealing with it closely, very closely. I have two different people working on it and, still, I'm not satisfied that I am doing all I should. One should always doubt one's own acts and see how to improve upon them."

"But why do you think that it is so dangerous?"

"Ideas can be dangerous. The Church recognized that simple truth centuries ago, and that is why we have only a small number of canonical sacred texts. I can measure the danger of an idea based on its destructive power. That in this case, the danger is of staggering proportions is easy to judge: I'm sure you are aware that you haven't answered my question – for the third time in a row, and that shows you," Le Fevre added, speaking gravely.

CHAPTER 50

Asti, Italy. July 2009

Eva drove for the third time through the picturesque city of Asti – but she wasn't enjoying the view. She wished that she had a GPS or, at least, that Hawthorne's instructions had been more precise. "From the city center, take *Corso Dante*," he had said, "and head up north. At the last roundabout, turn right and then straight out of the city." Hawthorne had supplemented those instructions with directions that were supposed to get her to an isolated house owned by an operative of Hawthorne's organization. The house was sporadically used as a basis for Service activities, and she would be safe there until they came to pick her up. She had attempted to follow directions but had twice fetched up at an industrial area and dead-ended there. She stopped at a traffic light and took a sip of her third, already cold coffee from the lidded Styrofoam cup. She needed to be more focused to escape the vicious circle in which she had been caught up.

She drove slowly, and when she reached the end of the boulevard, at the roundabout, this time she took the right exit, and five minutes later she fetched up in open country. Navigating in the countryside didn't turn out to be easier than in the city, and half an hour and several false turns later, she stopped on the seemingly endless country road, switched off the engine, leaned forward on the steering wheel, and allowed herself to cry. All the tension of the past few days erupted, and she sobbed uncontrollably. After a while, the sobs stopped, and Eva's body relaxed. Some of the tension had been taken away with the tears, and she felt better.

A noise near her ear made her raise her head, and she was startled to see that a police car had pulled over next to her and a policeman, a young and tall *Carabiniere*, was knocking on her window. She quickly wiped away her tears and opened the window.

"Everything okay, Miss?" the *Carabiniere* inquired politely.

"Yes, yes, *mais je suis perdu*, I'm lost," she said, hoping he would understand.

"Oh, *vous êtes un touriste*, you're a tourist," he said, in reasonably clear French, and Eva's face brightened up.

"You speak French! That's wonderful. I'm so lost ..."

Eva opened the door and got out, smiling. The policeman's partner, who looked much older than the other, was apparently taking no interest in her problems. He had remained in the car and was busy writing on a pad. She concentrated all her substantial feminine power on the young officer.

"Where do you need to go?" he asked.

"I'm looking for a friend's house. It's called *Cascina Leone*. He explained to me how to get there, but I got it all wrong. I'm such a mess, I'm sorry," she said, wiping away a remnant of tears from the corners of her eyes.

"Don't worry about that. I know where it is. You did go in the wrong direction, and it's quite far from here. It can be very confusing driving around here. Look," he hastened to add when Eva's smile changed into an expression of dismay, "we'll take you there ... or almost there. When I signal to you to turn right, you have to turn, go straight for one kilometer, and then you'll see a small bridge on your left. Turn left on the bridge, and in two minutes, you'll see the house."

"That's wonderful! That's so kind of you! I could kiss you. Are you allowed to kiss policemen in Italy?"

Eva smiled brightly, and the young policeman turned purple.

"I'm afraid that regulations don't allow it. But I'm happy to be of service all the same."

The officer saluted with a broad smile and returned to his car.

The young policeman waved goodbye as Eva turned right on a narrow road, and she waved back. The police car drove on for a few hundred meters and then stopped.

"What are you stopping for?" asked the young policeman. He was peeved because the sudden halt had jerked him out of a juicy daydream involving the curvy French tourist.

"See here?" said his partner, handing him his writing pad. A notice was pinned to it, which said, "Alert for a suspicious vehicle. Don't stop but report whereabouts. Rental car. Fiat," and then followed a plate number.

"So what?"

"So that's the car of the young woman that we just saw."

"Are you sure?"

"I'm sure, and you would be sure too if you kept your eyes on your duty instead of sticking them on nice tits," he said, speaking reproachfully and shaking his head sorrowfully.

"And now what?"

"What do you think? Now I'm going to report it," said the older policeman, picking up the radio microphone.

"Don't you think that we should follow her? I'd say we should."

"You keep your hormones in check, okay? The order says 'alert,' not 'follow.' Our shift is over, and my wife is putting the pasta on the table. I'm going home now."

"Isn't an 'alert' order quite out of the ordinary?"

"No, it isn't. It means that she's done nothing that you can stop her for. You can only follow her activities."

"I'd like to follow her activities," said the young policeman, with a wistful smile.

"My food will be cold," said the older policeman and drove on.

Von Stoffen ended the conversation with his Italian agent and hung up with a smirk of satisfaction. Those Italians had to be prodded all the time, but at last, he was getting results. He dialed a number on his cell phone, and Joseph Mead's voice responded at the third ring.

"Forget Pavia," von Stoffen said, "I know where they are. Write down the address."

CHAPTER 51

Cascina Leone, Asti, Italy. July 2009

Cascina Leone looked pretty much like every other farm house that she had seen on her way there, and without the policeman's instructions, Eva would have never singled it out for her destination. She drove on the gravel path, which from the road led to the front of the house, and in passing the remains of an ancient gate, she saw a faded sign with the word "*Leone*" barely legible on it, which reassured her that she had reached her destination. She parked the car near a wooden door with peeling dark green paint and circled the house to the right until she found a rain pipe. She felt inside the pipe with the tips of her fingers and found the key, just as Hawthorne had said. She used it to open the door and found herself in a large, cold, and poorly lit room, furnished with odd pieces of furniture, which included a sofa covered with painted linen, assorted chairs of disparate origin, and a rustic table that marked the border between the living room area and a small kitchen. Wooden stairs led to the upper floor and to two small bedrooms with Spartan beds.

Eva went back to the car and brought her bag in. She took from it the plastic briefcase with the medical file and looked around for a place to hide it. She didn't know why, but she felt uncomfortable keeping it with the rest of her belongings. The house was so bare that it presented limited options for hiding places, and after considering every corner, she realized that she had to look elsewhere. Next to the house, she had seen a barn, and she headed there. She entered and waited until her eyes grew used to the striped lighting produced by the spaced boards of which the barn walls were constructed. The smell of farm animals mixed with hay was not unpleasant, and she took a deep breath. The floor was occupied by a few agricultural tools heavily covered with cobwebs but was otherwise empty. Hay was stacked on a loft, and Eva climbed the ladder that led to it. Her attention was attracted by a wooden chest in the farthest corner, and she opened it to reveal a heap of smelly clothes. Without touching anything, she dropped the plastic briefcase into the chest and closed the lid. The dust that the lid spread around when Eva let it drop went into her nostrils and made her sneeze and her eyes water. She was quick to climb down and get out of the barn, and then she stood in the open air, feeling relieved.

She checked her watch and saw that it was past noon already. Little wonder that she was famished, but luckily the bar at the gas station had sold sandwiches, and she had bought a few. She fetched them from the car, together with a can of Diet Coke, and sat down at the table inside to eat. Once her hunger was satisfied, she felt a little better and settled down to wait. She hoped that Hawthorne or someone from his organization would come shortly to get her. He wouldn't be more specific than "soon" when asked when they would come to collect her.

Eva had never felt comfortable in isolated places, and the silence and solitude were beginning to scare her.

Franco jumped up from the armchair in which he was seated as he heard the knock on the door. He rushed to open it.

"Thank God you're here!" he said when Kathia's familiar face appeared. "Come in, come in," he added, stepping aside.

Kathia walked in, followed by her companion and Franco gazed at him inquisitively.

"I'm glad you're safe," said Kathia, somewhat stiffly. Their latest conversation, back in London, hadn't been pleasant, and she didn't mean to let him forget that if he was in trouble, he owed it to his lack of cooperation. She made an indefinite gesture and added, "This is Dan Botti, my Italian counterpart. He's here to help."

"Hello," said Dan, shaking Franco's hand.

"Nice meeting you," said Franco.

"We shouldn't be wasting any more time," said Kathia, still keeping her businesslike manners. "Tell us what happened. Everything. Even the smallest detail may be important."

Franco nodded, sat in the armchair, and gazed at the floor to collect his thoughts. Kathia and Dan sat on the bed, waiting patiently for him to start.

"I'm afraid that I haven't been entirely candid with you about my weekend at Easby's place, but I'll tell you all about it in a moment. The mess I'm in started with a phone call from Easby. It was a rather innocent call, proposing to me to take a trip to Udine to retrieve an old document ..."

Dan and Kathia exchanged a glance as Franco lay back after finishing his tale.

"I don't mean to doubt you," said Dan, "but you will appreciate that this is not an easy tale to swallow."

"I know, I can't blame you. I have very little evidence to corroborate my story, but I do have this," said Franco taking a folded piece of paper from the inner pocket of his jacket and handing it to Dan. "It's my great-grandfather's letter. She hasn't taken that, at least."

Dan unfolded the paper and read slowly. "Yes, it checks out," he said at last.

"What do we do now?" asked Franco.

"We need to gather some information," said Kathia. "We will have to talk with our head office in Geneva, and also with Dan's office in Milan, and see if they can help us find out what has become of Eva. And maybe now I'll get some cooperation from Scotland Yard. I want to know what James Easby is up to right now."

"I'll find us a room in this hotel. This is as good a place as any other to get organized," said Dan. "Let's grab something to eat before all restaurants close, and then we can come back and start making phone calls."

"Italian to the last drop, aren't you? Food always comes first, right?" said Kathia. She liked to sting him.

Dan shrugged, obviously unconcerned. "Man's got to eat," he said.

CHAPTER 52

Cascina Leone, Asti, Italy. July 2009

Eva woke up from a fitful sleep. The cuckoo clock on the wall maintained that the time was midnight, which meant that she had been asleep for more than four hours. She had decided early in the day that she would not go up to sleep in one of the rooms; the house was too spooky, and she felt like an intruder. Instead, she had lain down on the sofa – just for a few minutes, only to rest a little, she had said to herself – and had fallen asleep.

She was now wide awake and fully aware of the many country noises outside, which surely would make further sleep impossible. She was a city girl, and to her, each and every unfamiliar noise sounded scary. But besides the owls, the crickets, and the distant dogs and cows, she heard a much more frightening and closer sound – someone was rattling the handle of the front door.

"Open up, I know you're there!" ordered a voice from outside. It was a familiar voice, and Eva could barely believe it, but she recognized that Teutonic accent and was almost sure that she knew who was out there.

"Who's that?" she asked.

A brief silence ensued, after which the voice said, "It's me, Heinrich von Stoffen."

Eva's tension was relieved at once, and she hastened to turn the key in the door lock. The door was pushed open from the outside, and the tall figure of von Stoffen appeared on the mat, followed by the burly one of Joseph Mead.

"Thank God it's you!" Eva exclaimed. "But how did James know where to find me?"

"I wouldn't be too quick thanking God if I were you," said von Stoffen. "You may find that he has failed to deliver."

Taken aback and still failing to understand the meaning of his words, Eva retreated from the door. At that moment, her gaze fell upon Joseph's face, and she recognized him.

"What's going on, Heinrich? Who is this man? Why are you here?"

"This is my man Joseph, and from now on, I'll be asking the questions. But before we sit down to get some answers from you, I need you to come and take a look outside."

"I'm not going anywhere, you understand? You know what will happen when James finds out about this ... Yeow!" Eva cried in pain when von Stoffen grabbed her hair and yanked. He walked to the door dragging her after him. Outside he stopped before the trunk of a big car.

"If Joseph has a flaw," von Stoffen said with a horrid smirk, still holding a teary Eva by the hair, "it is that he tends to take my instructions a tad too literally. I told him not to let anybody near the house before I got here, so he handled this gentleman in his own way. Do you know him?"

Von Stoffen opened the trunk and pulled Eva's head down until she came face to face with Richard Hawthorne's lifeless features.

"Oh, my God!" she cried.

"So you do know him. Who is he?" He pulled her up and brought his face close to hers.

"He ... he's from Scotland Yard. His name is Richard Hawthorne."

"You hear that, Joseph? You've done a Yard's man. That may cause complications. Go and get rid of him, but be quick about it. I need you here. Before you go, help me with Miss Thibault."

They went back into the house and made Eva sit on a chair and then tied her hands and legs to it. Joseph left, and von Stoffen dragged a chair toward Eva and sat before her. "Now, let's have a little chat," he said.

"Why are you doing this to me, Heinrich? What have I done to you?"

"This is not personal, my dear. I'm sorry that I need to cause you discomfort, but I have no choice. I have a vital goal to achieve, and I can't let anything stand in my way. So now tell me, where is your boyfriend, and what has he done with the papers?"

"I don't know."

von Stoffen edged a little closer and slapped her hard on the face.

"Wrong answer, my dear. I'm afraid that you haven't fully appreciated my explanation, so I'll point out that I won't tolerate any lies. For instance, I know that the car outside is the one that he rented, so he can't be far away."

"No, please," Eva begged, weeping. "I'm not lying; let me explain."

"Explain."

"I ran away from him, and I took his car. He had become obsessive about me, and I was afraid of him, so while he was asleep, I stole his car keys and ran away."

"I'm listening to what you say, but it doesn't explain the gentleman in the trunk."

"Richard has ... had a crush on me. I met him socially, and we dated a couple of times. I ... I didn't know who to turn to; my picture is everywhere, and after I ran away from Franco I didn't know where to go, so I called Richard, and he said that I could wait for him in this place that belongs to a friend of his and that he would come to pick me up and take me away soon, so I came and waited. That's all, I swear."

"Umm ... all right. Let's assume that you're telling the truth. That means that a phone call from you will make your boyfriend come running to you. Interesting. I hope for your sake that we can make him come here, because otherwise ..." He didn't have to explain what "otherwise" meant.

CHAPTER 53

Pavia, Italy. July 2009

Kathia and Dan sat in Franco's room, which they had turned into an operations center, but without much result. Their phone calls to Geneva and Milan had been of no help whatsoever and had only yielded vague promises to try to contact the Italian police to request cooperation. A fat lot of help that would be, Dan commented bitterly. Despite five phone calls placed with various people in London, Richard Hawthorne was nowhere to be found, so Scotland Yard couldn't be counted on either.

Kathia went through the list of action items that she had made during the day. She did that perhaps for the fifth time and got no ideas from reading it, but at least it felt like she was doing something. Dan had given up calling people after his second battery had emptied itself on useless phone calls and was keeping himself busy moodily picking up crumbs off his room service dinner from a tray that looked as messy as his hair. Franco was slumped in his armchair and felt thoroughly wasted. He eyed his two companions with much less awe and expectation than before. He wondered when and how all this would end.

"What's that?" Kathia asked. A muffled sound was coming from the jacket that Franco had hung in the closet after lunch. He did not care whether it got creased or not but had acted purely by sheer force of habit.

Franco jumped up, his body suddenly animated anew. "It's my cell phone," he said. He ran to the closet and quickly fished it out. "It's Eva, shh ..." he admonished.

"Franco ..." said Eva's voice.

"Where are you? What happened? You scared me to death! Where *are* you?"

"I'm sorry. So sorry for scaring you ... I need you to come to me. I ... I'm not well. I know that you'll forgive me for running away – you're my White Knight, don't I always tell you so? So please come quickly, will you?"

"But why did you run away? What happened?"

"I made a mistake, I'm sorry. Can you forgive me?" That Eva was now crying was evident from her trembling voice.

"Yes, yes. Don't worry. Of course, I forgive you. Now tell me where you are."

"Yes, but first, promise me that you'll bring the documents with you, the medical file. Don't ask questions, I beg you, just do it."

"But the documents ..."

"No questions, I said. Do you care about me?"

"Of course I do."

"Then just do as I say, my White Knight."

"Okay, give me the address."

Eva explained at length, and Dan, who was listening as close as possible to Franco's ear, wrote it down.

"I love you," said Eva. "Come quickly, please," she added, and then the phone went dead.

Franco remained silent for almost a minute, and then he nodded and said, "Something's terribly wrong. Did you hear that?"

"What seems to be wrong is that your girlfriend's head is not screwed on right. She runs away, and then she expects you to run to her because she says so. She steals your stuff, and then she says she's sorry, so everything must be forgiven and forgotten, right? She sounds like a spoiled brat. White Knight, ha!" Kathia sneered.

"That's exactly it. Eva never called me that. She joked and called me her Dark Knight. And she knows very well that I don't have the documents and that I know that she took them."

"Someone was listening to what she was saying, and she wanted you to know it," said Dan.

"And someone has forced her to make the call," said Kathia, speaking slowly. "I take back the spoiled brat comment – provisionally, that is. I think she's being held against her will, and she's probably in danger. She has managed to make them believe that you still have the documents, which is swell because they're unlikely to hurt her before they get at you. But we must get there quickly."

"Shouldn't we be calling the police?" Franco asked.

"The Italian police?" Kathia said, letting out a little laugh. "Give me a break. By the time we managed to explain some of this, your girlfriend's body would be stone cold, and whoever is holding her would have disappeared. No, if we want to get her and the documents back, we need to act now. Not that I'm happy to get involved, but I want those documents, and you want her, so let's stop wasting time and get moving."

"She's right, Franco, we're on our own," said Dan, squeezing Franco's arm in a friendly move. "Kathia," he added, "do you have your gun with you?"

"You know what? I don't. To arrange to take it on the flight from London was so complicated that I left it behind."

"Not a problem, take mine. I always pack a spare one."

"Thanks," said Kathia. She took the gun that Dan was offering and checked it. "Good piece," she said with appreciation, "and good quality ammo. Nine millimeters is my caliber. Let's go."

There didn't seem to be much more to say, so the three of them filed out. They didn't take their bags and didn't check out. They had no time.

CHAPTER 54

Udine, Italy. July 1894

The Honorable L. knocked on the door of the Cecchi house. He was in good spirits and, contrary to the past, didn't mind if anyone saw him going there. The youngster whom he knew was the woman's son opened the door and gazed at him inquisitively.

"I need to see your mother," said the Honorable L. "Is she at home?"

"Yes, Sir," said the youth, stepping back to free the way for the guest. He closed the door behind him and gestured to him to follow.

"I know the way," said the Honorable L., "but please announce me."

The youth disappeared into the living room, from which he reemerged immediately.

"Please," he said, holding the door open for the guest.

The Honorable L. stepped into the living room and approached the armchair in which Mrs. Cecchi seemed to be permanently seated. The hearth wasn't lit, and the room was cool but not cold. The sun's rays managed to get in through the thick curtains that were drawn as if to fend off the glorious summer day.

"Good morning, Honorable," said the Cecchi widow and waited.

"Good morning. You are undoubtedly surprised to see me here in broad daylight."

"Well, it's at least unusual, and of course, I wonder to what I owe the honor," she said, speaking guardedly.

"I think that I'm a fair man. In fact, I'm sure that I manage to be fair, at least most of the time. I make it a point to give credit where credit is due."

"So?" The widow was obviously still puzzled.

"I saw Evelyn yesterday. For the first time in weeks, she seemed better. She got up and went into the garden. She looked much better. Really better. Her spirit – and mine – was higher than it has been for a long time, and I think that I owe it to you. It looks like your endeavor is producing results. So I came here to tell you."

"I'm grateful and happy, but also a little surprised. I thought ... it is perhaps too early to draw conclusions."

"Nonsense! I know what I saw, and it was wonderful. Well, in any case, I wanted to let you know. I have to go now. Good day."

"Good day to you too," said the widow, without getting up.

The Honorable L. closed the living room door behind him and stood for a moment in the semi-darkness of the hall.

"Sir," a voice said, startling him. He gazed in the direction from which the voice had come and at first saw nothing, but then the widow's daughter emerged from the shadows and approached him, stopping at a respectful distance of three paces.

"You startled me, my dear," said the Honorable L. "You shouldn't be doing things like that to an old man like me." He spoke benevolently because, after their last meeting, he had taken a liking to this girl, who was able to pass on warmth and sensations of well-meaning with the touch of her hand.

"Sir ... I wanted to tell you ..." she stopped, and the Honorable L. waited for her to go on. When she didn't, he prodded her.

"Well, what was it that you wanted to tell me? I don't have all day, you know."

The girl swallowed, obviously embarrassed, and then she lowered her gaze. "She's not getting better, Sir," she finally whispered.

"What? What do you mean?" the Honorable L. almost shouted.

"She's not; I'm sorry. I've seen it. Last night they spoke to me, and I'm now sure. She won't get better."

"How cruel of you to say that! And how wrong! I've just seen her, and she's getting better. Much better. You wicked girl!"

"I'm sorry, Sir," she repeated, with downcast eyes. "I really am. I thought that I should tell you, but I was wrong. I'm sorry," she repeated almost inaudibly.

The girl took a few steps backward and then turned her back to him and ran away. The Honorable L. watched her go and then stood there for a long time, gazing into the darkness. She wasn't right, he thought. She couldn't be right.

But he did believe her.

CHAPTER 55

Cascina Leone, Asti, Italy. July 2009

The house was silent and dark, and Franco's every step made a loud noise on the gravel path – or so it seemed to him – despite his effort to tiptoe lightly. He walked slowly, and his heart beat wildly. He had never considered himself particularly courageous, and the events of the last few days had taken their toll on his nerves. Sneaking into other people's yards in the dark was more than he had ever budgeted for. Under any other circumstances, he would have turned around and run, but Eva was in danger and counted on him to rescue her, and that was enough to propel his recalcitrant feet forward, although each step sparked a renewed battle with his instincts. He hoped that Dan and Kathia knew what they were doing.

He reached the narrow strip of red tiles that separated the house from the gravel and stood before the door, reluctant to start something by advertising his arrival. A shuffling noise coming from within made it clear to him that his arrival had not gone unnoticed.

"Eva?" he whispered.

No answer came from inside the house, but the door opened wide, and a tall man appeared.

"Oh, good!" he said. "Here's our White Knight. Come on in."

Although sarcastically polite, the invitation was backed by a big pistol pointed directly at Franco's chest.

"von Stoffen!" Franco cried with surprise. "What are you doing here? And what is that gun in aid of?"

"If you don't step right in, right now, you'll find out. Turn on the light, Joseph," he added, upon which a pale, yellowish light flooded the room.

Franco took a step inside, and the first thing he saw was Eva, strapped to a chair with a large tape that gagged her.

"Eva! What have you done to her, bastards?" he cried. He started to move toward her, but Joseph placed himself in his path. A switchblade knife appeared in his hand as if by magic, and he placed its tip in Franco's nostril.

"Uh-uh," he said, shaking his head.

"Don't be a fool," said von Stoffen. "One more step, and you'll regret it. I'll have the file now, please."

"The file ... I don't have it on me," said Franco.

"That's too bad because if I don't get it in the next five minutes, Joseph here will start carving out little pieces of your girlfriend, beginning with the face. So where is it?"

"I'll tell you, but leave her alone. I don't care about it or any other old paper. I have no idea why everybody wants it, but I don't."

"Good. I like your spirit of cooperation. So where is it?"

"I hid it outside, on my way to the house."

"Where?"

"I need to show you. I don't know how to explain. It's dark outside, but I know how to retrace my steps. But let Eva go, first."

"I don't know if you've noticed it, but you're in no position to dictate. Now get out and show me. If you're a good boy, I may be generous and let you two go in one piece."

"All right, but don't hurt her. Promise me that you won't hurt her."

"You're repeating yourself and are starting to get on my nerves. I'll count to three, and if you're not on your way to show me, I'll tell Joseph to go ahead."

"No, no. I'll show you."

Franco grabbed the handle and opened the door. He moved fast and walked out, followed by von Stoffen, who still pointed the gun at him. As soon as he was sure that they were both out in the open, he threw himself to the ground as Dan had instructed him.

"Hands up!" he heard Dan's voice from his right.

Von Stoffen didn't hesitate to use his gun, and Franco heard a cracking sound, following which he waited for the bullet to hit him, but nothing happened. A second gunshot and then a third from his left made him close his eyes harder. His head seemed unable to process any rational thought, except for a prayer that this would end quickly and that he would be still alive when it did.

"It's over, Franco. You can get up," Dan said after what seemed to him like an eternity.

"I got the one inside before he understood what was happening to him," said Kathia. "And Dan," she added with admiration, "you were quick to hit the tall one."

"You were pretty good too. In fact, almost as good as you're beautiful. And when you hold a big pistol, you're even sexier."

"Don't start," Kathia admonished, but she was clearly pleased.

"'Excuse me," said Franco, sounding peeved. He climbed over von Stoffen's body, which blocked the entrance and pushed Dan and Kathia aside.

Skirting Joseph's body, he hastened to Eva and removed the masking tape from her mouth. Tears had formed at the corners of her eyes, and she gasped with pain when the tape came off with a ripping sound.

"Ouch!" she said, and then she breathed deeply.

"Sorry, sorry," said Franco, and then he kissed her, a long, emotional kiss.

"Untie me," said Eva when their lips finally parted.

"Sorry again," said Franco and kneeled behind her to work on the tight knots that held her to the chair.

"You've got some explaining to do, Miss," said Kathia, who meanwhile had joined them together with Dan. "We want to know what's going on. Explain your behavior."

"Do you need to interrogate her right away?" Franco complained. "Can't you see what she's been through? Get her some water – do you want some water, Eva? Questions can wait."

"I'm not so sure about that ... Ah!" Kathia cried, and then she collapsed, spurting blood from the groin, as Joseph's massive body rose with the switchblade knife in his hand.

"Jesus!" Dan cried. He dropped the glass of water that he was fetching from the kitchen and pulled his gun.

Two shots put a stop to Joseph's menacing move, and Dan ran to help Kathia.

"He wasn't dead!" said Franco with amazement but merely stating the obvious.

"He is now," Dan mumbled.

CHAPTER 56

Cascina Leone, Asti, Italy. July 2009

Franco finished untying Eva, and they both stood still, looking around them. The room resembled a slaughterhouse, with blood everywhere, Joseph's body at their feet and, nearby, Kathia's body, which twitched in a pool of blood as Dan kneeled beside her.

"Come here, help me!" Dan shouted.

Franco and Eva hastened to join him. Kathia's eyes were upturned, and only their white showed.

"What's happening to her?" Eva asked. She gazed at Kathia with horror. Dan had ripped her trousers open where Joseph's knife had cut her and was pushing his fist hard against her thigh. He seemed to have managed to stop the flow of blood.

"He cut her main artery, and she lost a lot of blood in seconds. Go get me a stone this size," he urged, speaking to Franco and showing his other fist. "You," he ordered, looking straight at Eva, "take the knife, find some strong piece of fabric, and cut a strip as long as you can. Quick!" he shouted when Eva kept staring at him without any sign of comprehension.

Overcoming her repulsion, Eva picked up the knife that lay beside Joseph's body, and then she ran to the kitchen table and cut a long strip from the tablecloth. She went back to Dan, who hadn't moved, just as Franco returned with a round stone. Dan glanced at them and nodded. "Good, leave the strip here and go fetch a table knife or a fork. Franco, wash that stone in the sink quickly and come back."

A minute later, Franco returned with the washed stone and Eva with a table knife. "Now we must do this right," said Dan. "Franco put the stone in the middle of the strip that Eva has cut and make a strong knot so the stone is cradled in the strip and can't move. That's good," he said when Franco did as instructed. "Now bring it here, close to my fist. When I lift my fist, put the stone exactly where it was, and push hard – don't worry that you may be hurting her. The stone must be plugged into the wound hard enough to keep the main artery sealed. Keep it there and keep pushing until I'm done tying the strip around her thigh. You understand?"

Franco swallowed and nodded in agreement, and then he knelt at the other side of Kathia's body and placed the stone next to Dan's fist.

"Now!" Dan ordered and lifted his fist. A gush of blood came from the wound, which stopped immediately when Franco pushed the stone hard against it. Dan passed the flaps of the strip around Kathia's thigh twice and then made a strong knot on top of the stone. He inserted the table knife into the knot and twisted it to increase the stone's pressure against the thigh. "That should keep for a while," he said after he checked that no blood was oozing from the wound, "but we must get her to a hospital quickly, or she will die."

Without a word, the three of them went to the kitchen sink and washed their bloodied hands. Then Dan became practical again. "My car is hidden far away, too far to take her there. We will need to use the one outside. Who has the keys?"

"I have them," said Eva.

"Good. You drive, then. I have to sit in the back with Kathia to keep the blocking bandage in place. Franco, take my car keys," said Dan, as he threw the keys that he had taken from his pockets toward him, "and drive back to the hotel in Pavia. I'll meet you there after

we take care of Kathia. Now help me carry her to the car. Gently!"
he cautioned when Franco started to lift her by pulling under her
armpits. "No brusque movements that can dislocate the stone."

They carried her gently to the car, and Eva opened the rear door.
They lay her on the backseat, and then Dan climbed in and sat with
her head on his lap.

"Let's go!" he ordered.

"One moment," said Eva, "let me say goodbye to Franco. I'll be
right back."

She took a few steps away from the car and hugged Franco,
putting her lips close to his ear. "You saved me, again, Dark Knight.
I owe you."

"But why did you ..." Franco started to ask, but she cut him short.

"Shh ... I can't explain now, but I was watching out for you, for
us. You will understand when I get a chance to explain."

"Yes, but ..."

"Listen. After we leave, go to the barn and climb up the ladder.
There is a box hidden behind the hay. The file with the documents
is in the box. Take it and get lost. Don't go back to the hotel; that
may be dangerous. You must keep the documents safe, and God
knows how many people are still out there trying to take them from
us. Do you understand?"

"Yes, yes. But how will I find you?"

An angry yell came from the car, "Get your ass over here!" Dan
ordered.

"I'll find you," Eva whispered. "Love you," she said, and then she
gave him a hard kiss, pushed him back, and ran to the car.

Franco stood there, watching Eva drive away. He wasn't sure that
he could trust her, but, on the other hand, he had little to lose doing
what she had suggested. And he wanted to trust her, despite past
experience. The car turned at the gate and disappeared, and he kept
watching the empty gravel path. He still felt the pressure of Eva's
teeth on his lower lip.

CHAPTER 57

Cascina Leone, Asti, Italy. July 2009

Franco easily found the box and the documents. He was thirsty and would have given a lot for a sip of water, but the idea of going back to the house and being alone with the corpses scared him too much. He tried an old water pump near the barn, but all he got from it were a few squeaking sounds. Resigned, he started to walk back to where they had left the car. His first priority was to get as far away as possible from that house and those corpses. It took him fifteen minutes to reach the car. He dropped the plastic briefcase on the passenger's seat, switched on the engine, and drove away without planning a direction. Ten minutes later, he felt that he had put a sufficient distance between the house and himself, so he stopped and killed the engine. He needed to think. The *Cascina Leone* was isolated, and he hoped that nobody had heard the shots, but he couldn't be sure.

Making an inventory of his situation didn't make him feel any better. He was alone in unfamiliar surroundings at 4 AM in the morning, with no place to go; his clothes were stained with blood, which meant that he had to keep away from other people; an unknown number of potential psycho murderers were looking for him. All that because of an old document to which he had attached no importance at first, but which obviously was of tremendous importance to someone – so much so that people were killing to get it.

First of all, he had to find some clothes, which obviously meant stealing them. A minute earlier, he had passed a cluster of farmhouses, and there had to be laundry hanging outside to dry in at least one of them. He turned the car and stopped near the first one. He cautiously circled it and couldn't believe his luck when, at the corner, he saw laundry hanging at a short distance, with what at the light of the moon clearly looked like men's clothes. He took a step in the direction of the laundry, and at that very moment, all hell broke loose. A dog that was chained near the house ran growling menacingly toward him, and when the chain stopped it in midair from getting at him, it started barking at the top of its voice. Numerous other dogs from neighboring houses joined in the chorus, and a light appeared in an upper window of the house. Without hesitation, Franco gave up the quest for clothes and ran back to the car, ignoring the "Hey, stop!" cries behind him. He frantically turned the key in the ignition and drove away.

Despite the bad experience, Franco had no choice but to persevere. This time he selected an isolated house. A sleepy dog was chained near the front door, and it took no interest in Franco's hesitant steps toward the backyard, contenting itself with emitting a few, half-hearted grumbles. The uneventful expedition produced a colorful shirt that he donned with a shiver because he had always been a stickler for fashion, and a pair of decent, black trousers, roughly his size. Back in the car, he emptied the pockets of his old clothes, and then he stopped by a group of trees in unfarmed land and stuffed them into a hole under a big stone.

Sitting in the car and at last rid of the bloody signs of the night, he could finally bring himself to think what to do. No matter which approach he took and from what angle he looked at his situation, a single name kept popping up: Easby. He had misgivings about Easby's management of the whole affair and had good reasons to believe that he shouldn't trust him, but with Kathia gone, he had nobody else to turn to. The hour was almost 5 AM, a bit early to call anybody, but he couldn't bother with niceties and, besides, it was Easby's fault, to begin with, that he found himself in such a tough spot. He flipped his cell phone open and was worried to see that only two lines of battery charge remained. He prayed for the battery to last long enough and for Easby to be available. After seven unnerving rings, he heard Easby's sleepy voice. "Who's that?" he asked.

"James, it's me, Franco."

"Franco? Thank God! You had me worried sick." Easby's voice was suddenly alert. "Are you back in London?"

"No. I'm in Italy. Listen, James, I'm in trouble. I need your help."

"I know, I know. We need to get you to a safe place. Do you have the document with you? The one that you and Marchetti went to get?"

"Yes," said Franco. *Everybody seems to be more worried about this piece of paper than about my welfare,* he thought bitterly.

"Where about in Italy are you?"

"I don't know. Someplace near Asti."

"That's good. I'm not far away from you; I'm in Switzerland. This is what you should do – wait a minute, you have all your travel papers with you, right?"

"Of course."

"All right. Then drive to the border crossing at Lugano, but don't get there too early. It will take you about two hours at regular speed from where you are, so drive slowly and try to get there around eight o'clock. That's a busy hour, and the border police are too swamped to ask too many questions."

"Why should I worry about the border police? I'm not wanted for anything, I hope?"

"Just a precaution, my boy. Because of that Venice business."

"Oh, so you know about that ..." So much had happened since they had fled Venice that he had almost forgotten about it.

"Yes. Once you are in Lugano, go and treat yourself to breakfast in one of the nice cafés near the city center. The shopping center is on *Via Nassa,* and that's where you want to go. I'll meet you there; when you're settled in the café, give me a call, and I'll come to you."

"I'm running out of battery. I don't know if I'll be able to call you again."

"It doesn't matter. It's a small place, and I'll find you anyway. Just get there as I said."

"I will," said Franco and hung up.

For the first time that day, he felt relieved. Switzerland sounded like a safe and peaceful place to go to, and God knew that he needed some quiet. He decided to reserve judgment on Easby. After all, the people who doubted him hadn't turned out to be too smart, knowledgeable, or reliable either.

CHAPTER 58

Lugano, Switzerland. July 2009

An apple strudel and a hot cappuccino made Franco feel slightly more optimistic. Until he got himself seated at a small table inside a picturesque café, he had been too busy worrying about all his problems to notice how hungry he was. Having now restored some of his blood sugar levels, he laid back and gazed at himself in the mirror that covered the wall before him. He looked disheveled, with the wrinkled, slightly faded, and too brightly colored shirt, the unshaven look, and the dirty, ruffled hair. He wondered what the waitress had thought of him; his was undoubtedly an uncommon look in that elegant quarter.

Crossing the border had been the work of a minute; the border police were apparently not watching out for him, and the officer to whom he had offered his ID had barely glanced at it. The real problem had been finding parking, and he had left the car in a parking lot far away from the city center.

His phone battery had gone dead just as he was about to tell Easby the name of the café, but he had explained where he had ended up clearly enough to be found, and presently Easby joined him at the table.

"Glad to see you, my boy," said Easby, shaking hands with him. "You must've gone through some rough times. You seem to be in a bit of disarray."

"I look like shit, and I feel worse than that. I haven't slept a wink, I haven't had a proper meal for ages, and I haven't washed after going through more than I care to remember. I must stink."

"There is perhaps a hint of odor about you, but don't worry, where we are going, you'll get a proper shower and clean clothing."

"Where *are* we going?"

"Oh, not far from here, about one hour's drive. You can sleep in the car."

The waitress approached them to take an order from the newcomer. Franco thought she had lifted an eyebrow, probably wondering what a distinguished gentleman like Easby was doing with a dreg of society like him. Easby declined the offer with a smile and, instead, asked for the bill.

"And what then?" asked Franco, continuing the conversation after the waitress left.

"We're about to complete the project. It's so lucky that you got here in time to see it. Where is the document, by the way?"

"It's here," said Franco, handing him the plastic briefcase, "but I mean, so much has happened since you last saw me ... I don't even know where to begin telling you. And I don't know where I stand because of what happened in Venice. I'm sure that I need to talk to authority, but I don't know to whom, in practice."

"Don't worry, we'll sort it out. I have friends in the right places. I'm so sorry that you had to go through an ordeal. I had no idea that my simple, humanitarian quest would stir up trouble. I still don't fully understand it, but I'm sure that, with time, we will find out what it was all about. Now tell me, where is Eva?"

Easby's fatherly manner and his overt concern for his and Eva's welfare were heartwarming for Franco. He was so tired – both physically and mentally – that he needed to feel that, at last, he was in good hands.

"Eva is fine," he reassured him. "She had to stay in Italy. It's a long story, and I'm too exhausted to tell it now."

"The important thing is that she's all right. You can tell me all about it later. Where did you leave your car?"

"It's in a public parking lot."

"You can leave it there. We'll worry about it later. Let's go now."

Easby took the change from the small tray that the waitress had brought back, and the two men got up and left. He had parked not far away, and in five minutes, he was driving the car toward their destination.

Franco, on the other hand, was already fast asleep.

CHAPTER 59

Ambri, Switzerland. July 2009

"Wake up, my boy. We've arrived."

Franco opened his eyes with an effort. They were puffy and sticky. Someone had opened his door, and a tall, heavy man stood beside him.

"This is Hans, my boy. He's been looking after the chalet since I bought it last year."

"*Willkommen!*" Hans barked.

Franco pulled himself up heavily and blinked against the sun in the cloudless sky. The car had stopped a short distance from the door of a typical rustic chalet. He gazed up at Hans and managed a courteous nod.

"I have a few things to do, but Hans will look after your needs. Hans," Easby added, addressing the other man, "please get some clean clothes for Professor Lorenzi and show him his room and the bathroom. I'll see you when you're ready, my boy," he concluded, turning again to Franco.

"James," said Franco, and his voice came out very thin, "I'm really exhausted. I must catch some sleep. Do you mind?"

"Of course not! How inconsiderate of me. I should have thought of it myself. Don't hurry. Sleep as much as you need and come down when you feel equal to it."

"Thanks, James," whispered Franco with the little strength that he had left.

Moving through a misty semi-dream, he followed Hans into the house and up the steps until they reached a door made of coarse pinewood, and Hans pushed it open.

"This your room, *Ja*? Bathroom at end of corridor. I bring clothes, *Ja*?"

With those enlightening words, Hans disappeared, and Franco looked around. The room was small, with a bed too short for him – a youth bed – but he would have gladly slept on the floor if he had to. He brightened up a little when Hans returned with a complete change of clothes in one hand and a towel, soap, toothbrush, and toothpaste in the other.

"This is *gut*? You call if you need, *ja*?"

Franco nodded a tired nod of gratitude, and Hans retreated. Armed with the cleaning gear Franco went out of the room, turned left, and, as he pushed open the door next to him, a cry stopped him.

"*Nein!*" Hans's voice bellowed. "Bathroom other way. This room *verboten*."

"Sorry," said Franco, too tired to ask himself what the big deal was. He had caught a glimpse of someone sleeping in the room, but that was all there was to it. His weary brain barely managed to guide his body to the bathroom, where he washed perfunctorily and replaced his clothes and underwear with the clean underwear that Hans had brought him. Then he went back to the room, flung himself onto the bed, and in a moment, he was asleep.

When Franco woke up, it was already dark – 8:17 PM by his watch. A noise outside drew his attention, and he opened the window and looked down. A new car had arrived, and Doctor Benini descended from it. Welcoming voices outside increased Franco's embarrassment that he had disappeared on his host for so many hours. He dressed quickly and went to brush his teeth. His head was light, and he felt completely rested. Feeling relaxed for the first time in several days, he tiptoed down the stairs to join the others.

The stairs ended in a short corridor, which led to the left into a cozy sitting room and to the right into a small dining room. Franco turned left toward the voices that came from the sitting room and stopped on the threshold. Easby, Benini, and the medium, Maria, were seated around a low table on which they had placed the plastic briefcase. They were examining the papers taken from it.

"It's just as you told us. Almost word for word," Benini said, sounding admiring.

"I told you so," said Maria.

The sound of Franco's steps made them realize that they were not alone, and they turned their attention to him.

"I'm sorry," Franco apologized. "I didn't mean to disturb you."

"Not at all. Not at all," said Easby. "Please join us. You came at the right time. I didn't want to disturb you, and I can't read Italian very well – certainly not that small, unclear handwriting, so I was waiting for Arturo to arrive and read it to me. And we've gone through the other documents as well. The only other interesting paper is Evelyn's Death Certificate. Here, look at it," he added, handing him a piece of paper. The place and date of death were "Ambri, Switzerland, 22 August 1894."

"I see," said Franco. "But why is this important?"

"Ah! You surprise me, my boy. I thought you would appreciate its importance immediately. Evelyn was twenty-six years old when she died. What would you say was the average life expectancy of an upper-class woman at the time?"

"Around seventy," Benini volunteered.

"That means that in the normal course of things, she would have died around 1938," said Easby.

"So?"

"So, my boy, this certificate will be our proof of success, our litmus paper. If we succeed in our project, it means that we have changed reality. Therefore, the date on this certificate of death must change to a date around 1938. It cannot remain 1894. Do you see it now?"

Franco, who until then had stood beside Easby's armchair, now sat heavily in an empty chair next to him and gazed at the floor. He was embarrassed, but he felt that he had to say what he really thought. His integrity demanded it. With an effort, he faced Easby and spoke softly but vehemently.

"But James, you don't really think that this is going to happen, right? You can't change the past. I'm sure you know that. I mean, it was an interesting mental exercise, and of course, it is particularly intriguing for me since my family is involved, but this has really gotten out of hand. People have been killed because of it – don't ask me why or how because I can't fathom any of it – but you are a rational person. Surely you must realize that the whole idea is unrealistic."

"Must I, indeed?" said Easby. He sounded annoyed, and his countenance had lost its fatherly and soft character. "I think that you are on the wrong track, my boy. Read this," he ordered, handing him a piece of paper.

Franco immediately recognized his great-grandfather's handwriting. The letters were uncharacteristically thick and the words difficult to read, and he read slowly. The words formed before his eyes, but his brain had trouble grasping their meaning.

"God forgive me for what I am doing," said the first line, and then it continued. *"I may burn in Hell for this, and I deserve it, but I don't mind the eternal punishment if my Evelyn is saved. When you read this, The One Who can Speak with the Dead will have found you. This you must do:*

1) Select a surrogate and select her well. She must be young and, God forgive me for sinning against my progeny. My blood must run in her veins.

2) Her body must be possessed by the same consumption that is devastating my Evelyn's body. Use an infected needle to propagate the malady.

3) She must lie in my Evelyn's bed when she dies. The One Who can Speak with the Dead will open the door between her and Evelyn, and her sacrifice will save my child.

May God have pity of my sins."

"Well," said Franco, "this is a bunch of superstitious nonsense. You don't plan to go and try to do anything of what's written in here, I assume. By the way, even if you wanted to, there is no female alive in my family. We're a small family, and I know everybody. Only men; sorry folks," Franco joked.

"You're right that we're not going to do anything ..." said Easby.

"Good!" said Franco, sounding relieved.

"... because we've already taken care of everything."

CHAPTER 60

Ambri, Switzerland. July 2009

Franco gazed at Easby with disbelief.

"But what? How?"

"The project has been ongoing for a long time now," Easby explained.

"But ... but you just read the crazy instructions a moment ago. How ..."

"Let me explain," Maria intervened. "I've known those instructions since I was a child. Reading them now simply confirmed what I knew beforehand and gave us confidence that we have been acting properly all along. My grandmother had a copy of those instructions that she kept together with your great-grandfather's letter. Her mother had received them by communicating with the spirits and had dictated them to your great-grandfather."

"Much more likely that they were the product of her diseased mind," Franco spurted.

"I suggest that you don't belittle my great-grandmother's power. She was quite powerful in her time, although my grandmother was even a stronger medium than she. But my grandmother was weak. She got it into her head that those instructions were diabolic and had to be destroyed, so she burned them. But before she did, my mother read and memorized them, and she passed them on to me and made sure that I'd memorize them too. My mother was made of much sterner stuff than her mother, and so am I. Then, one night I dreamt about it, and I knew that the time had come. I found Doctor Benini – I won't bore you with that tale – and here we are."

"I don't understand," said Franco, turning to Easby. "The instructions speak of a young woman. So why did you need me?"

"Oh, we've done the research. You see, we realized very soon that we were in trouble because your family has not been blessed with many females, and at first, we thought that the project would be a non-starter. But then Benini came up with the solution. If we read the instructions carefully, we see that all we need is for your great-grandfather's blood to run in the surrogate's veins. It does not have to be *all* his blood. Some is enough. Our surrogate's blood type is AB+, so that's why we needed to enlist the help of a member of your family who had an AB+ blood type: you."

"How ... how did you know?" Franco stuttered.

"We did research. How do you think that we knew about your incident with the peach? We've gone through all your medical records."

"So that séance ... it was all a lie!" Franco almost shouted, rising indignantly.

"An innocent ruse, really," said Easby. "I'm sorry if that caused you discomfort, but it couldn't be helped. We truly needed you on board."

"Discomfort? That was devastating! So she can't really speak with the dead," he said, pointing at Maria.

"She can, and she does, but we couldn't take chances with you and thought it wiser to stage your mother's speech than to prove Maria's powers to you otherwise. I'm sorry again. I apologize. I didn't mean to upset you, but we had to secure your help. And it's not much that you are required to do to help us. All we need is a little of your blood to give the surrogate a short time before she dies. Look upon it as a blood donation. I'm sure you've done that before."

"Do you mean to say that you're going to let that young woman die? I don't believe it!"

"It's out of my hand," said Easby, shaking his head sorrowfully, "it has been from the start."

"I don't believe you."

"You should. I'm telling you the truth. Tell him, Arturo," he ordered.

Dr. Benini had positioned himself far from them as if to signal that he was not a part of the argument. He stood next to the door and beside Hans, who had joined them so quietly that only now Franco noticed his presence. He now spoke without gazing at Franco. His voice was low, almost a whisper.

"James is telling you the truth, Franco. Sally was doomed from the start. She has HIV, and it had started developing at a quick pace."

"HIV is not tuberculosis. She's dying of tuberculosis if I understand this right."

"Tuberculosis is a common complication of HIV –"

"Tell him everything, Arturo. Franco has a right to know since he is going to play a central role in this."

"All right," said Benini, shuffling his feet. He stared at his shoes as if to find inspiration there, and after a long pause, he continued. "We have been testing students in a few universities, looking for a TB-positive one. We concentrated on faculties that had a large population of foreign students since we knew that TB incidence in Eastern Europe, Africa, and South America is the highest. We interviewed men and women, but the men were just a decoy since we needed a female for the project. Whenever we found a young woman who seemed to be a potential – one who didn't look quite healthy in a simple physical examination – we took biological samples and ran tests. We weren't lucky and didn't find anyone who tested positive for TB. We did find one of the right age, who tested HIV positive, however. We ran more tests and saw that the disease was advancing. She seemed oblivious to her symptoms and attributed them to poor nutrition, high study load, and too much alcohol. She was quite candid about it all and admitted to being sexually active – in fact, promiscuous – and practicing unsafe sex. Little wonder that she got herself into trouble."

Benini paused and gazed earnestly at Easby as if to plead for leave to stop speaking.

"Go on, Arturo. All the details," Easby ordered.

Benini swallowed a couple of times and continued. "We were quite desperate because Maria kept insisting that the time was near and that we would miss the window of opportunity if we didn't move fast. Then I had an idea. You should know that TB is extremely aggressive in HIV patients. It develops quickly and proceeds faster than in non-HIV patients because their immune system is compromised. In fact, many HIV patients die of TB. We knew that we would have a measure of control over it and that by giving her some antibiotic treatment, we would be able to prolong the course of the disease to get her alive to the critical date ... to now."

"I still don't understand. How could you be sure that she would develop TB? Not all HIV patients do."

Benini gave Easby a desperate glance, obviously seeking help, but Easby ignored him. Franco, on the other hand, saw it and understood. He took a quick step forward and grabbed Benini by his jacket.

"You son of a bitch!" he cried. "You gave it to her."

Hans took a step forward and pulled Franco's hand until he opened it. Benini, who had become red in the face, took a step back and avoided looking him in the eyes.

"You must understand: she was doomed anyway. So yes, I inoculated her with a resistant strain of *Mycobacterium tuberculosis*. Once we confirmed that she was actively infected, we signed her up for the experiment, of course, without telling her its real aim. I feel sorry for her, but I'm not responsible for her primary illness. It makes little difference for her whether she dies of tuberculosis or of some worse disease, but it will make a world of difference to Evelyn if we complete the project and save her life. *Mors tua, vita mea*, as they say."

"You're nuts! You're stark, raving mad! Evelyn has been dead for a hundred and fifteen years."

"Only in the current reality, not in the one that we are about to create. And besides, you've known that all along, my boy," said Easby.

"Yes, and as long as I thought that this was a futile exercise and that the only danger was that I would feel ridiculous at the end of it, I didn't mind. But I never budgeted for this. People have died, and this young woman is about to die in your pursuit of this crazy scheme." Franco saw that Easby remained placid as he spoke, and his rage mounted. "And I'm not your boy," he added, rebelliously.

"All right, have it your own way. It doesn't make a difference anyway. We are going ahead with the plan, and it looks like the big day is tomorrow," said Easby.

"And what will you do if I refuse to play? You said it yourself that I am indispensable."

"I feared that you might take such an unreasonable position. We will have to proceed without your cooperation, then, and I may assure you that it won't be pleasant. Hans!" he commanded, "Take Professor Lorenzi to the guest's room upstairs and lock him in."

A frighteningly large hunting knife had appeared in Hans's hand, and he showed it to Franco before using it to tickle his back while his other hand rested on Franco's shoulder.

"We go," he said simply, applying light pressure.

"Hans!" Easby called again.

"*Ja?*"

"If he gives you any trouble at all, you can tie him to the bed."

"*Danke!*" said Hans, and his facial muscles reassembled into something that could have been a smile.

CHAPTER 61

Ambri, Switzerland. July 2009

As soon as Hans locked the door behind him, Franco ran to the window and opened it. He immediately understood that there was no hope to escape from that route. The wall below was even and smooth, and any attempt to climb down would have certainly ended in broken bones if not worse. He sat on the bed and tried to think of a rational way to deal with the situation but soon realized that he was at a dead end.

He heard voices coming from the room next to his, which he assumed was where the surrogate was being kept. Every now and then, he would hear her coughing, but most of the time, people spoke in voices too low for him to understand what was being said. The wooden boards of the chalet's floor were squeaky, and every time someone walked along the corridor, it felt like the steps were right in the middle of his room. There seemed to be a great deal of activity going on, with people coming and going from the next room, and each time he wondered whether they were coming for him and what would happen to him. Obviously, they would not let him live when everything was over and they no longer needed him. He was too much of a hazard. He could have kicked himself for not playing the part of the enthusiast, as Kathia had warned him to do, but it was too late now to change it. They would never believe a professed change of heart on his part.

The key was turned in the lock, and Franco jumped up, ready for anything and prepared to sell his life dearly, but it was only Hans with a tray and Easby behind him. Hans placed the tray on the small table and then went to stand silently by the door, leaving the floor to Easby.

"Here, we've brought you some food," Easby said.

"I don't want it!" Franco blurted and immediately regretted it when the smell of a soup, coming from the tray, reminded his body that it had been a long time since it had a proper meal. The thought of food made his stomach rumble.

"Don't be absurd!" Easby rebuked him. "We're civilized people, and civilized people must feed properly. I'll see you tomorrow," he added and left.

Hans left after him and locked the door noisily. Franco soon realized that being caged had little effect on his appetite. Despite a vague notion that he should have shown it to them and fasted, he finished everything on the tray.

Feeling a little better with a meal in him, Franco returned to the window to search for escape routes that he might have neglected. He considered standing at the window and shouting for help, but the chalet was isolated, and it was unlikely anyone would hear him. Besides, Hans would be sure to come up and silence him before long. Tying bed sheets to lower himself along the wall didn't seem a practical option either, since the sheets were short and too thin to offer any assurance of strength. Disheartened, Franco lay down on the bed and, without turning off the light, lost himself in thought until, much later, he fell asleep.

The following day Franco got up late. He had slept fitfully, disturbed by frequent noises and moans coming from the room next to his. His throat was dry and felt like sandpaper. He banged rhythmically on the door until the key was turned, and Hans stepped in.

"Why noise?" he demanded.

"I need to brush my teeth. And I need something hot to drink. Coffee would be best."

Hans gazed at him thoughtfully, obviously weighing his prisoner's requests. After what seemed to Franco like a very long time, he said, "I agree. Come," and preceded him to the bathroom where Franco brushed his teeth and washed his face slowly, under Hans's watchful eye. He then returned to his room, and Hans locked him in again to return a few minutes later with a cup of coffee and two slices of buttered bread with *confiture de lait* on them.

"Thank you," Franco felt compelled to say, despite everything.

"Grrr," Hans answered and disappeared again.

The feeding routine repeated itself twice, at lunchtime and at dinnertime. There was no doubt that the monsters who were keeping him a prisoner were civilized monsters. Franco lingered over his food simply for want of anything better to do, but during the day, he mostly killed time watching the acrobatic flight of assorted birds and listening to the noises from the room next door. It was 10 PM by his watch when a sudden rush of activity made him become alert. He heard steps climbing the stairs quickly and excited voices coming from every direction. Then the door opened, and Benini came rushing in carrying a large bag, followed by Hans.

"It's time, Franco. Roll up your sleeve and lie down on the bed," he ordered.

"Now listen, Benini," Franco started to say, but Benini wasn't listening. He signaled to Hans, who grabbed Franco and held him forcefully against his body in a grip in which he was barely able to breathe.

"I did hope that you would cooperate," said Benini, shaking his head sorrowfully. He took a syringe from his bag and unceremoniously stabbed Franco's arm with it, injecting a large amount of liquid. The injection hurt, but Franco was unable to shout. Within seconds his legs gave under him, and his head swam. Hans dragged him to the bed and rolled up his sleeve. As Benini approached him with a blood donation kit in his hand, Franco found the strength to speak.

"What did you do to me?" he whispered, slurring his words.

"I gave you a potent sedative to make sure that you won't give me any trouble. It's time to give our surrogate a blood transfusion. It's okay, Hans," he added, "you don't need to hold him. He won't be able to move much for the next few hours."

Franco watched impotently as his blood flowed into the first plastic bag and then into the second. He was nauseous and had a pulsating pain in his temples. He wanted to speak, but all that came from his mouth were short gasps.

Benini collected his equipment, and he and Hans left without even bothering to close the door. Franco lay helplessly askew on the bed, one of his feet on the ground and the other on the wooden bed frame. His heel hurt, and he had to exert himself to pull it away from the frame. His consciousness drifted, and he couldn't be sure if the voices he heard came from the house or his head. Some sentences were complete and made sense, and those were probably only a figment of his imagination, but most of the time, the bits of conversation he heard were unintelligible.

Franco lost the sense of time, so hours could have passed when he awoke from one of his many blackouts and discovered that his limbs were working again. His hands and legs responded to the commands of his brain, and he tested them circumspectly, flexing his muscles slowly. He soon discovered that any activity involving getting even partially erect was out of the question. The mere attempt at sitting caused violent dizziness and nausea. Instead, he let his body slide to the floor and attempted to push himself forward. He had no clear idea about what he was going to do, but one thing he knew for sure: he had to get out of that room. After a few attempts, he discovered that crawling worked well. Apparently, the muscles responsible for the lizard-like movement that he was performing had recovered better than others. He crawled out of the door and past the room from which the voices were coming, until he reached the top of the stairs. He controlled his descent down the stairs by putting the hand he wasn't flexing forward and by applying pressure on the step with his knee.

The descent was painful and bumpy, but at last, he reached the corridor that led to the front door, where his journey was stymied. The door opened inwards, and the door knob was too far up for him to reach from his position on the floor. Franco looked around for something to help him reach the knob. A large brass umbrella holder held a single umbrella and a walking cane. His hand reached high enough to grasp the cane, and with it, he pulled down the door handle, and the door opened a crack. Pushing his fingers into it to swing the door open was painful, but Franco ignored the blood on his hand and pushed through the opening and out into the relative freedom of the graveled yard.

"Ha!" said a voice behind him.

Franco wasn't able to turn to see who had spoken, but he didn't have to because a moment later, a large, beefy hand grabbed his throat, and another put the big, spooky knife that he already knew before his face. He closed his eyes, waiting for the blow to end his life.

A cracking noise, like a shot, broke the silence of the night and a heavy weight pushed him hard to the gravel, thrusting a myriad of small, sharp stones into his flesh and taking his breath away. His vision was darkened, and consciousness left him.

CHAPTER 62

Ambri, Switzerland. July 2009

Hands touched him, and voices came from everywhere and blended into a chaotic vociferation. Franco opened his eyes and, in the yard's semi-darkness, glimpsed strange silhouettes running to and fro. Someone had turned him around, and he was lying on his back and facing the clear night sky. Eva's worried face looked down at him, and a man in uniform stuck a needle into his vein.

"Don't talk," Eva said. "The police doctor is taking care of you. You'll be okay."

"Yes, Professor. You have no major wound, but you've been drugged," said the uniformed physician. He spoke cheerfully as if treating people who had been drugged were a treat to him. "I just gave you a shot to help you out of it. See if you can get on your feet now. Slowly!" he cautioned.

Supported by Eva and the doctor, Franco got up and stood for a few moments, testing his equilibrium.

"I'm better, thank you. But what ..." he started to say.

"Later," said Eva. "You'll know everything later, but now we need to go inside and see what's going on there."

Franco looked around and saw several Swiss policemen in full combat gear standing at the house's corners with machine guns. Shouts and voices that only a moment before had come from within had stopped, and a strange silence enveloped the chalet. Hans's body lay still at a short distance. He had blood on his face and was clearly dead.

"He was about to stab you, and the captain shot him," Eva explained.

Franco nodded and averted his gaze from the body.

"Here, I'll help you," said the doctor, grabbing his arm, and the three of them walked into the house.

They took the stairs slowly, careful to let Franco walk with small steps without exerting himself too much. At the top of the stairs, three policemen kept guard outside the room next to the one where Franco had been held prisoner; they quietly moved aside to let them enter. As they crossed the threshold, they saw a strange scene. The room was much more spacious than the one that had functioned as Franco's prison, but nevertheless, it was overcrowded. A young woman lay in a bed that was the central piece of the room. In the near corner, two policemen pointed their guns at a handcuffed trio consisting of Easby, Benini, and Maria. Next to the bed, a civilian of distinguished aspect spoke in whispers with a police officer.

"Doctor!" the officer called. "Come here and see what you can do for this young woman."

The doctor approached the bed and carried out a quick examination, silently followed by everybody in the room. At the end of the examination, he turned toward the officer and shook his head.

"There is nothing that I can do," he said. "She's dead. She passed away while I was checking her pulse."

The distinguished gentleman, who until then had kept silent, turned to the police officer and said, "Then you can take them. They're all yours, Captain." Then, addressing Eva, he added, "This must be Professor Lorenzi, right?"

"Yes, Uncle David," said Eva.

"Uncle?" said Franco, baffled. "Who is this person?"

"His name is David Westmore. He's Undersecretary for Unplanned Research. It's a long story; I'll tell you later," said Eva.

She applied a little pressure to his arm as if to beg him to postpone questioning her, and Franco grudgingly kept quiet.

"Wait a moment, David," Easby said from his corner, and David Westmore gazed at him and lifted an eyebrow. "Please let me see the death certificate before they take us, will you? It's on the dresser over there."

"Why should I?"

"You owe it to me. For old time's sake."

"I owe you nothing," said Westmore, "but I can see no harm in letting you see it. Which of these papers is the one you want?"

"I'll show you," said Franco, suddenly animated. He picked Evelyn's death certificate from the documents scattered on the dresser and examined it closely. He fixed his gaze on the date of death, and for a moment, he thought that the figures were flickering; his vision still hadn't fully recovered from the effects of the drug. The place and date seemed blurred for a few seconds, and then his vision cleared, and there it was: "Ambri, Switzerland, 29 August 1894."

"It didn't work," he said. "See for yourself," he added, handing the certificate to Easby, who took it with both his handcuffed hands.

Benini read it over Easby's shoulder, and then a smile appeared on his face. "You see the date?" he asked. "It said, '22 August 1894' before. It has changed."

"I think you're right!" said Easby. His face lit up with excitement. "We've done it! We've changed the past. We've given her one more week!"

"You're dottier than I thought, James," said Westmore, snatching the paper from his hands. "Will you please take them out of my sight, Captain?" he concluded.

The captain nodded, and the policemen prodded the three prisoners into motion. As they passed near Eva and Franco, Easby stopped and gazed up. "Eva," he said, "I want you to know–"

"Don't speak to me," said Eva, raising her hand, palm forward. "Just don't speak to me."

Easby opened his mouth again as if to speak, and then he shook his head and moved on.

"Come," said the doctor to Franco. "I'm taking you to the hospital. I need them to run some tests."

Franco opened his mouth to protest, but then he saw Eva's worried expression and closed it again.

CHAPTER 63

Ambri, Switzerland. 29 August 1894

The Honorable L. waited by his daughter's bed in silence. Dr. Schmidt, who stood at the other side of the bed, held Evelyn's wrist. She breathed lightly, almost imperceptibly. She had stopped coughing for quite some time and hadn't opened her eyes for hours. The nurse waited dutifully at the feet of the bed, ready to perform at the doctor's command.

"Her pulse is slow," said Dr. Schmidt, as if speaking to himself. "I don't understand. She had improved so much last week that I was sure that she would get better." He shook his head as if to intimate that she had failed him.

"Get out," said the Honorable L.

He said it plainly and in a low key, but nobody argued. The doctor and the nurse left without a word and closed the door behind them.

The Honorable L. knelt by the bed and rested his head on his daughter's shoulder. The tears that he had imprisoned inside for months now flew freely from his eyes and wetted Evelyn's nightgown.

"I've failed you, baby," he said hoarsely. "Forgive me. Forgive me. Forgive me," he kept repeating.

But she could no longer hear him.

CHAPTER 64

Lugano, Switzerland. July 2009

"Breakfast is always a real feast at this hotel," said David Westmore.

To Franco, it should have looked more inviting than ever that morning since his last meal had been a hospital one, and breakfast elegantly served in the cozy privacy of a room was even better. Despite it, Franco eyed Eva with suspicion. She kept an embarrassed silence and wore an apprehensive look on her face, waiting by the table that had been laid near a window with a beautiful view of Lake Lugano.

"I see that you ordered for two," said Franco. "Who were you expecting?"

"She was waiting for you, Franco," said Westmore. "I called her from the hospital while you were getting dressed. Well, kids, I need to go now. Important state business ..." he added vaguely.

He kissed Eva on the cheek, shook Franco's hand, and before they could say anything, he was gone.

"Won't you sit down?" Eva asked.

"Yeah," Franco said, sitting stiffly at the table in front of her, "but you've got quite some explaining to do. You know that."

"I can explain while you eat," she said, and then she poured them coffee.

Franco drank some and bit into a slice of toast, but then he simply stared at her, waiting.

"You remember when I told you at first that my father committed suicide?" She paused and waited for a reaction, but Franco merely waited for her to continue. "Well, I was keeping up a necessary lie," she said simply.

"You don't say! *You*, lying?" Franco mocked her.

"Please, listen to the end. I was telling you the truth when I told you that my father didn't commit suicide. He was murdered by James. Father and David worked under James in the Secret Service for a while. Then James came into money and left. Father left too, officially, but in reality, he continued to work in the Service. When James started to get involved with all kinds of potentially dangerous individuals in Europe, Father was assigned to work undercover to keep a close eye on his activities. He reconnected with him and got involved in his organization. At that time, David and Father were very close friends, and we saw a lot of him – that's how I took to calling him Uncle David – but this may be what alerted James that Father was, in fact, spying on him."

Eva stopped, obviously emotionally affected by the memories that her tale was bringing back. Franco put his hand on hers, and she lifted her gaze and looked straight at him. Her eyes were moist.

"The official story was that he was depressed and that returning from a party where he had drunk too much, he had drowned himself. But David says that there was something else in his blood, some drug, and no way that he could have either driven to where he was found or gotten from his car to the river by himself, the condition he was in. It was murder."

"I'm so sorry," said Franco, pressing her hand.

"Yes," she said. "I knew nothing until last year when David told me the whole story. He thinks that James had kind of adopted me not out of remorse but to avert suspicion from himself. I was angry with David at first for letting me stay so close to James, who was responsible for my father's murder, but then I understood that I had been given a unique gift: the opportunity to get even with him. It wasn't easy, but I did it. Uncle David assigned Richard Hawthorne to be my contact, and he told me what to do. Poor Richard!"

"Why 'poor Richard'?"

"Oh, right, you don't know about it. Von Stoffen's man killed him. He was coming to take me away, and I got him killed. He had no reason to suspect that coming to the farm might be dangerous, and I did nothing to alert him."

"It wasn't your fault."

"Actually, it was. I was following instructions only up to a point. I had put you in danger for my personal vendetta, and I had to fix it. So I took the documents and left a message on James's answering machine telling him that I had them and that I had left you. I figured that he would call his killers away from you. As it turned out, the man in Venice had nothing to do with James."

"Yes, that got me confused. What was von Stoffen's role in all that?"

"From what I understood, listening to them while they were holding me, von Stoffen wanted to stop James from going ahead with his project. I don't know why. He didn't say."

"By the way, what became of Kathia?" Franco felt a pang of remorse that he had not inquired about her before. After all, she had been right about Easby all along – more or less.

"We got her to the hospital in time, and her condition is stable. Dan is sitting by her bed, holding her hand. I spoke with him this morning, and he said that she was coming around to his view that they were soul mates. I hope it works out for them. I feel bad about how she was wounded; after all, it was I who got everybody into trouble.

Franco raised his head and gazed straight at Eva. "You mean to tell me that you made yourself a target to move the killers' attention away from me?" he said. "That was a crazy thing to do."

"Yes. I guess I was crazy. So here I am. You know the rest. I got closure, at last."

"You did—big time. But there is one remaining point that eludes me. How did you find me in Ambri?"

"Look in the left pocket of your jacket," Eva ordered.

Franco fished into the pocket, and his hand emerged with a box of mints.

"Mints? You found me using mints?"

"The bottom of the box has a transmitter that sends out a very potent signal at long intervals. Poor Richard Hawthorne gave it to me so he would be able to find me if I got into trouble. I slipped it into your pocket when we said goodbye at the farm. Uncle David had the equipment needed to locate you."

"Wow! *Chapeau* to you for the presence of mind."

"I wasn't going to let you get lost, although ... have I lost you?"

"What do you mean?"

"You know what I mean."

Eva gazed out of the window as she spoke, and her eyes grew wetter than before. Franco got up and circled around the table, and then he pulled her up from her chair. He placed his hands on her shoulder and gazed straight into her eyes.

"We will always be close," he said.

"Close?" she said, pushing him back. "Close like, 'I'm letting you fall in love with me, so I can take you to bed'?"

"Not true! Not at all. I'm not taking advantage of you," he said.

"So where does that leave us now?" she asked.

Franco averted his gaze from her and looked out of the window. He spoke quietly. "I had time to think, you know, both in that chalet where they kept me locked and in my bed at the hospital. I think," he paused, "that I should take some time to be alone," he said at last.

"I see," said Eva. She sat heavily and then gazed up at Franco. "It was stupid of me to think that you might reciprocate. But it's better this way. If you're fed up with me, it's better to know it now."

"I'm not!" Franco protested. "Quite the opposite. I'm afraid that if I stay any longer with you, I might fall in love with you so hard that ... that ..."

"What's wrong with that?"

"You understand how I feel."

"No, I don't. It doesn't make sense to me."

"I'm scared, Eva," said Franco. He took a step toward her, but she got up and backed away.

"If you're too scared to live, you're not a man!" she threw at him furiously. "You're a ... you're a ... You can take your wretched personality and go away. I hate you!"

She was crying openly with her face buried in her hands. Franco got nearer and tried to hold her hands, but she wriggled out of his grip and remained standing without looking at him. Franco stood there, helplessly waiting for her to speak. When the minutes passed, and she didn't move or speak, he turned and left.

CHAPTER 65

London, England. July 2009

Franco's life had regained a semblance of normality. During the last week, since his return from Switzerland, he had not contacted any of his acquaintances, preferring to be alone. He had sat a couple of times in his office to work listlessly on an article but had accomplished little other than that. He had gone out to eat, most of the time, since he found the atmosphere of his apartment oppressive now and had employed some of his time to update his lectures for the next semester. But despite his efforts to keep busy, he felt hollow inside. So much had happened in a short time that he had changed in a way that he found difficult to understand. He had been plunged into a world where murder and treason were the norms from a slow-paced academic life. He had become a burglar and a fugitive and had done daring deeds together with a beautiful, funny, and intelligent woman, who wasn't shy to tell him that she loved him. He had been chased by murderers, drugged, and almost killed. Could it be that he was missing all those things? And if he wasn't, what was the meaning of this hollow feeling inside, of the sensation that something essential was missing?

He was immersed so deep in thought that the doorbell caught him unprepared and made him jump. He hastened to the door.

"Zoe!" he said with surprise, seeing who his visitor was. "What are you doing here?"

"I've been phoning you, but you never picked up. I want to talk to you. May I come in?"

"Oh, sorry. Of course," said Franco, blushing and moving aside to unblock the door.

Zoe went straight to the small sitting area and sat on the only uncomfortable chair as if to make a statement that she was not there on a social visit. Her back was straight, her body taut. Franco gazed at her; the short, curly black hair over the tanned complexion matched her black, piercing eyes well. She was beautiful but in a sort of didactically detached manner. He felt too fidgety to relax on the sofa, so he chose to sit on the corner of his massive coffee table, facing her.

"I've been thinking a lot," she said and stopped. Franco didn't react, and after a brief pause, she continued. "I have researched during the last two weeks, and I found several instances of cases similar to yours."

"I'm not 'a case'," Franco complained. He was irate and didn't mind showing it.

"Yes, you are. You're a clear case of degenerative Oedipus complex ..."

"We've been through this before, Zoe. I don't want you to psychoanalyze me, and I'm not interested in your theories."

"Let me finish. You owe me that much."

Franco resigned himself to listening. He knew by experience that Zoe was unstoppable until she had said her say and that the quickest way with her was to let her expose whatever new thought she had come up with.

"What you're doing is self-inflicted punishment. You are giving up happiness to atone for what happened to your mother. You're not shielding yourself from the unhappiness that looms in your future, as you would like to convince yourself and me – you're making sure that you're miserable right now, to pay for what you perceive as your sins. You're giving up love, rejecting the people who love you and are loved by you, and by the time you realize that, it will be lost forever. It-will-be-too-late," she emphasized, articulating each word, "love won't be waiting for you. I won't be waiting either. You must understand, Franco: it's now or never, and if you ..."

"You're right," said Franco, getting up with a jerk.

"Let me finish ... Oh, I am?"

"Yes, yes." Franco had picked up his jacket from his dinner table chair and was frantically going through its pockets, checking the contents of his wallet and his cell phone. Zoe watched him, obviously stunned by his peculiar behavior.

"Then you are ..."

She stopped in mid-sentence as Franco turned his back to her. "So sorry, I must go," he said and went for the door.

"But, but ..." said Zoe.

"Close the door when you leave, will you? Thanks a lot," he said and hurried out.

He ran down the stairs and out on the street, dialing a number on the way.

"*Oui?*" a musical voice answered.

"Eva! Can you hear me?" Franco asked, panting.

"Who's that?"

"It's me, Franco."

"Franco?"

In the silence that followed, Franco struggled to pout his lips. "*Je ...*" he said.

"What?"

"*Je ... Je,*" he struggled to say.

"Oh ... I see."

"Eva ..."

"You know what? Shut up and get your Latin ass over here," she said and hung up.

Franco smiled and flagged a cab. "St. Pancras station," he confided in the driver. "I'm on the next train for Paris."

EPILOGUE

Rome, Italy. July 2009

Monsignor Le Fevre's phone rang.

"Your Excellency, you have a call from London," said his young secretary.

"From London? Put him through."

After a short wait, a familiar voice said, "Hello."

"Hello," said Le Fevre, and even that single word carried much tension.

"I have good news," said the voice. "The project about which you were worried ... it was terminated. Finally terminated."

"Oh, praise The Lord!" said Le Fevre, and one could almost hear over the telephone line how the tension of the past weeks at once left his body. The silence on von Stoffen's part had been a constant source of apprehension for Le Fevre during the last few days, and now his head felt light from the intoxicating news. "Thank you so much for informing me. But are you sure? Is this official?"

"Definitely. Everybody involved is either under custody or has left this vale of tears. You need not worry. The information that you gave us proved very useful in dealing with this problem. We appreciate it."

"It is I who should thank you for your efforts and for your cooperation."

"That's what friends do, Monsignor. I'm happy that it turned out well for everybody ... except for the sinners, of course. Well, goodbye now."

"Be well," said Le Fevre, but he said it to a silent line.

London, England. July 2009

David Westmore took his gaze away from the boats that looked like toys in the Thames, twelve floors down from his window, and turned his attention to the two young people – a woman and a man, both in their early thirties – who sat rigidly in the chairs before his desk. They were clearly tense and nervous in their impeccable business suits – but that was little wonder since to them, Westmore was only a notch less potent than God Almighty himself.

"That was our friend from the Vatican, as you may have guessed," said Westmore. "An ally at times, and a pain in the neck more often than not. But he can be useful, occasionally."

He left the window and sat at his desk.

"So you were saying that you have DNA evidence ..."

"Yes, sir," said the woman, earnestly handing him a thin file. "Here you will see the results of my tests. She's unequivocally a direct descendant. We couldn't find any photographs of the epoch to assess resemblance, but as far as the DNA is concerned, there is no doubt."

"You know that we must be absolutely certain. We can leave no room for mistakes," said Westmore, speaking severely.

"Sir, John and I have done everything we could think of." She gave a side glance at the young man sitting beside her, who nodded dutifully in assent. Her voice grew more excited as she spoke. "We found Anna Stupp's grave, and that was no easy task. And getting an exhumation order from an Austrian court was a challenge. We had to use all of our department's expertise in document forging ..."

"I know. I authorized it. Go on."

"Our analysis confirmed the result of our research that pointed to the subject as the granddaughter of an illegitimate son born to Anna Stupp, whose existence had been kept secret. It was not determined who the father was and whether the boy was Adolf Hitler's half-brother, although the evidence points to it. After Anne Stupp's death, he was raised by her sister as her own son. It's all in the executive summary, Sir."

Westmore opened the thin file and read slowly while the two young people watched him apprehensively. He wasn't a poker-faced reader; his reaction included smiles, pursed lips, and head shakings. He read to the end, placed the file neatly back on the table in perfect alignment with the black leather desk top, and gazed at some object far in the back of the room, above the woman's head.

"Anna Stupp," he said as if speaking to himself, "Adolf Hitler's father's sweetheart .... Yes, that has potential."

MEET THE AUTHOR

Kfir Luzzatto is the author of eleven novels, several short stories, and seven non-fiction books. Kfir was born and raised in Italy and moved to Israel as a teenager. He acquired the love for the English language from his father, a former US soldier, a voracious reader, and a prolific writer. He holds a Ph.D. in chemical engineering and works as a patent attorney. In pursuit of his interest in the mind-body connection, Kfir was certified as a Clinical Hypnotherapist by the Anglo European College of Therapeutic Hypnosis.

Kfir is an HWA (Horror Writers Association) and ITW (International Thriller Writers) member. You can visit Kfir's website and read his blog at https://www.kfirluzzatto com. Follow him on Twitter (@KfirLuzzatto) and friend him on Facebook (https://www.facebook.com/KfirLuzzattoAuthor)